The Cottage on Lough Key

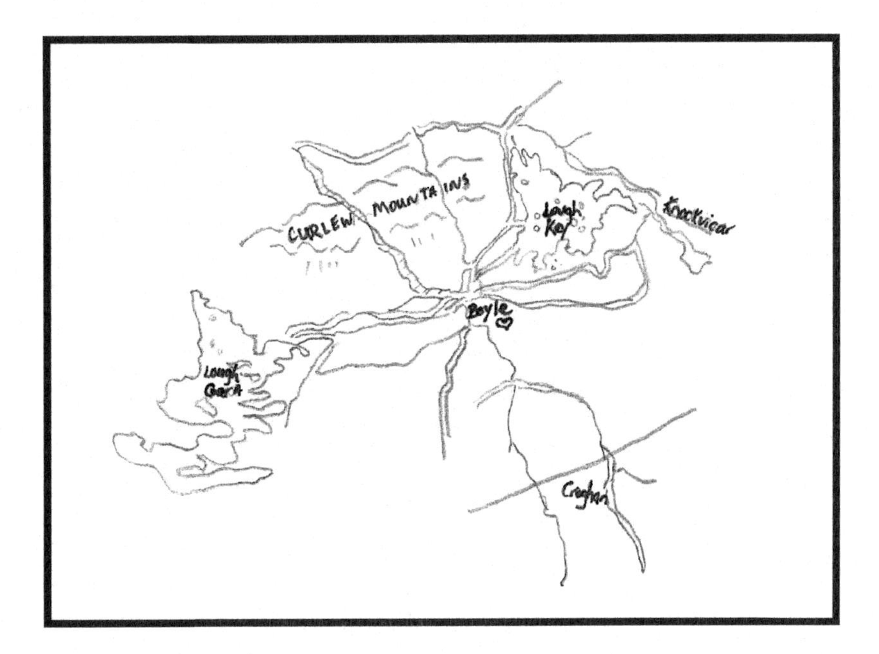
CURLEW MOUNTAINS
Lough Key
Knockvicar
Boyle
Lough Gara
Croghan

The Cottage on Lough Key

by

Anna Marie Jehorek

ISBN: 1523426217
ISBN-13: 978-1523426218

Dedication

For Bea Dunbar, Mom – my best friend and travel partner – you bought my first travel journal and told me to write it down and remember.

For Nicholas L. Dunbar, Dad - your parting message to me was, *Don't hide your light under a bushel, show the world what you've got.* You always believed in me, even when I didn't. I miss you and Mom beyond words.

For Jason and Connor – your love and support never wavers, your encouragement lifts me up.

And for Uncle Eddie, 'Ned' Mullany – I treasure the memories of sitting by your turf fire in Croghan and *yes*, I'm still minding my sheep.

Note

This story is fictional, but I do use the names of some real and not-so-real places. The real places mentioned in the story are written about fictitiously because it's fiction. The names and characters are completely fictional, any similarity to real people living or dead is coincidental.

Because the world can always use another love story.

The Cliffs of Moher

Chapter 1

I stand as close to the edge as I dare leaning forward slightly to see below. It's a hazy warm day, but the wind is persistent and my hair is hopelessly tangled about my head as I stand gazing across the water. A musician sits not far from me on the cliff. The soft melodic sounds of his violin float across the open space and become the soundtrack to my encounter with nature. It's here I'm convinced the theory of continental drift must be true for the grassy cliffs below my feet appear to have broken away from a larger rock than the one I now stand on. I close my eyes as I breathe in the fresh sea air and try to capture a mental picture to hold onto for eternity. People are milling about but I hardly notice because this is like no other experience I've ever felt. In this moment, at this place I am consumed by the spiritual beauty. The Cliffs of Moher on Ireland's west coast engage all my senses and won't let go.

Taking the bag lunch out of my knapsack, I find a spot away from the crowd past O'Brien's Tower and sit down on the grass to eat. I was a small girl the first time I came to the cliffs with my mother, father and brothers. We were visiting Grandma and Grandpa in Boyle but Dad decided an excursion to the west coast would be fun for the family so he borrowed Grandpa's car, piled us inside, and took off to see the cliffs. I remember being mesmerized by the breathtaking beauty. Growing up in New Jersey, I'd never seen cliffs like these and to me it was the most beautiful place in the world. As I sit here chewing a piece of brown bread I look around and think, this is *still* the most beautiful place I've ever seen.

Finishing my lunch, I reach for my knapsack, place it behind me and lie back using it as a pillow for my head. The breeze is still blowing but the daylight haze bathes me in its warmth. Clouds drift overhead trying to push the haze away. I study them as they move past. Shutting my eyes I listen to the soft violin music in the distance. I haven't felt so at peace in months. Recognizing this fact, I take a deep breath and exhale slowly before my thoughts turn to the reason why I've not felt calm in months.

Brad was coming home in three weeks. Three weeks and he would have been home with me - busy with the details of our wedding which was to take place today. This is supposed to be the happiest day of my life. I should be wearing the beautiful off-the-shoulder, candlelight ivory sheath dress with a swoop train and toasting to a happy future with my handsome husband right now.

Darn it, why do I do this to myself?

Breathe in. Take deep breaths, Gemma, and try not to think about it.

My eyes well up and I feel the sensation at the back of my throat which tells me, I can't stop the tears. I give up and finally a few spill out rolling down the sides of my face into my ears. Mom always told me not to cry when I'm lying down. "It adds to your fears when you put tears in your ears" she'd admonish. I used to believe her, but not anymore. I don't care about tears in my ears, I need to get them out anyway I can, regardless of where they land.

Not wanting to have a complete breakdown in public, I slip my hand into my knapsack, find my phone, plug the ear buds in and try to find a song that won't make me cry. Finally, the shuffle mode lands on an upbeat song. Success; U2, "Beautiful Day" comes on. How can I feel sad listening to a song called, "Beautiful Day?"

Once the moment of sadness is suppressed, I gather my things and head back to the car park. My detour to the cliffs has taken me out of my way. I'm an hour and a half from Galway and I promised my cousin Sorcha I'll spend the night with her.

I throw my knapsack in the boot of the car. Catching my American self as I begin to walk to the left side, I stop and turn right towards the driver's side door and climb in. I look in the rear view mirror and do a cursory inspection. Eyes are slightly puffy from crying and my hair is wild from the wind so I reach into the overnight bag sitting on the passenger seat and find my hair brush. Gingerly I manage to break through the dozens of tangles the wind has tied it in and sweep it back into a neat ponytail. Turning on the Ford Focus I release the parking brake and head down the road to make my way to the N67 towards Galway.

The haze has lifted for the most part and the sky is now a brilliant blue. The drive from the cliffs to Sorcha's in Galway is lovely. As I reach Lisdoonvarna I decide to stop in at Sweet Dreams Bakery and get something to bring for tea.

Lisdoonvarna is a quaint town famous for an annual matchmaking festival held each September. I know of the bakery only because the last time I visited Sorcha, I got turned about and stopped there for directions. Sweet Dreams has since become a favorite stop along the way. The brown bread is the best I've tasted and the owner makes lovely cupcakes that are just as good as the gourmet ones back in the States.

Pulling up outside the bakery, I put the blue Focus into park, take my wallet from the glove box and get out. Tiny bells tinkle against the glass door as I enter and breathe in the heavenly aroma permeating the small shop. A tall slender woman with light brown hair pulled back in a hair net is behind the cash register assisting an elderly woman purchasing a coffee cake. She looks at me and says, "I'll be right with you dear." I smile and nod then turn to study the treats encased in glass.

Gorgeous brown and soda breads, Banoffee pie, Irish coffee pie, Bailey Puff pastry, a custard pastry pie called "Tara" - my mouth waters looking at these treats. With so much to choose from, I have a hard time deciding. But, I know Sorcha's counting calories so I won't tempt her with anything too sinful.

"Thanks for waiting, what can I get ye?"

Looking up from the glass case, my eyes meet the woman behind the counter smiling at me. I clear my throat and respond, "I'll have a loaf of soda bread and a loaf of brown bread, please."

"Grand, I'll get that for ye straight away then."

As the shop keeper bends to open the case, the elderly woman with the coffee cake stops beside me and gives me a sideways glance. I smile to be polite, but I feel she's studying me. In fact, I feel like she is *really* studying me hard. Her persistent gaze is becoming a bit unnerving so I ask her, "Is there something I can help you with?"

She softens her expression and I see a twinkle in her eye. "No, nothing at all darling, but don't ye worry. Your heart may be broken, and ye miss him terrible, but the sun is going to shine on ye again soon."

Stepping back, I say, "Pardon me?"

"Don't ye worry, lass. He's coming to find ye soon and you'll smile again and your sad tears will be replaced with tears of joy."

She turns to walk away, lifting her wrinkled hand and patting me on the shoulder, "God bless, God bless ye."

I watch as she walks out the door and I'm dumbstruck. How does she know? Is it that obvious?

I snap out of my thoughts when the woman behind the counter reappears with my breads neatly packaged. "That gonna do it for ye? It will be three euro thirty."

"Yes, that's all." I say, clearing my throat to ask, "That woman who just left, she seemed to know something about me. Is she from around here?"

"Oh, Mrs. Dugan, she's a sweet old lady. Nothing to be afraid of dear."

"I'm not afraid, just a bit rattled by something she said." I hand her a five-euro note, she takes it from me and walks to the cash register.

As she keys in the numbers she continues, "Well, they say she's fey. There's folks all around who swear she sees the future. Swear she knows what's going to happen before it does. Many is the time what she sees comes true."

Handing me my change she smiles, "Thank you dear, and you needn't worry, she may be fey, but she's kind and would never tell ye anything to scare ye." I tuck the change in my wallet, walk to the door, push it open and as the bells tinkle against the glass she calls out, "Thanks a million, come again."

I walk to the car and put the bread on the back seat. My mind is a thousand miles away pondering what the *fey* old lady said to me. I start the car and drive off thinking of my Dad telling me stories of the things people believe in Ireland. Fairies, banshees, wee people, De Danann – all myths. Sure, the old woman may think she's fey, but this place is full of people who believe in myths and legends that aren't true. Like Dad says, "They're full of malarkey." As I return to the N67 I switch on Radio 2 and turn up the music. I should be getting to Sorcha's right at tea time.

❖

Sorcha greets me at her door wearing an old pair of blue jeans and a baggy Coronas concert t-shirt. She's got her sandy brown hair pulled up in a knot with wisps of hair sprouting out of it in all directions. Her carefree appearance is much like her approach to life. I've always admired her free spirit and I think that's why I'm drawn to her. At twenty-seven, she's eleven months older than I am, so naturally we paired up well as kids, but it's really her energy and easy going demeanor that make being with her fun. Even if we weren't cousins, I think we'd be friends.

"Ah let me get a look at ya." She lifts my arms to the side and inspects me from head to toe. "Aw feck girl. Are ye eating at all?"

"As a matter of fact, I had lunch and I've got bread for tea."

She eyes the package in my right hand and then turns her attention back to my slim figure. "Well, okay. But you look like you've lost a stone since I saw ye last." Taking me by the hand and pulling me into her flat, she grabs the overnight bag from me and throws it in the corner. "Sure enough it's been a rough go for ye, but I'm glad your folks convinced you to come visit your relations in Ireland for a while."

"Yeah, I'm glad too. I'll have to go back eventually, but it's nice to be away from everything for a while and clear my head."

Sorcha walks into the kitchen and turns on the kettle to boil the tea and calls back to me, "Have a seat Gemma, I'll get the tea ready. You relax."

I glance around the room. Sorcha's flat is adorable. She found it when she first came to Galway five years ago. She'd landed a job with a local medical devices company much to the dismay of her parents. My aunt and uncle wanted her to come back to Boyle and work in the family's chemist shop after graduating, but Sorcha being the free spirit, wanted to leave the small town and find her own life in a bigger city.

At first she tried Dublin, but she wasn't having any luck finding a job. She was forced to broaden her search and finally found a good company in Galway. It didn't take her long to find the perfect flat and once she did, Galway became home.

Moving a pillow, I sit down on the leather sofa and pick up a small photo album from the coffee table. I begin flipping through the pages – pictures of Sorcha and friends, family, her cat, Bono, and Sorcha with Liam.

Liam and Sorcha started dating a little over a year ago after meeting at a friend's St. Patrick's Day party. Liam is tall with blonde hair, chiseled features and deep brown eyes. I smile remembering her telling me about him over the phone. "He works at Galway Crystal. By God, Gemma he's a glass blower. Imagine what he can do with his mouth?!"

I call into Sorcha, "This is a great picture of you and Liam. So how's that going?"

She pops her head out of the kitchen and grins, "I think I'll keep chasing him till I let him catch me."

I smile and say, "Oh, so he's *the one*?"

Her reply is playfully coy, "Well, were he a fish I'd not be throwing him back in the Boyle River."

"I think that's wonderful, Sorcha. I can't wait to meet Liam. He sounds like a great guy from all you've told me."

"Aye, I only hope he's half as wonderful as your Brad was. God, I'm so sorry Gemma. He was grand, wasn't he?"

Looking down to hide my expression, I nod, "Yes, he was."

After a momentary silence, I look up. "So, will you be making me wear a sherbet colored bridesmaid dress anytime soon?"

Laughing, Sorcha gives a devilish grin. "You'll look lovely in lime sherbet taffeta and a fascinator, for sure. Maybe I'll have you carry a parasol instead of flowers."

We both laugh, stopping when the kettle whistles and Sorcha goes back into the kitchen. It's so good to have someone who knows how to talk about the proverbial elephant in the room without dwelling on it and becoming maudlin. A visit with Sorcha is just what I need. Away from the worried looks from Grandma and Grandpa. Away from the well-meaning advice from Aunt Francie and Uncle Tom. Away from the forlorn looks of the people in Boyle who know my story. Away from having to tell the story repeatedly of how Brad's helicopter was shot down over Afghanistan three weeks before he was to come home - three weeks before he was to come home and marry me.

Sorcha reenters the room carrying a tray with tea and bread. Bono's following behind her. He loves butter so we'll be fighting to keep the cat away from our bread. Putting the tray on the coffee table, Sorcha turns and shoos him away, "Get out of here ya fecker." Sorcha's never been one for pretenses and I love that about her.

"So, Gemma, it's Saturday night, you're a twenty-six year old, hot American in a foreign country, what do you feel like doing?"

"To be honest, I've not been in the mood for wild night life recently, but maybe a night out would be good for me."

"Grand! Then Myles Lee it is. I'll call Liam and have him meet us there around eight o'clock."

"Myles Lee? Have I been there before?" I ask reluctantly.

"It's the Dew Drop Inn, but we locals call it Myles Lee and for the life of me I don't know why. I'm just trying to help ye fit in. But on second thought, a fawn-haired Yank is exotic here so you'll have no trouble meeting a fella if you're interested."

Sorcha pours us both another cup of tea, but I'm lost in thought. I hadn't considered *meeting a fella* as she puts it. I'm still recovering from losing *the* fella. Funny thing, once I'd found the perfect guy the rest seemed so inadequate. I can't imagine finding anyone that will make me feel the way I felt about Brad. I sip my tea and consider the prospect of meeting another man. Gently placing the tea cup on its saucer, I shake my head.

"What was that? Were you saying no to something?" Sorcha questions.

I can be honest with her so I reply, "I was thinking about what it would be like to meet somebody new. I mean, Brad was the one. I can't imagine feeling those feelings for another person."

She pats me on the knee, "I don't know, Gemma. I've no experience with this sort of thing. I know it will never be the same, but maybe it will be grand in its own way. Maybe you'll know again just like you did with Brad. There will be a wonderful charming man who will love you and you'll feel excited to hear his voice, and happy to know he loves you. It's hard to say. I only know you need to be true to yourself. Don't settle, and don't take second best or good enough. You need it to be grand."

Tears fill my eyes. It had been "grand" with Brad. I'd found that once. The thought of finding it again seems like fantasy.

"Finish your tea. We'll wash up and fix ourselves to be the hottest young tarts at Myles Lee." Sorcha stands and carries the tray into the kitchen.

Dabbing my eyes with a napkin, I look down, eyeing Bono rubbing his black fur against my leg. Unable to resist, I put a little dab of butter on the end of the cat's nose. He happily licks it off and I swear it looks like he's smiling at me.

Chapter 2

Myles Lee is one of the best known pubs in Galway. Saturday nights are busy with locals and tourists alike and the fair weather has drawn a large gathering. Fortunately, Myles Lee has outdoor seating on Mainguard Street. June days in Ireland are amazing because it stays light out until eleven o'clock. The mild temperature and long days make it my favorite time to visit.

After much fashion consideration and several changes, Sorcha chose a pair of skinny jeans and a long cream-colored cotton sweater. She's been working hard to lose a few pounds and is proud and confident in a pair of tight-fitting jeans and three-inch heels. I on the other hand am more classic with my look this evening, opting for boot cut jeans and a black jewel neck long sleeve t-shirt with a lavender scarf. Knowing she looks good, Sorcha works her way through the crowd. Finding a couple taking their last sips of beer, she lays siege upon their table as they stand to leave.

Proud of her acquisition, she waves her arm in the air flagging me down. I suppress a giggle and weave through the tables to the corner and Sorcha.

"I still have the gift, Gemma," she says, moving the empty pint glasses to the other side of the table as she studies the seating area in search of a waitress.

"I'm impressed. Took you all of one minute to find a table tonight. That has to be a record, even for you."

Sorcha situates herself facing the crowd so I take the chair to her left. I'm not feeling sociable tonight, but I still want to see the faces in the crowd. As I pull out my chair, I see the table next to us from the corner of my eye. There's a couple who appear to be on a first date. Their body language tells me they don't know each other well, but their faces betray the fact they're happy to be out together.

Beyond them is a table with three guys who look somewhat out of the ordinary for Galway. I can tell they aren't locals because of their clothes. The polo pony stitched on the pocket of the button-down oxford shirt and khaki slacks on the man facing our table is a tad "preppie" compared to the rest of the patrons. There's a tall ginger fella wearing a pale yellow windbreaker and his friend beside him has light brown hair and a blue button down shirt.

As I sit down Sorcha glances over at them and back at me, "Were you checking them out?"

"Why, yes, I was. I always want to see who's around me. That's how I know how tightly to hold onto my purse."

"Very funny. What'll ye have? First round is my treat."

"Smithwicks."

Sorcha scans the area again in search of a waitress. Finally, putting both hands on the table, she pushes down and stands. "Well bugger, I'm going to the bar. Right back, Gem."

Left sitting alone, my anxiety level rises. I've never felt vulnerable before, but in my first *real* social situation since Brad died, uneasiness is giving way to sadness. *Hurry Sorcha, hurry back.*

Thankfully, a waitress approaches and begins removing empty glasses from the round table. As she wipes down the table top she looks at me, "What can I bring you?"

"I've got a drink coming, but thanks."

"Grand, well, my name is Yvonne if you need anything else."

As she gathers her tray of empty glasses and bottles and walks inside, Sorcha reappears with our drinks in hand. I break into a big smile as she raises the glasses in the air to proclaim, *Mission accomplished*! I note the guy in the blue shirt with the light brown hair looking in my direction as Sorcha returns and sits down.

"See, that didn't take long Gem, did it? What shall we drink to?"

She tilts her head in thought and finally says, "To Brad. God bless him and keep him and may he always be looking down on ye, Gemma. Love never dies." Our glasses touch and as I look down in the beer to take a sip my eyes fill once again.

The first sip is always the best. Cold and delicious. I swallow and look up at Sorcha. I imagine in time it will get easier, but profound sadness consumes me as I realize this new status without Brad in my life is forever.

"So, when is this Liam going to get here? I'm dying to meet him." Changing the subject, I stop myself from sinking further into thoughts of Brad.

"He'll be here any minute and I think he's bringing a mate with him."

The blood drains from my face and fear fills me to my core. Sorcha sees this and before I can say a word places her hand on my arm, "Oh God,

Gem, put your mind at rest. You don't think I'm such an eejit that I'd be fixing you up this soon, do ye? It's only a mate of his from school. He's known him practically his whole life – not a fix up, okay?"

"Sorry; it's just, so many well-meaning people want to make things better and I know there are several of the ladies in Boyle who've already asked your mum if it would be appropriate to send their sons around to say hello. That's the last thing I want right now."

"Gem, I can't imagine what you're going through, but if there is one thing I know, it's the fact that when the time is right and you're ready again, you'll be the one to decide."

"Thanks, Sorcha."

"There you are!"

I hear a booming voice from the curb and see what I know must be Liam coming in our direction with friend in tow. Liam Tully is just under six feet tall with blonde hair combed to the side. He has a warm smile and a twinkle in his brown eyes. Passing the waitress on his way to our table he gestures the number two with his right hand and says, "Black stuff." In instant recognition, Yvonne, the waitress, turns and walks back inside to the bar.

Noticing we need one more chair, Liam glances at the couple on their first date – leans over pointing at an extra chair, "Do you need this?" The couple stops their conversation and in unison look at the chair then back at Liam. "No, go ahead" the man nods and Liam grabs it, straddling the back as he sits down and gives Sorcha a peck on the cheek. I immediately see that Liam is perfect for Sorcha and already I like him, despite the fact he's a bit loud.

"And this must be the beautiful Yank I've heard so much about. Gemma, so glad to finally meet ye." Liam reaches out and takes my hand in his large mitt, but instead of shaking it as I anticipate, he gives it a gentle kiss. We all laugh at his chivalry and he turns to the tall dark haired friend now seated at the table with us, "Declan Gallagher, this is Gemma O'Connor from America."

Declan smiles and nods, "It's a pleasure to meet you, Gemma. Are you in Galway for long?"

His expression is earnest and he's very handsome. On first impression he seems shy, but I can't be sure if that's because Liam is so un-shy. His dark hair is slightly wavy and he has sparkling blue eyes and a strong build. I am pretty certain he's athletic because I detect a slight unnatural bend in his nose, probably an old sports injury. Declan is relaxed and unassuming, casually dressed in a navy blue long sleeved t-shirt which sets off his eyes. Smiling at him I reply, "I'm only visiting Sorcha until tomorrow and then I head back to Boyle where I'm staying for the summer."

"Ah, grand. Well, at least you'll have one night out with your wild cousin," Liam interrupts.

Turning in Liam's direction and smiling, "Yes, but I'll be back again if the craic is good."

They all three laugh at me. Apparently the sound of the word craic being said by a Yank is hilarious.

⁂

As I feel the effects of my first pint kicking in, I relax, allowing myself to have fun being out with people again. Liam has an infectious laugh and a great sense of humor making it close to impossible to stay depressed.

Declan turns out to be very nice, but far too soft-spoken to compete with Liam's boisterous nature. Clearly, these two have been friends for a long time and Declan is comfortable letting Liam be the life of the party, which is a charming quality. It also tells me Declan is secure in who he is and humble as well.

Liam and Sorcha are busy chatting about plans for their upcoming holiday at Kilkee, so Declan leans closer and in the kindest voice says, "Liam told me about your fiancé. I'm so sorry for your loss."

Completely surprised by his comment, I give a half smile and say "Yeah, it sucks doesn't it?"

I've never been big on using the word *sucks* for anything other than well, things that suck. But saying it out loud to Declan seemed okay and from his compassionate expression, he understands completely.

"Yes, it does suck." As he finishes his words, he lightly pats my hand which is busy rolling a damp piece of cocktail napkin into a tiny ball. I stop what I'm doing and look up at him as if to say, *thanks for understanding*. Smiling at me, he squeezes my hand and says, "Can I get you another?"

The pint in front of me is three-quarters gone so I consider his question. "Make it a shandy, but don't say anything to Sorcha. I'm a bit of a light-weight these days."

Patting my shoulder as he walks away from the table he looks down at me and gives a gesture right out of the movie *The Sting*, brushing his finger against the side of his nose letting me know it's our secret.

I watch him walk inside the pub and as I return my attention to our table Sorcha and Liam are getting up.

“We're just going inside to use the loo. Separate loos. Well, you know what I mean.”

As they walk off, I have the feeling of being abandoned and I'm uneasy. Before I slip into a panic, the guy in the light blue shirt from the other table appears.

“I couldn't help noticing you. You look familiar to me.”

As soon as he speaks, it's obvious he's American.

“I'm American.” I reply as if to say, “Maybe that's it.”

“I'm American as well.” He smiles a charming, handsome smile. “I'm here doing some post-graduate work at University College Cork.”

“Ah, that explains it.” I say smiling back. “You don't look like a local.”

He tilts his head in a questioning gesture, “Do I look *that* out of place?”

“No, it's just your clothes are slightly...” Struggling to not say the wrong thing because his clothes are fine... “from not around here.”

He looks down at the front of his shirt then back at me, “I'm Paul. I hope that was a compliment and not an insult.”

I feel heat radiating as my face flushes so I awkwardly gesture to Declan's empty chair, “Would you like to sit a minute?”

“Just a minute, I wouldn't want your boyfriend to come back and think I'm moving in on his girl.”

"Oh, Declan, he's not my boyfriend." Shaking my head, I take another sip.

As I say the words I wish I hadn't. I just telegraphed to this handsome stranger I'm available. There's a degree of safety in Paul thinking Declan and I are together.

"You look so familiar to me I thought maybe you and I had met at school." He says, taking a draw from his pint glass.

"Nope, I don't go to UCC. I don't get to Cork often at all. I usually stay in a small town in Roscommon called Boyle. I'm here visiting my cousin Sorcha. Her mom is my Dad's sister." I hope this guy isn't a stalker because I just told him too much personal information.

"Where are you from in the States?" Paul says as I look at his hand to see if he's wearing a ring. No ring visible, but that doesn't always mean they're single. It's all coming back to me. Being single and the games and all the other crap – I really don't feel like being single again.

I stop my train of thought long enough to answer him, "I live in North Carolina."

Paul's entire face lights up and he says, "Wilmington?"

I look at him with an expression I know is somewhere between perplexed and frightened. "Yes. I teach high school in Wilmington. Got my master's degree at UNC Wilmington."

"That's it! I teach at UNC Wilmington. You were an education major, weren't you?"

"Okay now you're freaking me out, Paul?" I say his name in a questioning tone to ask *Paul what?*

"Blair. Paul Blair."

I don't know what to say, but I'm curious. "Paul, I have to ask. How do you know I majored in Education? I did my masters work in Education."

Nodding his head as he takes another sip of his pint, "I was taking an elective class one semester. I think it was called Introduction to Shakespeare. There was a smaller class that always met in the room before my class. I'd see you coming out as I was going inside. I don't know how, but I found out it was a Masters level course. You had a bright red back pack and usually wore your hair in a ponytail.

"Wow. You've got a great memory. Any other details you care to share?"

Smiling, Paul says, "No, and I can see my photographic memory is getting me in trouble once again. Don't worry, I'm not a stalker. I have a gift. It serves me well usually, but sometimes I can come across wrong."

I tilt my head and allow my eyes to take another look at Paul. His face is friendly and he's definitely good looking. He's close enough for me to see his eyes are hazel. "You didn't come across wrong, Paul. You seem very nice. You surprised me, that's all."

From the corner of my eye I sense activity at Paul's table as his friends are standing to leave. Paul looks over and nods at them. Picking up his beer he takes the last sip of it and says to me, "It's been a pleasure finally meeting you....." He pauses and I jump in, "Gemma. I'm Gemma."

Paul reaches for his wallet, opens it and pulls out a business card. Turning it over he asks, "Have you got a pen?"

"I don't."

Looking around, he sees Yvonne walking by with an empty tray tucked under her arm and asks her for a pen. As he writes on the back of the card he says to me, "Gemma, if I haven't frightened you and if you're in Cork say in the next two months, I'd love to see you again. Maybe you'd like to go to lunch or out for a pint."

Handing me the card he smiles, "I won't ask for your number so you don't have to worry. You seem like a sweet person so I'll leave it up to you. Nice finally meeting you."

As he and his friends walk off I read the card. "Paul Blair – Associate, Department of Archaeological Studies University of North Carolina Wilmington." Turning it over, I read the number he's written on the back. It's obviously a Cork number.

Declan sees me eying the card as he returns with our drinks. Sitting down he notices Paul and his group of friends leaving. "They didn't upset you did they?"

I tuck the card in my purse and smile at Declan, "No, not at all. One of them is kind of an old acquaintance."

I take the shandy from his hand as he sits down and ask him, "Shall we drink to something?"

I lift my glass and think of what I'd like to drink to, but before I come up with a toast, Liam and Sorcha return from the restroom and Liam chimes in, "Slainté!"

Our glasses touch and Declan and I repeat, "Slainté!"

Chapter 3

Oh, thank goodness. Just a dream.

The first thought I have when I realize I wasn't rushing to return keys to a rental office. I was only dreaming. Dreaming about being at Myrtle Beach with Brad and hurrying to check out of the condo we rented before incurring a late check-out charge on our bill.

Damn it.

The second thought when I realize it's just a dream and Brad isn't with me anymore and never will be again.

Oh bugger.

My third thought as I look around Sorcha's flat – remembering where I am and how I spent the night on her sofa so she and Liam could have the bedroom. Bleary-eyed, I spot the clock on the wall. 5:01 am.

Not bad, but I'd hoped to sleep a little later since we were out until almost midnight. Rare for me these days.

Brad died in February and ever since, sleeping has been fitful at best. In the beginning, it was all I wanted to do. After the initial shock wore off and people returned to their *normal* lives, I crashed. I think I'd been running on pure adrenalin those first days. The adrenalin ran out and I hit hard. I couldn't eat a thing and sleep was all I wanted. I would wake up at noon and be ready to call it a night by seven o'clock.

As the days after Brads' death turned to weeks, I started getting back into a more acceptable routine, but I still wake up each night and lie staring at the ceiling. Sometimes I cry. Other times, I just stare and think.

Sorcha and Liam probably won't be up for a while. I glance down at my feet. Sitting on top of my blanket is Bono. He's sleeping soundly so I decide to try and do the same. I close my eyes and make a concerted effort to lull myself back to sleep by thinking sleepy thoughts, but as if to taunt me, I hear the first bird of the morning chirp.

Opening my eyes and looking to the clock – 5:15 am.

I guess to the Galway magpie five-fifteen is the official start of the day, regardless of whether it's a Sunday morning after a pub night Saturday.

I spot a copy of *Hello!* magazine on the coffee table. Stretching my arm while trying not to topple Bono off of my feet, I manage to snatch the magazine from the table. I only look at it a moment before conceding my eyes aren't awake enough to focus on reading so I toss it back on the table. At this, Bono's eyes open and his head pops up. Once eye contact has been made, I know it's over; I'm forced to get up and feed the kitty.

Bono is close on my heels as we tip toe into the kitchen. I stop in the middle of the room and put my hands on my hips surveying the layout. *If I were cat food, where would I be?* I begin opening cabinets as Bono purrs and aggressively rubs against my leg. Finally, I open the cabinet beside the stove and see a bag of cat food inside.

Bono acknowledges my discovery by purring louder. As he dives into the bowl while I try to pour the food, I can't help chuckling. I stand observing his glee for a few seconds then put the food back in the cabinet.

When I turn around, Liam is standing in the kitchen doorway watching me.

“Jesus, Mary and Joseph! Liam, you scared the feck out of me!”

In a defensive motion, Liam throws his hands up ready to block a punch, “Sorry Gemma, I thought I heard something in the kitchen. Why on earth you up so early?”

“I guess I was done sleeping. Besides, there's a magpie outside the window who felt I'd slept enough.”

He puts his hands down, walks past me, and begins making a pot of coffee. It's nice seeing how at home he is in Sorcha's place so I smile.

“What ya thinking that's funny?”

Keeping my voice low, “Just how nice it is Sorcha has met someone special.”

As he fills the coffee maker with water I acknowledge he really is a good looking guy and for all his volume last night, he obviously has a softer-spoken side to him.

“Will you ask her to marry you?” I say as I pull out a chair and sit down at the table. I’m surprised at my bluntness.

Pushing the on switch, he turns to me and says, “I've asked her to marry me every day since our first date. She tells me one of these days she'll get back to me.”

“That's kind of how it was with me and Brad too. She must be scared.”

“Scared of what? I've not given her a bloody reason to be scared.”

"That's what she's scared of. At least that's what I was scared of."

Joining me at the table he sits down. I'm comfortable with Liam so I continue. "Sometimes when you've had bad experiences or met the wrong person in the past, you keep waiting for the *Gobshite Moment*.

Seeing his perplexed look, I add, "You know; *Gobshite*. Socially inept. Initially a guy seems nice and normal, but then something happens or they do something so bizarre it breaks the deal. Like the time her date took her to a nice restaurant and then started picking his teeth with a matchbook at the table. Something happens and you know it's all wrong. Sorcha and I call it the *Gobshite Moment*."

Liam lifts his eyebrows as he considers what I've said then replies, "Well, I've not done anything she's called a *Gobshite Moment* yet, but I'll be careful."

Liam walks over and takes two mugs down from the cabinet and pours the piping hot coffee. He looks over his shoulder, "Milk and sugar?"

"Just milk."

As he carries our mugs back to the table and sits down, I take one from his hand and begin blowing to cool the coffee. Before I take a sip, I glimpse over my mug and say, "She's close, Liam. I've never seen her like this before. She's close."

He takes a deep sip of his coffee, smiles a big smile and says, "Yeah, I know."

When Sorcha finally wakes up, I've already showered and gone down the street to buy the morning paper. I love getting the morning paper in Ireland. At home I'd simply log on my computer and pull up the news online, but here there's something special about getting the paper. Upon my return, I find Sorcha seated at the kitchen table looking a bit fatigued from last night.

"Good morning, Sorcha, how ya feeling this morning?"

"Oh, ya know. Like I should have switched to a shandy like you did, but a little breakfast will perk me right up."

How did she know I switched to a shandy? I must really be predictable. Note to self, try and be a little wilder.

Looking at me Liam asks, "You can come to Declan's for brunch, can't ye?"

"You guys were serious about that last night?"

"Absolutely. Declan can cook. His parents are both chefs at Jury's. Aye he's an awesome cook, you have to come. Sure he's probably up cooking now. He'd be sad if ye didn't come."

"Well, as long as I am on the road by half one. It's a good ride back to Boyle and you know Grandma and Grandpa will have tea waiting for me."

We drive over to Declan's in Liam's car. As we leave the city and get closer to Salt Hill I stare out the back window at the beautiful scenery. I wonder if the people who live here truly appreciate how beautiful Ireland is. I take a quick peek down to make sure my camera is close at hand. Lately, I've felt like taking pictures. I've always been a shutter bug, but taking pictures has been something I've especially enjoyed since I arrived.

As the car turns onto the gravel drive to Declan's house, one thing becomes apparent -Declan isn't struggling to get by. His house is a sprawling bungalow situated on a point overlooking the water. Curiosity gets me, "Is this Declan's family home?" Surely he can't live in this big house all by himself.

Sorcha leans across Liam to sound the horn announcing our arrival and casually says, "Nope, Declan had it built himself. He's got a wicked awesome job. The youngest Chief Financial Officer for Kingsley International. He's a business wonder-boy."

Kingsley International? It doesn't sound familiar, but to be only thirty and the CFO of anything international is pretty impressive.

Liam is his boisterous self as we enter and exclaims, "Wow, something smells wonderful. I'm so hungry, I could eat the arse off a farmer through a tennis racquet."

Declan appears wearing a bright green apron with the words, "When Irish eyes are smiling there's usually something cooking," printed on the front. I giggle and instantly he glances down at the apron. Blushing slightly, he looks back up and smiles. "It was a Christmas gift from mum."

"It's lovely."

I continue into the kitchen and settle myself on a stool at the counter. Sorcha and Liam climb up on the stools beside me and Liam booms, "Well, what's for brunch, Declan?"

"I'm making a frittata."

"A fri wa wah?" Liam says in a playful voice.

Turning to me Declan says, "Gemma, you know what that is, don't you?"

I bat my eyes and use my best Southern belle drawl. "I do, but back home in North Carolina we just say it's an eggy mess."

Declan returns to the stove - looking like a natural in the kitchen, he deftly cracks open the eggs using just one hand. It's obvious his parents shared their love of the culinary arts with their only son. Being in the kitchen puts a bounce in his step and I surmise cooking must be an outlet for him.

I'd imagine being so young and successful, cooking must be a form of relaxation. A stress release. Another thought that pops in my head - Why isn't there a Mrs. Gallagher or at least a hot girl friend? I mean, he's got a lot going on for himself. He's smart, handsome, financially well-off, and seems to be a genuinely nice guy.

Why am I wondering about his status? Am I interested for general knowledge or am I asking for myself? Wow, the inner thoughts are running wild this morning.

Sorcha snaps me out of my pensive mood when she pops off the stool and says, "Come on Gem, I want to show you around Declan's bungalow."

"I'd love to see it. Is it okay with you, Declan?"

Looking up from his work he grins and says, "Yes, it's absolutely okay and thanks for asking." Giving a broad grin to Sorcha he adds, "It's so nice to have someone with manners around."

"Oh, feck Declan. I've got fecking manners," Sorcha laughs as we leave the room.

The house is impressive. The view of the water from the living room is absolutely gorgeous. Sunlight dances across the water's sparkling surface as birds swoop down in search of a meal. Sorcha takes great pride in telling me how Liam and Declan met when they were nine years old and played on the same rugby team.

"I knew it!"

"You knew what?" Sorcha says tilting her head to the right.

"I thought Declan must have been athletic. That's all."

Sorcha looks at me with scrutinizing eyes and whispers, "Do ya fancy Declan?"

Her question surprises me so I wave my hand back and forth as if it's the most preposterous thing I've ever heard, "No, no, and NO. I simply noticed he looks like an athlete."

"Ok. Just checking,"

Continuing on, we find ourselves in his bedroom. The room is masculine, but still, there seems to be a bit of a woman's touch to the décor.

"And this is Declan's sanctuary." Sorcha pronounces. Leaning out of the doorway and speaking loudly for Declan's benefit she shouts, "This is Declan's bedroom where all the magic happens."

"Now, why did you do that Sorcha?"

"He loves when I have fun at his expense. Don't worry Gem, he's a good sport."

"I suppose, but geez."

Declan appears in the doorway behind us, but instead of the flush in his cheeks I saw a few moments ago, he has a devilish look in his eyes and turns to me. "You'll have to forgive your cousin Gemma, she's been madly in love with me for two years now but knows I'm more man than she can handle. That's why she's with Liam."

Without missing a beat, Sorcha counters, "I think it's the other way around, Declan. You've been pining away for me, suffering in silence while another man romances your dream girl."

Not knowing what to say I simply add, "Well, whatever you two tragic lovers have going on, your home is lovely, Declan."

"Thanks, Gemma. I appreciate that. Sorcha is always telling me her Yank cousin has great style."

Our eyes catch and I see he's sincere, not just saying it out of obligation. I say, "You're very kind, Declan."

From the corner of my eye, I see Sorcha's eyes flashing from him to me and back again. Before Sorcha's able to utter the words I see her thinking, Declan saves us. "Well, come now, brunch is ready. I thought we'd eat and then take a walk along the shore and enjoy this gorgeous day."

With that, he leads us from his sanctuary and back to the dining room where Liam is seated waiting to taste his first frittata.

Liam dominates the conversation as we eat, but nobody seems to mind. His cheerful, booming voice fills the room without being overwhelming. We all laugh and smile and for the first time in a long time, I'm genuinely having fun. I don't feel different. I feel like my old self and not the new grieving, pitiful Gemma I've been for the past months.

"Shall we go for a walk now?" Declan says as he pushes back his chair.

"But what about the dishes? I don't mind staying behind and cleaning up," chimes Sorcha.

Turning to Liam with a look that says, *Follow my lead, Liam,* she continues, "The two of us will clean up. Declan worked so hard he deserves a break and Gemma's never been here before so she should go and walk the shore. We'll stay and do the dishes, won't we Liam?"

Liam is momentarily confused and disappointed, but catches on. His eyes widen with mischief, "Ah yes, Gemma, you go and let Declan show you around. We've seen it all before."

And with that, Declan removes the apron, walks over to my chair, and as he helps me up whispers, "I don't think we have a choice." It's my turn to blush now. My face reddens as I sheepishly follow Declan out the door.

We start down the path leading to the shore in silence. I know I'm tailing a little too closely because I nearly slam into Declan when he stops abruptly. Turning to me he picks up my hand, leans in and whispers, "They can see us from the front window. This will give them something to talk about."

Looking into his eyes, I sense him moving in closer. Oh my gosh, is he? Is he about to kiss me? Now I'm looking at his mouth. His lips look very kissable. But wait, he wouldn't do that. He's too proper. Declan's a gentleman from everything I've seen. He wouldn't be so brash or bold. Would he?

Just as I'm resigned to the fact I'm about to be kissed for the first time since… Well, since Brad, I panic. My heart's pounding. I hear the blood in my ears. I'm not ready for this. Not yet, not now.

Declan is as close to me as possible when his hand reaches up and tenderly brushes a piece of hair from my forehead and tucks it behind my ear.

I'm still conscious, but barely aware as he tips his head, looks at me and grins. "That will keep them talking for hours."

Releasing my hand he turns and walks towards the shore. I gaze over my shoulder to see if he's right about Sorcha and Liam. The moment I turn around, I spot Sorcha diving below the window. I look back at Declan, who is now a few steps ahead, with new appreciation. He may be quiet, but he's a keen observer.

Catching up to him I ask, "How did you know they'd be watching?"

"Didn't you see Sorcha's eyes darting between us when we were in my room?"

"I did notice that. Sorry, she means well."

"Oh, I know that. She's been trying to fix me up with various friends since the day she and Liam started dating."

"Has she had any success yet?" I shock myself at my prying question.

Declan takes my elbow to guide me over a rocky area and smiles down at me, "No. She means well, but I guess I'm just not ready yet."

As we make our way to surer footing he releases my elbow. That was nice. Wait, why did I have that thought? Maybe because he's a gentleman. That must be it. It was a refreshing gesture. But it came so naturally to him. As if... as if he cares about me.

After a brief silence, I ask, "What do you mean you're not ready yet?"

"Well, Miss O'Connor, I think Liam and Sorcha were eager for you and me to meet because we have something in common.

"We do?"

"We do. You see Liam was best man at my wedding seven years ago."

For a moment I'm not comprehending what he's saying. If he got married seven years ago, where's Mrs. Gallagher?

Stopping, he looks into the distance as if trying to find the words out on the water. "My wife died four years ago of leukemia."

I wince at his words, "Oh, my God. I'm so sorry."

After what feels like a minute of silence, I reach up and pat his arm, "Now I know why you know it sucks."

Without another word he glances down and smiles, gesturing with his head to keep walking - we do. We don't say anything else until we're almost back to the house. I'm enjoying the silence and the company of a man. Declan makes me feel safe with him and now that I know his story, I somehow feel he's my friend.

As we approach the house, he takes my hand again and says, "Thanks for walking with me. It means a lot to me."

I must have a curious expression on my face because he smiles and lets out a slight laugh. "I don't get to take walks with beautiful women very often."

Looking down at the ground, searching for words again, he lifts his head and looks into my eyes, "Hey, I know we just met, but if you ever need to talk, I'm here. I know our situations are different, but I have an idea what you're going through."

His blue eyes are sincere and I feel the urge to hug him, but I don't know why. Maybe because I miss being held, maybe because he understands or maybe because it's so nice to meet a gentleman. Before I can say anything he leans in and hugs me.

Holding on awkwardly, at first I'm uncomfortable, but I find myself letting go, hugging him back and letting his strength pour into me as I bury my face in his chest.

"If you're like me, you miss the hugs. A lot."

Letting go I look up at him. A tear escapes and rolls down my cheek as I answer, "I think I'm a lot like you."

Chapter 4

Waking up, I roll over and peek at the clock. Seven-thirty.

Yes! Later than yesterday at Sorcha's. A small victory to start this Monday.

Stretching, I can see the room isn't very bright. It must be a misty morning.

I throw on my robe and walk out of the bedroom to the main room. The tiny cottage is cozy and charming – this place is perfect for me. I glance down, and for Tippy too.

The black and white Border collie looks up at me licking his chops to say, *Oh yes, breakfast-time*. Tippy is Grandma and Grandpa's dog and he is the smartest animal I've ever known. I think that's part of the reason they let him stay with me. He looks out for me almost like a person would.

Brad died in February so I took a month off before I decided to get back to teaching. I returned in April and struggled through the last month of school. My students were wonderful and understanding, but I was half way through my first day back when I knew it was too soon. I was only going through the motions and I was scared. I knew I needed a change of scenery so I called Mom and Dad that night and told them I was thinking of spending the summer in Ireland. They both said, "That's a great idea!" at the same time.

I bought the plane tickets the next day and marked the calendar. I at least had something to look forward to.

When I first arrived, I must have looked rather pitiful. Grandma only wanted to feed me and Grandpa only wanted to tuck money in my pocket. "Go get yourself a soda," he'd say.

They were so concerned, but after a few days of their worried looks and heavy sighs, I was feeling suffocated. I couldn't have been more relieved when at Sunday dinner that first week Uncle Tom suggested I stay at his cottage on the lake.

"You know Gemma, I've been so busy at the chemist shop lately the cottage isn't used much anymore. Would be grand to have someone stay there to keep the pipes working and prevent the place from looking abandoned, how'd ya like to stay out there and mind it for me this summer?"

Aunt Francie smiled and said, "That's a wonderful idea Tom. You're always saying you mean to let it out during the busy season since you rarely get to use it anymore. Why, Gemma would be the perfect tenant and she'd keep it up for us."

Uncle Tom's an avid fisherman and he bought the cottage at Lough Key when the kids were small as a place he could get away and relax. When the boys were young, they'd take long fishing weekends, just the guys. But lately with Fergus off at school and Sorcha moved away, there's only Martin at home and he's busy with football - not interested in fishing with his Da.

"Are you sure you won't be wanting to use the cottage, Uncle Tom?" I said it as if I didn't care one way or another, but I really wanted to stay there.

"Nah, nah, I've got so much going on in town. Besides, even if I did get a chance to fish it would probably be only a couple hours. You'd be doing us a favor."

"Well that settles it, Tom." Aunt Francie turned to my Grandmother who looked like she'd been out maneuvered and was losing her prize boarder, "Mary, isn't that lovely? Now Gemma will be out of your way, but still close enough to pop in for meals."

Grandma looked at me and seeing I was happy with the arrangement looked down a moment and said, "Will you at least take Tippy over with you at night? I'd feel much better and I know your Ma and Da would too if you had company."

I couldn't argue with that. Tippy is no bother and is actually very sweet. Besides, he does make me feel safer.

The next day Tippy and I arrived at Lough Key and made ourselves at home.

The cottage is cozy. It sits on the edge of the lake surrounded by tall cypress trees. It has a stone fireplace and a tin roof, two rooms and a loo with a shower. There's what I call a kitchenette with a nice cooker and small fridge to one side of the main room, a drop leaf table, a love seat and a recliner – perfect for me.

I walk to the sink and fill the kettle for tea then make my way to the cupboard where I keep the dog's food and pour a small amount into his bowl. Tippy darts toward the bowl as if he hasn't eaten in weeks as I turn on the radio. The cottage has most modern conveniences, but no television.

I decide to make a hard-boiled egg and bread for breakfast this morning. Grandma sent some brown bread home with me after tea last night so I turn on a pot to boil as the radio blasts a Robbie Williams song.

Tippy and I take a stroll around the lake before I head back to shower and get dressed. I promised Grandma I'd help in the office today. She's been trying to cut back her hours at O'Connor Taxis. I really don't want to, but she seemed happy I suggested coming in and working with her.

When Tippy and I walk in, Grandma is already busy on the phone with her large ledger book in front of her. As soon as she sees us she wraps up her call, "Aw, ya look grand this morning. Ready for fun?"

Fun is not exactly how I'd describe a day at O'Connor Taxis, but I guess I'm ready.

"Yep, Tippy and I are reporting for duty."

O'Connor Taxis was started by my Grandpa's father in the 1950s. He had one old DeSoto that he drove all over the city and countryside. Grandpa took over the business when his Dad got too old to handle the work. I think Grandpa was sad my dad decided to immigrate to America instead of staying in Boyle. He must have had dreams of his son taking over the family business just like he did.

You wouldn't think there would be much need for taxis in a small town, but there's always demand. Folks that don't have cars or elderly who don't drive anymore who need to get around keep Grandpa and his drivers busy all day and into the night.

A couple years back, Grandpa added a coach bus and each morning the O'Connor coach leaves town heading for Dublin. It was a big deal the first day he added the Dublin express. People drew numbers to be on the first trip and the Chamber of Commerce had a big celebration.

The people of Boyle now had a bus going to Dublin daily and folks from all the nearby town lands would wait at the top of the Crescent by the clock in town to travel into the city. The bus and taxis have made a lovely living for my Grandparents, but who knows what will become of it when they decide to retire.

"What can I do to help, Grandma?" I know she won't let me help with the books and I ask her this question already knowing most likely what her answer will be.

"Well dear, if you could sit at the phones and take calls then radio the drivers with the fares that would be perfect."

"No problem, Grandma. Deidre not coming in today?"

Deidre is the daughter of one of the drivers. She comes in and helps a few days a week while she attends beauty school.

"No, she's taken a long weekend and gone to a concert down in Cork. I think she's coming back today."

I sit down at the desk beside the phone and wait.

Mondays are busy at O'Connor's so time sails by for me. It isn't very challenging work, but it keeps me busy and prevents my mind from wandering. Before I know it, I'm picking up my purse to head back to the cottage.

"Will ya stay for tea, Gemma?" Grandma calls from the back office.

"No thanks, Ma'am. Not this evening. I've got to take Tippy for a nice long walk and I'm hoping to get some pictures of the sunset out at the lake."

"Ah, ya love taking pictures don't ya? You're always the one with the camera at the ready."

"Yes, I am. Ever since you gave me that old Polaroid when I was little, I've loved taking pictures."

"Well enjoy the sunset."

She lifts her head from her work and peers over her glasses. "You know, you should talk to Brendan O'Neill about entering some of your pictures in the Arts Festival coming up next month. I bet you're not too late to add an entry or two."

"Nah, I just take pictures for fun."

"But I've seen your pictures, they're quite good. I'll talk to him myself then."

My grandmother can be persistent so I simply leave her comment hanging and bid her goodnight. I know she's made up her mind so I make a mental note to choose a few of my favorite pictures and be prepared for Mr. O'Neill's request for my submissions.

One thing I've learned in life is to pick my battles.

Chapter 5

As the weeks go by, I'm spending more and more time taking pictures. Boyle is an amazingly beautiful town with so much to photograph, I start to plan my days around photography.

Mornings are spent capturing sunrise. I start first at the lake and move on through the Forest Park. Evenings the light is breath-taking as the sun sets beyond the Curlew Mountains. Daytime, the town is a beehive of activity and the pastels of the buildings and the brightly colored shop signs draw me to capture the day-to-day lives of the town's people.

Grandma and Grandpa initially were concerned about me spending so much time alone, but I put them at ease when I began showing them the pictures. They cheered immensely when I joined the Boyle Camera Club and began getting out and spending time with people instead of Tippy.

I'm absorbed in my oldest hobby and it's therapeutic for me. Looking at old familiar sites from different angles and seeing locations I'm well acquainted with through the camera's lens with fresh perspective invigorates me. In the evenings, I rush home to download my days' work.

One afternoon, I spent two hours taking pictures of the Boyle Abbey – the shadows and light hit the arches and crevices of the ancient stone edifice in the most spectacular way. With each picture I took, I'd see another angle or perspective I simply had to capture.

It's a genuine labor of love and I find myself, dare I say, excited to get up in the morning. I never imagined feeling this sensation again, but

I've found something, however small, to look forward to and somehow I no longer feel as if I'm only going through the motions.

One Sunday evening at dinner, my cousin Fergus was visiting and with a mouth full of spuds he asked, "What are ya doing with all the pictures you're taking?"

"Nothing," I said.

I'd never given it consideration, so I had no good answer.

Sipping his water and swallowing his food, Fergus pointed and said, "Nah, ya can't just do nothing. You need to post em and share em. You're a bloody awesome photographer, you should at least put them on one of those photo sites or better yet, start your own website."

As soon as the words left his mouth he was reaching for the pot roast and carrots, but his suggestion struck me like a bolt of lightning.

I kept a blog while Brad was deployed so I knew how to find my way around creating a website. Maybe Fergus' idea wasn't such a crazy one. That evening when I returned to the cottage at Lough Key, I began creating my own photography website, PhotosbyGemma.com.

It only took a short time to get it up and running. My uncle's friend at the print shop made me some business cards using one of my favorite pictures I'd taken of the Boyle Abbey as the background and voilà! I'm in business and preparing for my first exhibit at the Boyle Arts Festival.

"Hey, Gem!" Sorcha beams on the other end of the phone. "Ma tells me ya got some of your pictures on display at the festival this year. That's fecking great!"

"Yep, Mr. O'Neill convinced me to enter a few of my better shots." I say with tongue firmly planted in cheek since I know Grandma had more to do with my entry than Mr. O'Neill's convincing me.

"Well, listen, we're going to come for the last weekend of the festival. It will be good craic."

Everything is good craic with Sorcha, but I love that about my cousin.

"I'm glad you'll be coming. Tell Liam I'm looking forward to seeing you both."

"I will and maybe we'll have a party out at your fancy cottage on the lake."

"The more the merrier, the sofa is a pull out and the recliner, well, it reclines. You and Liam are more than welcome to crash with me and Tippy."

"We'll see ya soon then. Bye for now." I hear Sorcha hang the phone up before I can say goodbye, but that's pretty standard for our conversations. When Sorcha is done talking, she's done talking.

I finish adding a few more pictures to my website and call it a night. Walking into the bedroom, I think of Brad as I pull down the covers and crawl into bed. I can remember his smile, but the image is starting to fade. It's been over five months since I last saw his face as we talked on line. He was excited to be coming home. If only I could see his face clearer in my mind, but inevitably the memory is beginning to fade.

I open the nightstand drawer and pull out the picture of Brad I took at Myrtle Beach. I stare at it in hopes it will help me to remember him better. Thank goodness I took so many pictures. I can't bear the thought of the memory of his face becoming less clear in my mind. I struggle to see him as he was, but my mind won't allow me to hold the image clearly and with time....

I interrupt myself as I begin to feel a tear welling in my eye.

Stop, Gemma. Brad would be very proud of you right now. You're enjoying your hobby, you've got an exhibit in an arts festival and you've started your own website. Look at your accomplishments and be happy. He'd want that.

I give his picture a little kiss and slip it back into the nightstand drawer. "Goodnight, my handsome Brad. I love you and I miss you."

I slide down into bed, reach for the light switch and lie quietly in the dark until Tippy climbs up with me right on cue. It's as if the dog knows I need a hug.

Chapter 6

Friday is the big event at the King House where my pictures are on display. It's exciting having my pictures included with the art and photographs comprising the visual arts exhibition at this year's festival.

King House was built in the early eighteenth century and was the home of Sir Henry King and his family. The King family was one of the most wealthy and powerful families in Ireland.

Later, in the nineteenth century, King House was converted into an army barracks and after that, fell into a state of disrepair. When I was an infant, King House stood behind scaffolding as renovations were made to revive the old building. Today, it's restored to its grandeur and is once again a beautiful, stately Georgian home and landmark the town is quite proud of.

I decide to wear a simple black, sleeveless, V-neck crepe dress with the pearl earrings Brad gave me for my twenty-fifth birthday. I put a few curls in my hair and stand back to look at myself in the mirror.

The dress is a little looser than it was when I bought it, but it's not hanging off of me as my mother would no doubt claim.

I tilt my head, scrutinizing and considering my hair. It looks nice hanging down over my shoulders, but my earrings are hidden. Compromising, I pull the front pieces of hair back in a jeweled hair clip leaving the majority of the curls to fall softly.

I put on some red lipstick and wrap the soft blue pashmina I purchased in town around my shoulders. Standing in front of the mirror I take one last glance at myself when I feel a wave of emotions about to hit.

I loved to dress up for Brad. From time to time he had formal events he was required to attend. I sigh thinking about how handsome he was in his Marine Corps dress blues. Gosh, he was hot.

I grin remembering his look of approval the first moment he'd see me all dressed up to go out with him. His expression couldn't have been more genuine. His entire face lit up, his eyes would sparkle - it made me fall in love with him all the more.

I loved being the girl who made Brad light up like that.

This is going to be harder than I thought, but I can't think about that right now. I'm going to have a wonderful time visiting with friends and meeting new people and it will be a fun evening. If I repeat this over and over I may actually convince myself to have a good time.

The photography displays are in one of the large rooms off of the grand hall. I've been to King House several times, but this evening it's even more elegant than I remembered. The string quartet and piano playing by the ornate fireplace add ambiance and richness to the occasion. I scarcely believe I am one of the *artists* being honored in these regal surroundings.

I make my way to my pictures which have been beautifully matted and mounted. I'm particularly proud of the black and white photo of Boyle Abbey and the color picture of the clock at the top of the Crescent in town. Ordinarily, I would have ordered the prints online, but Uncle Tom insisted on developing them at the pharmacy. He could see I was reticent so he handled them himself.

I spot Uncle Tom and Aunt Francie heading my way and Uncle Tom is carrying a glass of champagne in each hand. He hands me one of the glasses when they arrive and says, "Cheers, Gemma! I say, you look stunning this evening and your photos are magnificent."

"Thanks Uncle Tom, and I have to give you credit. They really turned out nicely. You did a marvelous job. The prints are brilliant."

He smiles and says, "Slainté! Here's to my beautiful and talented niece. May God have all good things ahead for ye."

Before I can finish taking the sip of champagne, I hear Liam Tully's deep voice above the din as he and Sorcha approach. Trailing a couple of paces behind wearing a pair of jeans, a light blue dress shirt, and a navy blue blazer is Declan Gallagher.

"Well, well. If it isn't the female Ansel Adams!" Liam teases as he leans in and kisses my cheek.

"Hope ya don't mind Gem, I persuaded Declan to come with us." Sorcha whispers in my ear as she greets me with a peck on the cheek as well.

Finally joining us, Declan grins and says, "Hope you don't mind my tagging along Gemma, but Sorcha has been talking up the Boyle Arts Festival for weeks and convinced me to experience it myself."

Before I can speak, he picks up my free hand and gently kisses it and as he puts it back down gives a little squeeze and says softly and directly, "You look lovely."

"Thanks, Declan."

Thanks, Declan? Thanks, Declan? A handsome man pays me a compliment and that's all I come up with?

Before I let my inner voice take over, Sorcha exclaims, "Wow, Gem! I knew you were talented, but I had no idea just how talented. These are absolutely amazing. Brilliant!"

She pulls me closer to the pictures and says, "You look beautiful. So proud of you."

Behind us, I hear Liam taking care of the introductions between Declan and my aunt and uncle, but I'm taken aback by Sorcha's words. It wasn't so much her words, but her sentiment. Her eyes were telling me more than her words and I knew she meant she was proud of how I've been getting on and moving on. I feel tears in my eyes and she wraps her arm around my shoulder and hugs me. Our heads touch for a moment and then the moment is over and Sorcha is back to her old self.

"Feck, I had no idea my cousin was such a brilliant photographer, excuse me, artist. Isn't she brilliant Declan?"

"Aye, indeed. You should be very proud Gemma."

Declan steps closer, studying the pictures. The display is a compilation of several of my favorite places around Boyle. In addition to the clock at the Crescent in town and the Abbey, there's one of the old stone bridge at the Boyle River, a picture of some sheep near Cavetown Lake, a black and white picture of the gates at Rockingham and my favorite shot of some wild flowers in front of the abandoned church at Easter Snow.

After what seems like several minutes, Declan steps back crosses his arms and says, "I'm trying to think of what *you* were thinking when you took each one of these."

I don't say anything for several seconds, mainly because I haven't a clue what to say so I take a sip of champagne in hopes the bubbles might jolt my mind into action.

Alas, nothing pops into my head, but mercifully Declan lifts his right hand to his chin pondering and says, "You're an observer. You're a bit quiet, but that's nothing to do with being shy. Mind you, you're a bit shy, but you're more about taking things in and thinking about what you see. It shows in your pictures."

"Really, you can see all this in a few pictures?" Okay, my mouth still works and those were fairly intelligent words I managed to string together.

"Well, Miss O'Connor, I guess knowing you for all of a couple days now, I've got a slight advantage, but yes. You see, I can tell by the subject of these pictures that they've been photographed thousands and thousands of times. However, you, with the lighting and shading and angles, somehow manage to show them from a unique perspective. You're an observer."

Returning with champagne glasses in hand is Liam. I watch him hand Declan a glass as I tilt my head in consideration. I'm still thinking of what he said when Sorcha holds up her glass and toasts "To my cousin Gemma. She's talented, beautiful and brilliant!"

I'm not used to being the center of attention so I demurely dip my head, but when I look up Declan is looking directly at me. He tips his glass towards me and drinks to the toast. Feeling my cheeks getting red, I do the only thing I know to do. I tip back my glass and take a sip.

Chapter 7

Saturday mornings used to be for sleeping in. When Brad's schedule permitted he'd come from his base in Cherry Point to see me in Wilmington. He'd arrive late on a Friday night so we'd stay in bed until at least noon - sipping my tea in bed with my handsome, strong Brad beside me.

Saturdays are always tough for me now, but I'm trying not to dwell on the past. I was once in the Elf Inn, a pub in the town of Elphin, when an old man I'd never seen before turned to me and said, "You know the trouble with the Irish? They're always living in the past."

That was it. That was all he said before going back to drinking his pint. I've always been one of those girls to look for the deeper meaning. I've never believed things happen by coincidence or by fluke. I've heard those called God winks. Those moments in life where it's as if God himself is winking at you and letting you know he's up there watching.

It was such an odd moment, but his words were profound so I took the old man's message to heart as something I was meant to remember. This morning, I find myself thinking of his declaration.

Maybe he was right. It's okay to look back, I just can't stare.

I shake off my thoughts of the old man in the pub and reflect on last evening as I drink my tea. It was a fun night at King House and I was surprised I enjoyed myself as much as I did. I was nervous at first, but everyone was so jovial and upbeat, it made me relax and forget my nerves.

Today promises to be much more casual. Sorcha, Liam and Declan spent the night in town at Aunt Francie's and Uncle Tom's, but tonight we plan to stay out late and return here.

Putting my empty cup down on the table, I look around the cottage, "I'm not sure where we're going to put everybody Tippy, but we'll figure things out, won't we?"

Tippy looks up with his big brown puppy dog eyes as if he understands, but I know he only wants me to feed him. I get up and feed him, wash my empty tea cup, and as I'm returning it to its place in the cupboard the phone rings.

"Hey Gem, we'll be by in ten minutes to pick you up. We want to get to the Moving Stairs and grab a table before they fill up. Lots of great bands playing there today for the festival."

"Okay, Sorcha. I've already showered and dressed so I'm ready."

Hanging up, I look down at what I'm wearing. A pair of black jeans, black ballerina flats and a royal blue jewel neck long-sleeved t-shirt. Brad always liked me in royal blue, he said it made my eyes sparkle.

Sigh, stop living in the past.

I hear the words in my head, but they're in the old man's voice so I smile.

Tippy and I are outside when I see the steel blue Mercedes driving towards the cottage. I take note of the car since I know it's not Sorcha's and I've been in Liam's Toyota. This must be Declan driving. As they pull into the drive, I see Declan behind the wheel wearing a pair of aviator sunglasses.

A thought pops into my mind, Brad used to wear aviator sunglasses. An image of my handsome Brad flashes through my mind. It's the little, unexpected things that knock me off balance. I take a deep breath and exhale slowly.

Sending Tippy back into the cottage I grab my purse and head to the back door of the car when the window slides down and Sorcha leans her head out.

"You're riding shotgun, Gem. Liam and I are back here, love."

If I didn't know better, I'd swear Sorcha is trying to force me upon Declan. Okay, I'll play along. I mean, it's harmless, right? I'm going back to America in a couple weeks and he's fun to look at. I'll be honest with myself about that. I can appreciate a handsome guy, no harm in that whatsoever.

Climbing in the front seat I say, "Thanks for coming to get me. I could have driven myself, but I appreciate you coming out to get me."

"Not a problem at all," Liam declares from the back seat. "Parking will be a fit in town so we'll just leave the car back at Sorcha's parents and walk to Moving Stairs. Besides, this way Declan knows how to get us back here when we're too shite-faced to remember later tonight."

"That's my man, always thinking ahead," Sorcha says sarcastically as she pats Liam's knee.

"It's lovely out here Gemma. I see why you like staying in the cottage." Declan turns to me and smiles.

"Yes, it's such a peaceful spot. I've certainly enjoyed my time recovering here."

Recovering? Where did that come from? It's not like I had surgery.

"The country is a beautiful place for getting over life's tragedies. I know my bungalow on the water has been tremendously soothing for me."

As he says this I almost wince because I'm reminded he's felt this way too. He's lived through these moments. Moments of firsts. The first time going out with friends, the first time going out to eat, the first time going to a party – without that special person.

Note to self; you haven't cornered the market on grief. Lots of people have pain and sorrow they're living with and recovering from. It's okay to say recovering. Losing a loved one is the most devastating thing anyone can live through. Recovering is the perfect word.

❖

The Moving Stairs pub sits at the top of the Crescent in town and it's a favorite place for music, food, and as Sorcha would say, craic. We walk in as the first band is setting up to perform and just in time to grab the last open booth.

Sorcha and Liam climb in one side so I head to the other. Declan slides in beside me and signals to the waitress who appears and immediately seems to be flirting with Declan.

She's just being friendly, it's her job and how she gets good tips. Why are you feeling.... feeling... what *are* you feeling? Are you, jealous? Should she really put her hand on his shoulder? Is that necessary? No, you're just imagining she's being flirtatious.

"A shandy, Gemma?" Snapping out of my thoughts, I hear Declan ask again, "Gemma, you want a shandy?"

"Oh yes, thanks. That would be nice."

When the waitress returns with our drinks I'm busy studying the menu. I didn't eat breakfast and it's almost one-thirty - my stomach is growling. I know what I want, but I keep studying the menu hoping something healthy will appeal to me. I don't want Declan to think I'm a pig.

I'm hungry, not a pig and why do I care what he thinks of my eating habits?

Sorcha and Liam order first then the waitress turns and looks at me and Declan. He shifts in the booth and says to me, "Would you like the plaice?"

How did he know I was going to order plaice?

"Yes, I'll have the plaice with chips."

Declan turns to her and says, "Make that two."

My curiosity has the best of me now. "How did you know I was going to order that?"

"I'm an observer as well, Miss O'Connor."

"Hmm, well you're good at observing because I don't recall mentioning flounder or plaice or whatever you call your flat fish in Ireland."

"You didn't, I saw you studying the menu and your eyes locked in on the plaice."

Warm, I feel my face getting warm. I'm not at all deep and mysterious, I'm actually easy to read, an open book to this guy.

Thankfully, the band begins playing before I can come up with a pithy remark about plaice so I sit listening and sipping my shandy. Our food comes and I eat in the most lady-like manner I can considering my hunger. We listen to the band playing U2 and Snow Patrol cover songs as we finish our meals.

I'm much more relaxed now that the formal events surrounding my photographic entries in the festival are over. The mood is festive and I'm enjoying the atmosphere and company. For the first time in a long time, I'm light-hearted and carefree.

The pub is quickly becoming packed with people as day turns to evening. After my second shandy, I need to use the restroom so I lean in and whisper into Declan's ear, "I hate to bother you, but I need to head to the loo."

He steps out of the booth, "Me too. Great timing." He turns to Liam and Sorcha and says, "If you'll excuse me, I'm going to escort the lady to the loo." He places his hand on the small of my back lightly as he guides me through the crowded pub.

Brad used to do that. In fact, that was one of the first moments I knew Brad was special. He guided me through a crowd...... Stop, stop, stop looking back. He's not Brad. But he is a nice guy, isn't he?

Declan, now shouting over the band which has resumed, leans in and yells, "I'll be right here when you're done."

Sure enough, he's standing outside the ladies room door when I reappear. Once again, he guides me through the crowd and as I sit back down in the booth, Sorcha is looking at me like the cat who swallowed the canary. She doesn't speak, she only winks.

Next, I feel a kick on my shin under the table.

I glare at Sorcha.

Yes, Sorcha, I know what you're thinking - now knock it off.

The next band begins playing songs with a country flair. The pub goes mad when "Friends in Low Places" the Garth Brooks standard is played followed by an old Randy Travis tune, "Forever and Ever Amen." We're having a lot of fun and the crowd is really into it, but then the unexpected happens.

The female singer in the band steps up to the microphone and says, "Now, for a lovely song by Trisha Yearwood called, 'How Do I Live?' from the film *Con Air*."

I choke on my shandy when she says this. I swallow hard, place the glass on the table, and wipe my mouth with the back of my hand as the band begins the slow tune.

The weekend after Brad's funeral, I went home with my parents to spend a couple weeks with them. I was exhausted and all I wanted to do was sleep. Escaping my parent's deep concern for a while, I went up to my old bedroom, climbed into bed and turned on the television.

I began flipping through the channels and stumbled upon the movie, *Con Air*. Surely, this wouldn't be anything too deep and heavy. This would be an easy way to take my mind away for a while.

It was working for a while, until the end of the movie when this song came on. Without warning, the emotional flood gates gave way and I began sobbing. Not just crying, but gut-wrenching sobbing as I listened to the words I'd heard before, but now they meant something different to me.

It was like the lyrics opened the spout on a keg and everything came spilling out at once. To this day, I vividly remember crying harder than I'd ever cried before and sobbing so deeply it physically hurt.

The singer steps to the microphone and begins the sad lyrics and I brace myself for the inevitable wave of sorrow. It's just a song and she has a pretty voice, knock it off Gemma. Pull yourself together.

Sensing a change in me, Declan reaches over and puts his hand on my knee. Not in a copping-a-feel way, but in a comforting-gesture way. Abruptly, he grabs my hand and says to me, "I want to dance. Come on."

Dance? To this? Well, there *are* others slow-dancing, but this is the song I cried my heart out to. How on earth can I think of dancing? Yet, I'm getting up and following him. He's got my hand and is leading me to the dance floor. Oh my, I'm actually going to dance with someone...... someone who isn't Brad.

He lifts my right hand and puts his right hand lightly on my waist. My reflex is to place my left arm on his right shoulder. I look up at him, my eyes pleading, *Why are you doing this to me?*

Leaning closer, he says in my ear, "Hope you don't mind. I needed to get up and get moving. The words to this song kill me if I sit and listen to them."

"Me too. This song opens the flood gates for me." I reply sheepishly.

You did it again, Gemma. You're not the only person that's lost someone she loved. Declan lost his wife. This song is just as painful for him as it is for you. He gets that. He gets that about you too. He understands what you're going through.

I'm beginning to look at Declan differently now. He's farther along, but he's recovering too. I notice how it feels to be dancing with him. He's strong and it feels good to be with someone stronger than I am right now. I lean in and rest my head on his shoulder. He squeezes my hand and bending his head slightly, gently brushes his lips across my fingers in a soft kiss.

He completely understands.

Chapter 8

The moon is shining brightly on the lake as we pull up to the cottage. "Hey Gem, let's sit at the picnic table and star gaze like we did when we were kids. I bet we'll see a falling star for sure tonight."

"Great idea, Sorcha. Why don't you bring your bags in the house and I'll let Tippy out first."

I turn the lights on as I enter the house. Tippy is relieved I'm home or is about to be because he shoots past me and out the front door.

"Whoa there boy." Liam playfully shouts as he walks past Tippy.

"Hey Gem, I know you offered me and Liam your room for tonight, but that was before you knew we were bringing Declan so I'll understand if you prefer to keep your room. Liam and I can use the pull-out sofa. Declan can sleep in the recliner."

"Did I hear my name?" Declan walks in the house carrying a backpack over his shoulder.

"I was just telling Gemma that Liam and I will take the pull-out sofa and you can sleep on the recliner."

Declan eyes the recliner, walks over beside the chair and drops his backpack beside it on the floor.

I look at him and back at the chair and say, "I can't let Declan sleep in that chair. It's comfortable, but it's not built for a six-foot tall man. I'll sleep in the recliner and Declan can have the sofa. You and Liam take my room."

The words are still hanging in the air as I become aware of the implications of what I've said. Without thinking, I've offered to give away the comfort of my own room, my own PRIVATE room, to sleep in a faux-leather recliner in the same room as a man I hardly know..... A man who isn't Brad.

"God love ya Gem, you're a peach!" Liam blurts out in the split-second that's passed since I made my unforced error. He pushes his hips forward and begins rubbing his lower back with his right hand as he continues, "Sorcha and I appreciate you letting us sleep in your room. I need a nice firm mattress since my years of playing rugby. Isn't that right Declan?"

"Aye, yes. Liam took some nasty blows back when we were playing. Now, he's a wimp and needs to sleep on a special goose feather mattress to support his sorry aching arse."

Hearing Declan come as close to swearing as I've heard him the entire time, I laugh. He turns to me, "You think I'm kidding. He's soft. Not half the man he used to be."

"Aw, feck-off, Declan," Liam mutters under his breath as he heads to the kitchen and picks up the bottle of wine he and Sorcha brought. "Come on, let's head out to the picnic table and watch the stars."

"It's getting a little cool, let me grab my sweatshirt. I'll be right there." I go back in my room and pull Brad's gray USMC sweatshirt out of the drawer and begin walking back as I pull it over my head. When my head pops out and I'm standing in the front room, Sorcha and Liam are already outside. Declan is waiting for me.

"Hey, Gemma, you don't have to sleep in the recliner. I'll be cool for one night."

I lift my hair from inside the sweatshirt, flip it over my shoulders, and reply, "Really, it's no big deal, Declan. I've slept in it before, it's not that bad." Again, I give up comfort. Why am I so darn polite? I'm an over-achieving people pleaser! He said he'd be fine for one night.

"If you insist, but if you're uncomfortable with a strange man in the room you'd tell me, wouldn't ya? I don't think I snore and I promise I won't....." He trails off, searching for the right words. "I just want to assure you, I'm a gentleman. That's all."

He looks almost boyish as he speaks. He's worried about me being worried about him being inappropriate with me - I think.

"I know you're a gentleman, Declan. It's part of what makes you so charming."

I look down at my sweatshirt and see the Marine Corps emblem emblazoned on front. I instantly remember Brad, but look up at Declan and smile. "I feel safe with you."

I mean it. I feel safe with Declan. A man makes me feel safe. A tall, dark, strong, smart, handsome man makes me feel safe....... and he isn't Brad.

Outside I hear Sorcha call, "Hey Gem, grab the radio on your way out, would ya love? We need some music to go with our wine."

"No problem," I shout back, grabbing the radio and the camping lantern. Declan reaches for the door and again, places his hand on the small of my back to lead me. He's not joking about being a gentleman. He's quite good at it. Effortless with him.

Liam has already poured the wine into the small juice glasses from the cupboard and is looking up admiring the stars. "God, it's perfect out here at night, isn't it? No, ya can't see stars like this in Galway with all the city lights. Can ya, Dec?"

"Aye, so true, Liam. One of the things I love most about living on the water in Salt Hill is seeing the stars at night" he says as he sits down beside me on the picnic bench.

For a while we sit quietly, enjoying the wine, the stars and the soft music, but when "These Arms of Mine" by Otis Redding comes on the radio, Liam takes Sorcha's hand and without a word they get up and walk inside the house.

It's a beautiful song, but now Declan and I are awkwardly alone knowing full well what Liam and Sorcha are up to. Now what?

Mary Gemma O'Connor - now what are you going to do?

Think of something, Mary Gemma O'Connor.

"You know, my name is Mary Gemma O'Connor. Gemma is my middle name," I blurt out.

"Yep, named for my Grandmother." I blurt again.

I begin to fidget with the hem of my sweatshirt as I search for more brilliant tidbits to add to this intellectually stimulating conversation.

"Well, technically named for Mary, the mother of Jesus, but also Mary my Grandma O'Connor."

Where is this coming from? Why doesn't he say something? Why do I keep talking?

"Yep, when I was born, Grandma and Grandpa O'Connor came to America to visit. Originally, my name was going to be Gemma Mary, but when Grandma heard she said, 'No granddaughter of mine will be called that.' "

"Why? What's wrong with Gemma Mary?" Declan asks.

Finally, he's participating in this conversation.

"She told my parents, 'Now, ya can't be putting another name before the name of the Mother of our Lord, can ye?' That sort of settled the name. Mary Gemma it is. Who can argue with that, right?"

I can't see his face, but I hear him laughing. Is he laughing at the story or is he laughing at me. It's too dark, I can't tell.

"No, that's very sound logic. You can't argue with sound logic like that. Although, I do find it coincidental your Grandmother's name is Mary. Perhaps she was wanting a name-sake."

He grabs my hand, "Come on, let's take a little walk. I'll bring the lantern so we don't fall in the dark, Mary Gemma."

I can see his face now in the lantern light. He's being sarcastic, isn't he?

"Are you making fun of my name?"

"Not at all Mary Gemma. On the contrary, now that I know the full story of your moniker, I think I'll use it more often. It's not as formal as Miss O'Connor, but certainly not as informal as Gemma."

"Okay, now I know you're making fun of my name. Look I was just...."

Cutting me off, he finishes my sentence, "Making conversation. I know, I know."

"Well, yes. I was making conversation. I notice you don't often initiate conversations so I thought I would."

Gee, that sounded kind of harsh. He initiates conversations, just fewer when Liam is around.

"That didn't sound right. I mean when Liam is around, he and Sorcha seem to dominate conversations, in a good way."

"In a good way." He says, mocking slightly. "You don't initiate many conversations yourself. That is, when Liam and Sorcha are around, I should say. You should speak up a bit more yourself, I like hearing what you have to say, Gemma."

He takes my hand again leading me down to the water's edge. There's an old log lying on its side where he proceeds to sit down. Tapping the spot on the log beside him, he says, "Have a seat, Mary Gemma."

He holds the lantern so I can see the log below me and I sit next to him. "Thanks. Isn't the moonlight beautiful on the water?" I hear myself saying the words, but I'm not sure if this is my inner dialogue or I'm actually speaking.

We're quiet for a while. Watching the ripples in the water, the gentle lapping against the shore is the only sound. I'm completely at peace, for a change. After a moment, I feel Declan's gaze focused on me. Finally, he tenderly speaks, "You know, it *will* get easier with time. I've noticed an improvement just since the last time I saw you."

I know what he means, but I ask anyway, "What do you mean?"

"You looked terrified the night we went out in Galway, but last night and today, you looked confident. I think you had fun too. You're coming along, and it will get easier."

I pick up a stick from the ground and begin fiddling with it, peeling the bark away.

"Oh, that. Yeah."

"If you ever just want to talk, I meant what I said before. I'm happy to help. It kind of helps me too."

I've peeled all the bark from the stick so I toss it and wait to hear the tiny plop as it hits the water then I turn to face Declan, "Thanks. It's nice. This is nice. You're nice."

Nice? Nice? Well it is nice. He's nice and he understands.

Declan stretches his long legs in front of him before changing the subject. "So, I hear you're doing big things with your photography – I mean besides the Boyle Arts Festival."

"Oh yeah, I've started a website." Sitting up tall, I say the name. "PhotosbyGemma.com." Before he responds, I continue, "I've spent hours downloading tons of pictures I've taken since I got here. I've sold a few online and in town, and, I'm even going to be taking some pictures for the Boyle Tourism Board to use in advertisements. I've got a full schedule for the rest of the summer. I'm pretty excited about it all."

"That's grand, Gemma." He answers softly. I keep getting the feeling he wants to say something else, but he doesn't.

I look up and take note of the large number of stars visible in the sky tonight. With my head still tilted up, I add, "I've got to make it over to Castle Island before I go back to America. I want to get some early morning shots. The light is perfect early in the day for taking pictures on the island."

"Where is this Castle Island?" he says as he shifts to turn and face me.

I reach over and lift his hand. Folding his fingers so just his pointer finger is out, I direct his hand to point towards the lake. "It's over in that direction in the middle of the lake. It's too dark now, but there's a castle out there and a legend as well."

I put his hand back down on my lap, but I don't let go. We sit in the moonlight side by side not saying a word, with me holding his hand. Maybe it's for security, maybe because I can feel his strength, maybe because it's nice holding someone's hand again.

"Well, Miss O'Connor, it's getting late. We should head back now, shouldn't we?"

"Yes, I hope Liam and Sorcha have finished....well, hopefully they're asleep now."

Awkward, but hey, we're both grownups and we know what they were doing, right?

Declan helps me to my feet, picks up the lantern, and leads me by the hand back to the cottage. When we reach the door he stops, turns to me and says, "Oh, just so you know, you looked stunningly beautiful at the King House last night. Just so you know."

With that, he opens the door and I walk inside. I can't say a word. He's left me speechless.

I gather my pajamas which Sorcha so kindly left in the recliner with a blanket and a pillow and when I come out of the bathroom, I find Declan making the sleeper sofa into his bed.

He's wearing a pair of cotton pajama pants and a white V-neck t-shirt which really shows off the definition of his muscles.

Playing it cool, I climb into the recliner and toss the hand-knitted blanket over me. I must look pitiful trying to cover myself because Declan walks over and reaches for the blanket, "Here, I got it. Stay still. I'll cover ya."

I push the recliner back and he gently tucks the blanket all around me. He fluffs the pillow and I lift my head so he can put it behind me. "There ya go Miss Mary Gemma O'Connor, nice and snug. Sweet dreams Macushla"

And then it happens. He leans in and kisses me on the forehead.

A kiss on the forehead......hmmm.

He called me Macushla.

Macushla, that's Irish for *darling*.

A man, who isn't Brad, kissed me on the forehead and called me Macushla.

"Goodnight, Declan, and thanks again."

I shut my eyes, but my mind isn't ready to rest so I lie in my faux-leather recliner remembering the night. I can still feel Declan's kiss on my forehead as I drift off.

Chapter 9

Opening one eye, I see it's early morning. The room is no longer pitch black, but a dark blue. The sun will be appearing soon so I shut my eye and turn slightly to get more comfortable. I take a deep breath and as I breathe in I smell fresh coffee brewing.

I pop open both eyes now and look towards the kitchenette. It's Declan. He's wearing jeans and a polo shirt. Up and dressed before the sun?

As I begin stretching, he notices I'm awake, crosses the room and squats down beside the arm of the recliner. "Good morning sleepy head. You need to get up and get dressed," he whispers.

"What? Why?"

Gosh, he's awfully close for this early in the morning. Don't exhale Gemma. Whatever you do, don't exhale. You haven't brushed your teeth yet.

"It's going to be a beautiful sunrise so I thought we'd take advantage and go to Castle Island. I've got a thermos of coffee brewing and I see the row boat is down at the slip. Quick, throw on your clothes and we'll go."

He's really a morning person.

My clothes from the previous day are neatly folded on the coffee table. Not wanting to intrude on Liam and Sorcha's sleep, I shrug, take them into the bathroom where I brush my teeth and dress.

I comb through my hair and pull it into a pony tail. I have a small tube of peach- colored lip balm in the medicine cabinet so I sweep it across my lips. This will have to do for our morning excursion.

When I reappear he smiles, "Ah, Gemma how do you make it appear so effortless?"

Again, not sure if that is sarcasm or not.

"Not completely effortless, but thanks. Has Tippy been outside?"

"Fed and let loose for a quick wee in the yard. Come on now, we've got to move before we miss the sunrise."

I grab my camera case and ball cap from the peg by the door as we walk outside. I put the cap on, working my pony tail through the gap in the back, and Declan slips into his windbreaker as we amble down to the row boat waiting at the shore.

Declan rows us out onto Lough Key. I admire how easily he manages to row and speak without the slightest sign of being winded. He obviously keeps in shape.

"Do you work out?"

I roll my eyes at my ridiculous question. Of course he works out.

"We've a wonderful gym at my office and I run a couple days a week. I used to work out all the time when Liam and I played rugby."

"Ah. No wonder you make rowing look easy."

The morning is cool. Declan sees me shiver and my teeth chattering so he stops rowing to pick up the thermos of coffee. "Here, let me pour you some coffee to warm you up."

He opens the thermos and the steaming hot liquid flows into the plastic cup. He must have found the cup at the cottage, though I don't recognize it at all. I wrap my cold fingers around the mug and hold it until my hands begin warming. I blow a bit before I decide I can safely sip without burning my tongue.

He's studying me and once again, he puts down the oars, takes his jacket off and drapes it around my shoulders.

"You don't need to give up your jacket for me. I'll warm up soon."

"Actually, you're doing me a favor. That jacket was really hampering my rowing efforts," he winks and smiles at me.

"That's lovely and so is the coffee. It's colder this morning than I thought it would be, but I didn't want to barge into my bedroom for warmer clothes since Liam and Sorcha are still asleep."

"Yes, I considered that too. Hope you're not too cold, Gemma. I figure since Liam and Sorcha are young and in love they could use some time alone this morning."

"Yeah, smart thinking on your part, but then again I've been told you're brilliant."

Laughing at my comment, he says, "Well I don't know about that, but you got me thinking last night about seeing the sunrise on Castle Island." He pauses and looks at me. "Think I'll have a cup of coffee too. Okay if we stop a minute?"

"Absolutely. I can take a few pictures of the island from here."

I put my coffee down beside me and retrieve the camera from my bag. The sun is rising. The sky is lighter and painted with narrow streaks of pink and purple so I commence taking pictures. Declan doesn't make a sound, but I'm aware of him watching me. It's a bit unsettling at first. I'm not accustomed to being watched while I work, but in a minute or two I'm too involved in the pictures I'm taking to be distracted by his gaze.

After several minutes, I put the camera down on my lap. Declan's still looking at me so I smile at him. He really has a nice face. His jaw line is angular without being sharp or severe. His eyes are almost azure and the blue polo shirt he's wearing sets them off making the color more intense.

"Will you tell me the legend, Gemma?"

"Legend?"

"You said there's a legend on that island, remember?"

"Oh, that. The legend of Úna Bhán. Yes, it's the story of two lovers; really quite tragic."

"Have you time to share it with me?" Reaching over to me he slips his hands inside the jacket draped over my shoulders and pulls his sunglasses out of the pocket. The sun is rising higher and rather than turning the boat so the sun isn't in his eyes, he puts on the glasses.

Before I get too lost staring at Declan in his sunglasses, I start telling him the story of Úna Bhán.

"Well, the way I've heard it told is there was a chieftain of Moylurg in North Roscommon, a Celtic king by the name of MacDermot who had a beautiful daughter named Úna Bhán. She was named that because of her long blonde hair. MacDermot had a neighbor by the name of Tomás Láidir Costello. Tomás and Úna Bhán fell madly in love with each other, but her father would have no part of it. He didn't think Tomás was good enough for his beautiful daughter so he forbid them from seeing each other."

"Oh, dreadful. Terrible, isn't it?" Declan smiles then gestures with his hand for me to continue.

"MacDermot banished Tomás from the area and he had his daughter Úna Bhán confined on Castle Island right here on Lough Key." I point my finger towards the island to add emphasis.

"As you can well imagine, Úna Bhán went into what they called a deep melancholy and was dying from the grief. When Tomás heard about the situation, he rushed to see her and upon his leaving vowed that if MacDermot didn't send a message for him to return by the time he got to the river he'd never return again!"

I stop and take another sip of coffee, but Declan is intrigued. "Well, go on, finish the story. Did MacDermot send a messenger?"

"He did, but too late. The messenger didn't reach Tomás until after he had crossed the river. Naturally, being a man of honor, Tomás couldn't break his vow so he never returned."

"What happened to Úna Bhán?"

"Not good." I shake my head, "She died of a broken heart and was buried on Trinity Island here on Lough Key. Tomás Láidir Costello was so grief-stricken he used to swim to the island every night to keep vigil at her grave until he finally came down with pneumonia. He knew he was dying so his dying request of MacDermot was that he be buried beside his true love, Úna Bhán. His request was granted and they were finally united - but they were dead."

Declan with a slight frown on his face softly speaks, "That's a terrible legend. Where's the happy ending?"

"Well, I told you it's a tragic love story, didn't I? Anyway, tradition says, two trees grew up over their graves to form a lovers knot standing guard over their graves."

"Oh, well now, I feel a little better" he says as he pats my knee and picks up the oars. "Promise me one thing."

"What's that?"

"Next legend you tell me, make it have a happy ending. You and I've had enough of our own tragic love stories, haven't we now?"

I take his request as more of a rhetorical request as he begins rowing us closer to Castle Island. But he's right, the legend is pretty terrible, aside from the trees forming a love knot, it's really quite sad.

I sip my coffee in silence as he moves us to the shoreline of Castle Island. The grass is wet with dew as I step from the boat onto the shore. I'm regretting wearing the ballet flats, but my boots were in my bedroom so I'm just going to endure damp feet for a while.

We stroll around the island which is somewhat over-grown with tall grass, weeds and trees. It's difficult walking and from time to time we pause and I take more pictures before moving on.

At one stop, I see some wild flowers covered with the morning dew. I zoom in tight to catch the tiny drops on the petals in the early sunlight. Moving on, I notice a pair of ducks standing on the shoreline, oblivious to our presence. I squat down and snap, snap, snap the shutter, capturing their every move as they waddle back into the water.

"Stand up there now, Declan. I want you in one of my snaps," I say joking with him.

He stops and leans against one of the big cypress trees and I snap several pictures.

"Come here, Gemma. We need a selfie of our trip."

I hesitate for a second, but he gestures with his arm for me to come over to him and I slide beside him, hold the camera up and snap the picture.

"Let's take a look Gem," he says taking the camera from my hand and turning it to see the display.

"Not bad" I say.

"You'll have to send me a copy of this one," Declan says, handing the camera back to me.

Continuing on, we head up to the remains of a castle. We carefully navigate through the vines and tall grass that grow around the ruins. As we approach, I tell Declan, "The history books in the area show a castle was present on the island as far back as the 1100's. The King of Moylurg lived here, but these remains are what they call a folly castle which was put here sometime in the nineteenth century."

"So this isn't the castle where Úna Bhán grew up then?"

"No, but if you like, maybe we can row over to Trinity Island and look for two trees growing together in a love knot?" I say with a touch of playfulness in my voice.

"Now, that's more like the wise-cracking Yank I've come to know and love."

Declan stands for a moment with his hands on his hips looking at the castle before turning to me and saying, "We'll have to save that trip for another day." He takes my left hand to help me over a large stone. "Why don't you take a few more pictures and we'll head back."

I take a few more snaps. First, of the sun rising behind the castle, and then of the ivy-covered stone wall which was once a grand entrance. Looking up, I see the sun is higher in the sky. "You're right, the sun will soon make picture taking more difficult."

Removing the camera strap from around my neck I gently place it back into the case and put the strap on my shoulder. "You ready?"

"Yep, let's go back. Our dinghy awaits."

Declan's a short distance ahead of me so I take quick steps to catch up with him. "Hopefully, Sorcha and Liam will be done sleeping together when we get back."

I feel my face getting hot. "That isn't what I meant. I meant done sleeping with each other. Sleeping, but not sleeping together. Well, I don't know what I mean, but you know what I meant."

Declan laughs out loud as I try to compose myself. "God, you're an angel, really." He takes my hand to help me into the boat and as he climbs in behind me he gently kisses my forehead. "Truly you're an angel, Gemma."

This time I don't know what to think or say so I remain silent most the way back. Finally, from nowhere I hear myself ask, "Was she sick long?"

I bite my bottom lip, but the words have already left my mouth. He was in a good mood. He was laughing and smiling. Why on earth would you bring up his dead wife?

He's quiet for a few seconds, but answers me, "No. It was fast. Three weeks, that's all. She woke up one morning covered in horrible bruises. Three weeks later, she was gone."

Instantly, I've got an awful, sick feeling in my stomach. "I'm so sorry, Declan. I don't mean to pry, it's just you called me an angel and well, that made me think of our angels, yours and mine. Brad and ...." I pause because it dawns on me, I don't know his wife's name.

"Sheila. Her name was Sheila and it's okay, Gemma. I told you if you want to talk, I'm here for you. You've done no harm, honest."

I can tell by his voice he means it. I say the only words that come to mind. "Thanks, Declan. I don't talk about it much, but when I'm ready to open up, I know it will be with you."

PART II

Wilmington, North Carolina

Chapter 10

The humidity is stifling this morning on Front Street so I welcome the cool rush of air conditioning blowing my sundress as I enter the coffee shop. I take a look around and see Sue waving to me at a table near the back. I wind through the labyrinth of tables to greet her.

Sue Cartwright and I met in grad school at UNC Wilmington. We had so many classes together, it felt like we'd known each other for years. First, we'd meet for study groups, then we'd go to movies, and before long we were best friends.

Sue is one of those people who always makes you feel good about yourself. She's what I call an encourager. She's always promoting me and my abilities, fun to be around, and always happy to see me. I need that, especially now.

Standing to hug me, she enthusiastically squeezes tight and says, "It's so good having you back home!"

"It's good to be home," I say as she sits back down.

It's good to be back, but the heat and humidity makes me wonder why I ever left my little cottage on Lough Key.

I hand Sue a gift wrapped in bright pink and purple polka dot paper. She takes it from me and her eyes brighten in anticipation with each tear of the paper, "What's this?"

"It's a small souvenir from Ireland for my dearest friend."

Sue pulls the matted and framed photograph from the paper and exclaims, "Oh, Gemma, it's gorgeous! Thank you!" She studies the picture of dainty wild flowers and asks, "Did you take this?"

I nod my head in affirmation.

She looks at me and then back at the picture before saying, "I know exactly where I'm putting this. I've been looking for the perfect picture for the wall behind the bistro table in my kitchen. This is perfect. I love it!" She jumps up again and gives me another embrace.

I'm delighted she likes the picture and say, "I thought of that when I saw the colors of the flowers – ideal for Sue's kitchen."

Sue gives me a shooing gesture with her hand and says, "Go get some coffee and come back and fill me in on your summer."

I approach the counter and place my order for iced tea, I can't handle hot coffee this morning. As I return to the table, Sue is smiling up at me. "Gosh Gemma, I can't get over how good you look. Ireland must have been just what you needed. You look like your old self again."

"Yeah, my family were great and I got to spend some time on my own sorting things out in my mind. I feel refreshed and ready to get back to work."

"I know it hasn't been easy, but you're a survivor, Gemma. I'm positive good things are coming your way and Brad will always be looking out for you," she says patting my hand.

I pick up the cup of iced tea. Beads of condensation drip down the side as I take a sip. I place it down on a napkin to absorb the moisture. "So, do we really report for the new school year Monday?"

"Ugh, yes! The summer has flown by, but I'm kind of excited for the new year. Did you hear? In addition to a new Vice Principal this year we're also getting a new football coach."

"No. Other than your e-mails, I've not had any news about Cape Side High. Have you met either of them yet?"

Sue takes a look around the coffee shop as if she's about to divulge a state secret. Leaning in close she whispers, "Well, the football coach is nothing special, but the new Vice Principal is in his early thirties, blonde hair, blue eyes, five-feet-ten or eleven, and extremely good looking. I can already guess some of the single ladies at work will be making extra trips to the office just to see him."

"Oh, no. Thankfully, I won't be one of those single ladies. I'm going to be nose to the grindstone this year, but by all means Sue, if you think he's your type, you should make some extra trips to the office."

"Ha! No, no thanks, you know I'm waiting to meet my millionaire down here on the water front. One of these days a great big yacht will pull up and my Prince Charming will find me and he's not going to be living on a vice principal's salary."

"I love that about you Sue, you know what you want and you're not willing to settle for less." I laugh and take another sip.

Sue's quiet for a moment as she studies me, "You know Gemma, and don't take this the wrong way because I mean it as a compliment, but you look so calm and pulled together. You should go to Ireland more often."

"Thanks, I think."

"I can't put my finger on it exactly, but you've got this confident air about you. You were confident before, but it's different this time. It's like you have new perspective and purpose. Oh hell, I don't know what I'm saying, but it looks good on you."

"I think the time away was good for me. I had a change of scenery, tried new things, and made new friends. It was a pleasant summer, despite the fact I was supposed to have gotten married."

"I thought of you all the time, but especially on that day. I hope it wasn't too terrible for you Gem."

"It was sad, but my cousin and her friends made sure I was distracted that day."

"Good. I'm glad to hear it."

We spend close to an hour talking and catching up. Sue's excited about taking over the drama club at school this year in addition to teaching history. I fill her in on my photography website and tell her all about the Boyle Arts Festival.

She's excited when I tell her about the pictures I sold. "You got 350 euros for one!"

"Yes, 350 euros - cash - for one picture!"

"Did you meet the person who bought it?"

"Nope, all I know is the person showed up right when the exhibit was opening one morning, told the receptionist he wanted to purchase one of the pictures, handed her an envelope of money and told her, 'Please make sure this gets to Miss O'Connor.'"

"Well, did she at least give you a description of the guy?"

"She was hung over from the party the night before so all I got was, he's tall and has brown hair. So, pretty much could have been over half the men in Ireland."

"When we go to work Monday, I'm going to insist you start a photography club at school." Lifting the picture I gave her she adds, "You'd be terrific, Gemma, and the kids love you. It's a wonderful idea!" Sue exclaims.

I've always admired Sue's enthusiasm. It's hard to stay down when she's around so before I know it, I'm telling her, "Why not? It will be fun."

"I'm so glad we could get together and that you're doing well, Gemma." Sue smiles and I sense she's about to get up and leave. "Well, I'll see you at school Monday. I'm off to the grocery store. I've got nothing to eat in my house."

I give her a farewell hug and decide to stop in the restroom before walking home. She waves to me and departs and I head to the ladies room. When I come back out and begin walking to the door, I see a man seated at a table looking at me. As I approach his table, he stands and says to me, "Galway."

"Excuse me?"

"Didn't we meet in Galway?"

I look at him more closely and realize where I know him from. Before I say anything, he says, "The Dew Drop or Myles Lee. The pub? Remember? I'm the guy from Wilmington."

"Of course, I remember. You're Paul, the archaeologist."

His eyes dance when he sees I remember our meeting and he adds, "That's right. Paul, Paul Blair."

"Paul Blair. You're from here. You teach at UNC Wilmington, right?"

Looking relieved that I remember our first meeting, he asks, "Are you in a hurry or can you sit and have another cup of coffee?"

"Make it an iced tea and I'll say yes."

"You got it, Gemma," he says as he hops up and walks to the counter and orders an iced tea.

When he returns, he sits down placing my drink in front of me and smiles, "You never called, guess you didn't make it to Cork while you were in Ireland, did you?"

"No, unfortunately I didn't make it down to Cork this trip."

"This trip, so you go to Ireland fairly regularly?" he asks as he closes his laptop.

"My father is from Ireland so I have plenty of family and friends over there. That's who I was with that night, my cousin and her boyfriend."

"I see. It must be great to get to visit so often. I was only there for a summer program at Cork University, but I had a blast. Hope to get back again."

I study him as he talks. He's confident, but not arrogant. He's handsome and his hazel eyes are bright and kind. I think he's a nice guy, but having only met him twice, it's hard telling.

"How long did you stay in Ireland, Gemma?"

"I was there from the beginning of June up until last Thursday, so I'm still feeling a little jet-lag."

"Oh, wow, that was a nice long visit. I was only there for a four week program, but we still managed to see a lot of the country."

Should I tell him the reason why I was in Ireland? How does one lightly drop that into a conversation with someone you don't know? Well you see, I was there to get over the death of my fiancé - Doesn't exactly flow with the conversation, does it? Best to hold off, really not necessary to say anything at the moment.

"Are you waiting for someone or just hanging out?" I ask, hoping to steer the discussion as far away from Ireland as I can for the moment.

"I'm doing a little work. I met with a couple students earlier, but they left so I decided while I'm here I'd stay and get some work done. How about you?"

"I was catching up with a friend I hadn't seen all summer. We go back to school Monday so she was filling me in on all I've missed in Wilmington this summer."

His expression is kind as he listens intently, like he really wants to hear what I have to say. I know I've just met him, but he looks at me as if I'm the most beautiful thing he's ever seen. Stop, Gemma, you can't tell that's what he's thinking. Maybe he's had too much coffee. Maybe he's got gas. Quit over analyzing.

"I'd better get going, I've got lots to do to get ready for next week," I say, taking the last sip of my iced tea. "Thanks for the tea. It was nice meeting you again, Paul."

Wow, that was abrupt. What's the rush?

Paul looks genuinely confused but says, "Sorry you've got to go. Maybe we can do this again sometime. We've run into each other twice now. I take that as a sign we were supposed to meet, don't you?"

Feeling flustered, I pick up the strap to my purse and as I place it upon my shoulder I reply, "Hmm, I hadn't thought of it that way, but maybe."

"Gemma, may I ask for your phone number? If it's okay with you, I'd like to call you and ask you out."

Boom!

Now what?

I say the only thing I know to say as a chronic people-pleaser, "Do you have a pen?"

I write my name and number on the back of one of his business cards and he hands me another to keep. Tucking his card into my purse, I stand and thank him again. He stands up to see me off and says, "If you'd be more comfortable, maybe we can make it a lunch date. That way if you don't have fun you can go home, or if you do have fun, we can hang out till dinner."

And with this he has officially charmed me so I smile and say, "That sounds great, Paul. Thanks, see you soon."

Oh my, I've just consented to the idea of going on a date. A real date with a man. A man who isn't Brad.....

Chapter 11

The entire first week of school is chaotic. Getting the classroom ready, meetings, preparing the syllabus – I'm swamped. By the time the students arrive for their first day, I'm relieved to be done with the busy work that comes along with the job.

I majored in Elizabethan English, which admittedly is a pretty niche market when one ventures out to look for a job, but I always knew I'd end up teaching so I wasn't worried. I'm delighted to be teaching a class called Major British Writers this year in addition to the standard Freshman English I've been teaching since joining the staff at Cape Side High School.

The name of the school is what drew me in initially. I wanted to stay in Wilmington after grad school so when I saw they were recruiting teachers at Cape Side High – the same name as the school on the TV show *Dawson's Creek* – I had to apply. My friends back in New Jersey teased me because when I was little I had a crush on the actor who played Pacey, Joshua Jackson. It's a good school so I could totally justify my choice. However, I still think of Pacey walking the halls from time to time.

At our first staff meeting Sue and I decide to introduce ourselves to Mr. Payne, the new Vice Principal. He's definitely a good looking guy, but perhaps not quite as handsome as Sue initially made him out to be. Nevertheless, within seconds, despite her earlier protests about looking for a millionaire, it's apparent she's more into him than she'll admit.

I can always tell when Sue is trying a bit too hard to play it cool because the complete opposite is what happens. She becomes painfully uncool.

We're talking with him and she starts talking loudly and gesturing wildly. So much so, I have to fight back giggles.

She does manage to brag to Mr. Payne about my photography which seems to impress him. He even suggests starting a school camera club. Sue jumps in immediately telling him she had the exact same idea. She gushes about what a coincidence they both thought the same thing.

I'm starting to feel embarrassed for Sue. She has no idea how over-the-top her flirting has become and I can see Mr. Payne looking for an exit opportunity. Finally, maybe to escape Sue's effervescing, he excuses himself. I politely tell him, "It was a pleasure meeting you, Mr. Payne." To which he replies, "Call me Rich."

After he's completely out of ear shot, I grab Sue's arm, pull her aside and whisper, "He just told me to call him Rich instead of Mr. Payne. Do you know what this means, Sue?"

Sue furrows her brow, "No, what does this mean?"

"His name is Richard. Richard Payne!"

Still bewildered Sue replies, "So?"

"It means his parents are cruel. They named their son Richard Payne – what's short for Richard besides Rich or Rick?"

Finally grasping, Sue lets out one of her big laughs that sounds like a horse whinnying. "No, Gemma, No! You've ruined him for me."

She leans in and whispers, "But thanks, Gemma, I was flirting with a man whose name is Dick Payne!"

"Well, I wouldn't exactly call what you were doing flirting, Sue, and I don't want to discourage your attraction, but I did want you to be aware before you start picturing yourself as the future Mrs. Dick Payne."

❖

It's the second week of the school year and I'm starting to get into a groove. I've put an announcement on the school website about the formation of the Cape Side Photography Club. I've started reading Hamlet with the Major British Writers class, and Sue and I have plans to attend the first Friday night football game. Things are looking up and life isn't as desperate as it was seven months ago.

I'm turning the key in the door knob of my condo when my cell phone rings. I don't recognize the number so I let it go to voice mail. Putting my laptop bag down on a chair, I go into the bedroom to try and figure out what to wear to the game tonight.

I really want to wear shorts because although it's September, the weather is still hot and muggy. But decorum prevails and I decide to wear a pale blue sundress instead. I have this thing about wearing shorts in front of my students. Even though I'm only twenty-six, I think back to my high school days and can't imagine seeing any of my teachers, besides the gym teachers, wearing shorts at a school function. I give a physical shiver imagining Mr. Berman the band teacher in Bermuda shorts. His ears are full of thick black hair and his shirt collar fights to contain what appears to be small shrubs underneath. I don't want to know what his legs are like.

I slip on the dress, pull my hair into a braid and tie a light blue ribbon at the top. "There, instant school spirit. Go Cape Side Gulls!"

I walk into the kitchen, picking up my cell phone from the table, and check the messages. As soon as I hear the voice, my heart beats a little faster.

"Hi, Gemma, this is Paul. Paul Blair, from the coffee shop and Ireland. Listen, I know it's short notice, but I wanted to see if you'd like to meet for lunch tomorrow down at Elijah's. Give me a call back if you get this in time. I'd love to see you."

I stand staring at the phone in my hand then look at the clock over the stove. Should I call him? It's just after five o'clock, he must be at home or leaving work. I look again at the phone and see his number. I can't decide whether or not to call him so I pour myself a glass of water and walk into the living room, sit down at the desk and pull out my laptop.

Thoughts shoot through my mind as I begin over analyzing the situation. I know, I'll call Sorcha. I boot up my laptop. As the computer starts, I glance at my watch again doing the mental math to figure out the time in Galway. It's a little after ten o'clock.

Finally, the computer is up and I see she's not on line.

I bet she would know how to handle this.

It's Friday night, of course she's not online.

I sit staring at the "friends list" when I notice the most recent addition to the list is online. "DecSaltHill" has a green light next to his handle. Declan is at his computer.

He did say if I ever need to talk he's happy to help, but I'm not sure dating advice is what he meant.

But.... maybe dating advice from someone who's been there is precisely what I want or need.

I keep staring at his name until my hand drags the mouse lightly over DecSaltHill and I click. Up pops a message box and I type in the words, "Hi Declan it's me, Gemma. Got a sec?"

I read and re-read the message. *Oh, why not?* And I hit the enter key.

The sound of the reply message startles me. That was fast.

"Sure, how can I help?"

Now what, Gem? What do I want to know? What do I want Declan to help me with? Am I going to ask him if I should go on a date?

My fingers tap away, "I'm in an unusual situation and I'm so sorry to impose upon you, but Sorcha wasn't home"

Backspace, backspace, backspace......... That sounds like he's your sloppy second choice.

Not knowing what else to say, a new thought pops into my head. "It's hard to type about, can we talk on Skype?"

"Sure, hang on and I'll call you."

I sit up straight, adjust the straps on my dress and press my lips together. Yep, still feel some lip-gloss. It's only Skype, Gemma, nobody looks pretty on the computer - don't go overboard.

The familiar sound of the incoming call begins and I click *answer*. There's a tiny flutter in my stomach as his picture appears on the screen.

Damn, he looks good, even online.

Declan's wearing a navy blue t-shirt with University College Galway written in white letters across his chest. He smiles when he sees me on his screen, "You look lovely, Gemma. How are ye?"

"I'm well, thanks Declan. You look good too."

Well he does, I'm only paying an honest compliment.

"Aw, you're sweet to say so, Gemma. Gee, it's been what? Over a month since we last saw each other?"

"Yes, I left on the eighth of August. I've been back teaching now for almost three weeks."

"It must still be warm over there though. Is that a tank top or a dress you're wearing?"

I'm surprised he's asking, but stand up and twirl, "It's a sun dress. The only form of comfort in the muggy South. September is as hot as July to me."

"Miss O'Connor, you look amazing. You're holding up well in the heat and that blue looks fantastic on you." He stops and tilts his head to the right before adding, "So what's eating ya? It must be something big if you've come to me and not Sorcha."

I find it impossible to fib, "Sorcha wasn't home."

Declan laughs as he picks up a mug sitting next to him, takes a sip and places it back down, "Your honesty is refreshing. I only hope as your second choice I'll be able to give the insights your first choice would have."

I feel the wave of crimson rising in my face, but ignore it in hopes he can't see that much detail on his computer. "I didn't mean for it to sound that way. I do want to talk with you and I appreciate your insights. It's just that this has to do with...."

Before I'm able to finish he says, "A man?"

I glance down and let out a sigh before connecting eyes with Declan again. "There's this guy and he's left a message on my phone. He wants to meet for lunch tomorrow and I'm not sure what to do. That's all."

"Gemma, you're a beautiful young lady - men are going to be attracted to you. It's going to happen. Men will especially find you appealing because from what I've seen, you're entirely unaware of how beautiful you are. The question isn't should you go? You will and you know Brad would expect that. The question is are you ready?"

Declan keeps surprising me with his insights. The way he immediately drills down to the issue and tackles it, I can see why he's successful in business. He's cut to the chase, knows precisely what's eating me, and in the same breath paid me the most flattering compliment.

"How do you do that, Declan? How do you so quickly know what people are thinking?"

"It's a gift and also a skill I've honed in my work. I have to cut out the extraneous information and deal with the concrete facts, or numbers, at hand."

Taking another sip, he places the cup back on the desk before continuing. "However, you've got such an honest and open face, Gemma, you make it easy to figure out what's eating you. Let's see what we need to figure out by asking some questions. First, where did you meet this guy?"

"We met in Galway the night we all went out. He's an American and lives here in Wilmington full time, but was over there for school during the summer. We ran into each other a couple weeks ago at a coffee shop here."

"I see." Declan makes a grim expression as he takes a deep breath. "Do you fancy him?"

"He seems like a nice guy, but I don't know much about him. He's cute." He's cute. Okay now I sound like I'm back in middle school.

"Cute is important. I like cute too." He smiles into the camera and I laugh at his playful reply.

"What would keep you from saying *yes* to a lunch date?"

Declan has gone directly to the question with the most impact.

"He's not Brad."

I hear my words before I've even thought about what I've said. When the sound hits my ears and my brain processes what I've uttered out loud, my throat gets tighter and my eyes fill up as if a dam's about to burst.

Softly Declan says, "No. No Macushla, he's not. He never will be. So, the question isn't should you go out to lunch? The question is, are you ready? How long has it been?"

Barely audible, I push out my answer, "Seven and a half months."

"Does this guy.... what's his name?"

"Paul. His name is Paul."

"Does Paul know your situation? I mean, does he know you've just lost your fiancé?

I look down and using my index finger, I start to remove dust from the keyboard. I stop and finally answer, "I haven't told him. The right moment hasn't come up. It's awkward bringing up the subject."

"You're right. People are uneasy and don't know how to react. They're not being rude, they just don't know what to say." His tone is reassuring.

"Declan, do you think I'm silly? He's only asked to take me to lunch."

Declan gives a loving smile and answers, "No, you're being true to Brad's memory and that's a beautiful thing. One of many admirable qualities about you, Gem."

"Thanks, Declan. You have a way of putting me at ease."

"Well, I'm not sure I've helped much, but if you want my opinion here it is. You're ready to go out again Gemma. You're young, beautiful and you're gradually returning to the land of the living. But you're afraid. Afraid to be back out there dating. Afraid of leaving Brad behind. Afraid of caring for someone new. Afraid of letting yourself go. Afraid of caring so strongly for another. Afraid of ever hurting so much again."

Yes, yes, and yes. Spot on analysis.

After a brief pause he continues, "Go. It's only lunch like you said. You'll know in your heart when you're ready for it to be more. The only thing I tell you is to be mindful not to doubt your own instincts. You're wounded Gemma, so mind yourself not to make major decisions till you've had time to heal more. You'll never be fully over Brad, but give it time. Time will change your perspective so don't get caught up in a moment. It would break my heart to see you unhappy with choices you make before you've mourned long enough."

I reflect on his advice and say, "Are you saying this to me or to yourself?"

"Ah, my brilliant Gemma. Touché. Is this where I ask you how you know *me* so well?" He laughs, but then turns serious, "Just promise me you'll take your time. Go have fun, it's just lunch, but be true to yourself. Don't settle. You deserve to be madly in love with someone. I know right now you probably don't think it's possible to be head over heels again, but I've been around you enough to know it will happen for ya. Just give it time."

"I will, I promise, Declan."

"Good, and remember, there's a big difference between who we love, who we settle for and who we're meant for."

I don't respond, but I take a mental note to remember his words because they're profound.

"Will you lie and tell me this has helped?"

"I don't have to lie. This helped. It helped a lot. You're right, it's just lunch."

"Good. Is there anything else I can assist with?"

"No, not now. I've got to go to a football game tonight at school. I'm about to head out now." I hesitate a second and smile, "I'm glad you were home."

"Me too, Gemma. It's lovely talking to you."

"The Internet works in both directions, you know. You can always call me. Just remember, I wake up five hours later than you do."

"Understood. Have fun, Gemma, stay safe now. God Bless."

"Goodnight, Declan and thanks."

I wait for him to hang up and sit staring at the screen a few seconds, remembering his sage advice. I'm blessed to have met someone so in touch with the torrent of emotions I've been feeling.

Before I leave for the football game I pick up my cell phone and hit re-dial. Paul isn't answering so I leave a message, "Hi Paul, it's Gemma. I'd love to meet for lunch tomorrow. I'll see you at Elijah's at twelve - thirty. If that doesn't work call me - otherwise I'll see you there.

Chapter 12

An early morning rain storm eases the humidity and the sun is making its way onto the scene so I go for a run to clear my head. I used to run several days a week, but like so many things, I lost interest after Brad died.

I run down Water Street past the old historic buildings before turning to head up the hill towards home. I can tell it's been a while since my last run, but it feels good to get moving again. Maybe I'll build up to my old levels. Small steps, small steps.

I think about my conversation with Declan last night. He's so insightful and grounded. It doesn't seem right he hasn't met anyone special yet. Maybe he doesn't want to meet anybody else. Maybe Sheila was the only one for him. Loyalty appears to be one of his character traits. I can see him being a one woman guy.

I also think about the game last night. Sue and I had a lot of fun and went out for pizza with a group that included the new Vice Principal, Mr. Payne. I mean Rich.

Sue did much better around him than the other day at school. She was calmer and her gestures were kept to a minimum. No wild gesticulating this time. She was still trying a little too hard, but there were a couple teachers vying for his attention last night so I can't blame her for wanting to stand out.

I think about my lunch date too. Am I really about to go on a date? I thought I was done going on first dates, but life had different plans for me. What should I wear? I don't want to look eager. I'll wear something casual.

My mind races and before I notice how out of breath I am, I'm climbing the steps to my building. My run has given me time to ponder my look for the date. I've decided to keep it simple - khaki shorts, a camisole and a pink tank top. I'll pull my hair up into a knot for a laid-back, carefree style.

❖

Elijah's isn't far from my house so I walk there. As I make my way down the hill on Ann Street, I see Paul waiting outside the restaurant. I wave. Recognizing me, he smiles, waves back, and walks towards me as I cross the street.

"Wow, you look beautiful!"

His face lights up as he speaks. I can't help feeling flattered.

"Thanks, Paul. You look handsome yourself."

The collar on his white, short sleeved polo shirt is popped up. He's got on navy blue shorts, Sperry's and a pair of Oakley's sunglasses. He looks preppy. *Very* preppy. I'm not sure I'm a fan of preppy. Brad was athletic, but always managed to dress in a classic style.

You're on a date with Paul, Gemma. Quit comparing him to Brad.

"Shall we go inside and get a table?" Paul opens the door and I step inside.

Smiling at the hostess he leans in, "We'd like a table on the deck if you've got one available."

He turns to me, "Is that okay with you, Gemma?"

"Oh, absolutely. It's such a pretty day, it would be a shame to be inside."

We wind our way through the restaurant, past the bar and outside to the deck. The weather has brought many of the diners outside so we're fortunate to get the last table under an umbrella.

The hostess leaves us and we're joined shortly by our waitress. "Hi, I'm Mandy and I'll be taking care of you today."

I always smile to myself when they say they'll be taking care of me. Really? If they were really going to be taking care of me today, they'd be buying my meal.

I must be smiling because Paul looks at me and smiles back. We send Mandy away with our drink orders and he finally says, "You've got a great smile, by the way."

Okay, so far he's told me I'm beautiful and that I have a great smile. He's winning points.

Mandy returns with our drinks and takes our order. Paul is looking around us and adjusts his collar several times. I'm not sure if he's worried about being seen with me or if I make him nervous, so I come right out and ask him, "Paul are you nervous?"

I can't believe I just asked him that question since I'm the one who's nervous.

Finishing a sip of iced tea, he places the glass back on the table and slowly answers, "Yes, I am nervous, and I don't know why."

"Well, if it helps, I'm nervous too. I haven't been on a date in a long time."

Ugh, why did I say that? I just opened the door to the questions.

Paul places both hands on the table and looks squarely at me for a moment before saying, "I find that hard to believe. You're a pretty girl, you just spent an entire summer in Ireland, and you expect me to believe you didn't go on a single date?"

I guess now is as good a time as any. Let's see. How shall I slide this into the conversation?

"I didn't go on any dates the entire summer. I have to be honest with you, Paul. There's something I need to tell you."

His eyes widen and he leans in. He's ready and waiting for me to tell him some shocking news. Something that would change the tone of the entire date. Something like I just got out of prison or I'm really a dude.

I see his apprehension, so I shake my head from side to side and smile, "No, no it's nothing earth-shattering, Paul. It's just.... it's just that, I was engaged and I'm not anymore. My fiancé was killed in Afghanistan and this is the first date I've been on since..."

I look down, waiting for him to respond. When he doesn't, I glance up to check his expression. He's looking into my eyes, but I can't figure out what he's thinking. His face isn't giving me any clues so I begin to ramble. "I'll understand if you don't want to finish the date."

Finally he speaks, "Why wouldn't I want to finish the date?"

"I just figured you might not want to go out with me if you felt I'd withheld a huge piece of information about myself. And judging by your silence and the look on your face..."

Before I finish my thought, he reaches over, takes my hand, and says, "You've gotten it all wrong. I'm silent because I'm surprised. I'm honored. I had no idea what you've been through and the fact you'd say *yes* to going on a date with me; that's really something. Thank you."

Letting out a sigh I say, "I was afraid you thought I'd been dishonest with you. I hadn't, but I didn't exactly know how to bring up the subject."

"I tell you what, I know now and it doesn't change a thing. I still think you're pretty, and smart, and nice, and I'm glad I asked you out."

The tension I felt between my shoulder blades leaves me and I'm able to enjoy my meal. After eating, we spend a long time getting to know each other. Paul tells me how he grew up in the mountains of North Carolina, but fell in love with the coast when he came east to go to college.

I tell him about growing up in New Jersey and moving here for my graduate studies and how I fell in love with the coast as well. He's fascinated to hear of my family in Ireland and how I spent the entire summer in a cottage on a lake.

He listens attentively making me feel like I'm the most important person he knows. After what seems like only minutes, but clearly has been much longer, I look around and see empty tables. We're the only table of diners left. Mandy our waitress has been patiently waiting for us to leave, but finally brings our check and explains she needs to close out so they can begin preparing for the dinner crowd.

"I guess we've monopolized this table long enough. How would you like to take a stroll along the Riverwalk, Gemma?" Paul pulls my chair out for me and we walk to the boardwalk and continue talking.

I'm surprised at the level of comfort I'm feeling with this person who is essentially a stranger to me. It reminds me of the night I met Brad. We were at the House of Blues in Myrtle Beach to hear a band. I was on a girl's weekend with a couple friends from grad school and Brad had a weekend off and was with a few of his Marine buddies.

Brad caught my eye when he arrived, but we didn't talk until I was walking to the ladies room and he was exiting the men's room. A rowdy drunk guy fell into me as I was approaching the ladies room, pushing me right into Brad. Brad caught me, asked if I was okay, and when I said *yes,* he bent down, picked up the drunk, and physically tossed him aside, and told him, "Apologize to the lady for your rudeness."

The drunk was so shocked he whimpered, "Excuse me," and skulked away.

I thanked Brad and continued into the ladies room, but when I came out, he was waiting for me. "If it's okay with you, I'd like to make sure you get back safely to your friends."

He walked me back to my table, but my friends were all up by the stage dancing so he asked if he could sit down for a few minutes. We shouted over the band the rest of the night and I think I knew then and there he was the one. It was magic - that feeling when you know. You just know this is going to be the most important person in your life.

Just as I'm about to get lost in my thoughts, Paul takes my hand and says, "Let's go across the street to the Reel Cafe and have a beer. You want to?"

We're halfway across the street by the time I answer him, but I'm having fun. I sarcastically say, "Sure I'd love a beer" as he pulls me into the patio area and we sit down at an empty table facing a giant TV.

September is college football season and I smile thinking of how much Brad enjoyed watching the games. He'd played football at the Naval Academy so each fall, when it was possible, he made the trip to Annapolis for at least one game.

Paul and I enjoy our beer and I can tell I'm really having fun when he convinces me it's okay to have a second. "Two more Highland Gaelic Ales," he says to the waitress as she smiles and heads inside to the bar.

I notice a small finch hopping around the ground in search of crumbs. “He’d make a cute picture if I had my camera with me.”

Paul’s eyebrows rise slightly and he replies, “You like taking pictures?”

I proceed to tell him all about my recent photography triumphs. He's interested when I tell him all about the website. He even suggests I bring the camera club to his dig site before the end of the fall. This guy is really nice, smart, and handsome; it's pleasant being out with a man. I never wanted to be doing this again, but I think I'm going to be okay. I take the last sip of my second beer. Placing the glass on the table, I look at the sky and the fading sunlight, then I glance at my watch.

"Uh oh, I saw that. Either you're thinking, 'Gee, this has been so much fun I can't believe how the time has flown, or you're thinking, 'How do I get the heck out of here?’"

"Aw, you caught me. Actually, I was looking at my watch thinking, 'I can't believe how time flew by."

"I think that's good, right?" He's leaning into me and smiling the most adorable grin.

"Yes, it's a very good thing. I've had fun."

"Good. I'm glad. Maybe we can do this again sometime?" he asks with uncertainty in his voice.

Our waitress returns and interrupts us. Paul asks for the check and after paying, he walks me towards Ann Street. When we get to the corner and I'm about to start up the hill towards my place, I stop and say to Paul, "Thanks for a really nice time."

"Thanks for coming out with me, Gemma." He looks down for a second and puts his hands in his pockets, "I know I may have sounded like I was kidding earlier, but I wasn't. Do you think you'd like to go out again sometime?"

I'm confused. I want to say *yes*, but my heart is still Brad's. I feel like I'm cheating on him, but I know I'm not. Then out of nowhere I have another thought.

What would Declan say to do?

He'd probably tell me to go out with him, wouldn't he? He'd say he's a great guy and he seems to like you, just take it slowly.

"I'd like that. We should do this again sometime." There, I said it. I said it out loud. Declan would be proud.

"Great. I'll give you a call soon. Thanks again, Gemma."

He takes his hands out of his pockets and placing one on each of my arms, he moves in and kisses me on the cheek. "Goodnight, Gemma, I'll talk to you soon."

"Soon," I repeat and turn and cross the street towards home.

Chapter 13

"Watch your sleeve, Gemma!" I hear Sue from across her lawn as she teeters over in her high heel black pumps to where I'm pouring punch.

Looking down, I see the white sleeve of my angel costume dipping precariously close to the red liquid. "Thanks, Sue."

Sue's dressed as a witch, but I have to say her costume is a little more *Elvira Mistress of the Dark* than Glenda from *The Wizard of Oz*. The bright red lipstick she's wearing accentuates her big smile as she shouts over the noise, "That's what friends are for."

It's obvious she's already had several cups of punch so I know I'd better be careful with this concoction I'm ladling into my cup.

"Hey, isn't your friend Paul coming tonight?" Sue is well aware he is, but is making a point of bringing him up.

"Yes, he had a late meeting on campus, but should be here shortly."

"I can't wait to finally meet him."

Sue's such a dear friend and I appreciate her eagerness to meet Paul, but I really hope she won't get too excited. She has a tendency to be effusive when she's meeting someone new she wants to impress. I'm reminded of the day she met Mr. Payne.

"Sue, this is only a third date so please, please, don't make a fuss when Paul gets here. He's very polite and understands my situation so I'm glad he's taking things slowly."

Sue's smile droops a little, but she perks right up, "Don't worry, Gemma. I may be dressed as a witch, but I won't frighten him off."

I'm placing the punch ladle back in the bowl when I feel a hand on my shoulder. "May I have a cup of punch, please?"

I turn around to see Paul standing there. He's wearing a white shirt, black slacks, a red cummerbund, and a red cape. In his hand is a pitch fork and on top of his head are two little red horns.

I immediately start laughing. "Oh my, you are the best devil I've ever seen!"

"Why, thank you. You are indeed the prettiest angel I've ever seen."

From behind me Sue loudly clears her throat.

"Oh, forgive me. Paul, I'd like you to meet my friend and co-worker, Sue. Sue Cartwright this is Paul Blair."

"How do you do, Paul? It's an honor meeting you. Gemma has said so much about you."

Oh no, Sue's using her charming voice. The one she uses when she wants people to think she's sophisticated enough to have descended from British royalty. It's really bad.

"I hope it's all been good." Paul replies.

Could this conversation get any more clichéd?

Sue and Paul banter back and forth with inane small talk. She tilts her head back and laughs hysterically at something he's said. I sincerely doubt what he said was funny enough to require that exaggerated laugh.

Just as this little scene is about to reach a new low, a voice shouts from the refreshment table. "Sue! Sue, are there more potato chips for the dip?"

She's visibly disappointed to have to tend to her hostess duties, but I'm relieved.

"If you'll excuse me. We'll have to continue our conversation later, Paul. It's a pleasure meeting you and please help yourself and enjoy the party."

As Sue leaves us, Paul gives a polite tip of his head and says, "Thank you, I will." But Sue is already across the lawn flitting about the refreshments before he finishes his words.

Turning to me, he takes my hand and gently kisses it, "My, you are a lovely angel."

It's hard for me to not enjoy his flattery and attention, but I'm incredibly awkward with my responses so for lack of anything equally charming to say in return, I grabble for words, "You're one hell of a devil."

He gives an inquisitive look and we both start laughing.

"Okay, well I tried, but you have to admit, it's not exactly easy complimenting the devil."

"I'll give you that. Now, is there anything to drink other than this red punch with what appears to be plastic spiders floating in it?"

"Come with me."

I lead Paul towards the back of the yard where Sue has placed a large cooler full of soda and beer. He plunges his hand into the ice and fishes out a bottle of Amstel Light.

There's a hanging swing between two trees a few feet away. Pointing with the bottle, he leads me to it and we sit down.

I watch as he pries the cap off the bottle and takes a draw of his beer. He swallows and looks up at the sky. It's a clear night and although it's late October, the temperature is mild. There are a few stars out which makes me wonder what lens I could use to capture the beauty of the sky in this light.

This is our third date. We went to a football game together one Friday night and we've talked on the phone several times. I'm beginning to feel comfortable with Paul, but tonight feels more like a true date and I'm a little nervous.

Paul breaks the silence first, "Are you warm enough?"

Glancing down at my layers of chiffon, I look back up at him and smile. "I'm fine, it's really not too cool tonight."

Despite my assurance that I'm warm, he reaches behind me with his left arm and wraps it around my shoulders sliding me closer to him as we gently swing. It's as if we're the only ones here. The rest of the party is carrying on, laughing, and dancing, but Paul and I are in our own little world.

We spend the entire evening on Sue's swing in deep conversation and moments of comfortable silence. He tells me all about the archaeological dig he's involved with. His work's fascinating and he loves what he does. He's positively exuberant telling me about a clay pipe he found that's believed to have belonged to the pirate, Blackbeard. I know it's only been three dates, but maybe Paul is exactly the guy for me.

He isn't needy. In fact, he's quite casual in his pursuit of me, and that's good. He has his career and other things keeping him busy so he doesn't seem to be pressured to get into a serious relationship.

After spending most of the night sitting on the swing, Paul leans in and whispers in my ear, "I hate for this to end. I'm having so much fun, but I've got an early morning tomorrow. Will you walk me to my car?"

It was Paul's idea to come to the party separately and now I'm kind of glad he suggested it. I'm afraid the moonlight, his warm embrace and those hazel eyes of his would render me vulnerable. I'm pretty sure he could sweep me off my feet tonight.

"Yes, I'd be happy to escort you to your car."

Hopping down from the swing, he takes my hand and guides me to where Sue is chatting away with Vice Principal Payne. As we approach, I can't tell if he's enjoying talking with Sue or if he's relieved we're interrupting.

"Excuse the interruption," Paul smiles at Sue. "I've got an early morning so Gemma is going to walk me to my car, but I wanted to say thank you, Sue. It was so nice meeting you."

Sue has clearly had several more cups of punch, leans in and gives Paul a hug. She feigns a whisper, but it's so loud both Rich and I hear her as she puts her lips to Paul's ear, "Thanks for coming. You take care of Gemma. She's a good girl and she deserves to be happy. We all care about her and if you hurt her, well. Well, I may have to hurt you."

"Goodnight, Sue!" I shout. "I'm heading home too."

We take our leave and cross the lawn, making our way to the street where our cars are parked. Dew is beginning to form on the grass and my feet are getting wet. I'm looking down at my shoes as I walk, my hand still in Paul's, when he stops short. I stop too and in one swift move, Paul lifts my chin up to his and kisses me.

This is no ordinary kiss.

This kiss is passionate.

This kiss tells me he wants more than a kiss.

At first I don't know what to do, but with the moon light, the chill in the air, and the way we've spent the evening I realize I want to be kissed.

I need to be kissed.

I kiss him back.

Paul's a good kisser. He's strong and forceful, but still gentle.

I want to keep going, but he stops, lifts my chin and looks into my eyes, "Gemma, Sue's a little tipsy, but I want you to know I respect what she said. She cares about you."

He pauses and looks at me. My head's swimming. My mind is caught up in the hot kiss. I search his eyes for an answer, *Why did you stop?*

His words are soft and his voice cracks a little, "I won't hurt you."

I can't tell from his tone whether he's making a statement or trying to convince himself.

Looking into his eyes, I decide it's the former. I want to believe him. I think he means it, but I know the truth.

Brad never intended to hurt me either. Hurting me was the last thing Brad would ever do, but his dying hurt more than anything in the world. It hurt because I loved him. When we love we *will* eventually get hurt. It's a package deal.

This could be a good thing for me. For us. For me and Paul. I may finally be giving myself permission to be happy. Permission to carry on with my life. Permission to move on. The question is, will I allow myself to be hurt again? Will I allow myself to love?

It's still too soon to know.

Chapter 14

"Gemma, can I help you with anything?"

I glance up and see Mom craning her neck to see me in the kitchen from her corner of the sofa where she's watching football with my father and brother Aidan. I laugh under my breath thinking of Dad and how he's come to love American football as much, if not more, than the other football we call soccer.

"No, Mom. I've got this." I pick up a can of cranberry sauce and begin turning the can opener. I pry the lid off and shake the can aggressively until the can-shaped sauce finally plops into the serving dish below.

I say I've got it, but I don't have her convinced. It's my first Thanksgiving and she's having a tough time letting go. Since they arrived last night, she's been a bundle of nerves which isn't helping me relax.

"Mom, when I invited you guys for Thanksgiving it was so you wouldn't have to worry about a thing. Now, please, let me cook. If it helps, have a glass of wine. It's a holiday after all."

My parents have been incredible since Brad died. I know it's hard for them watching their only daughter go through this. But sometimes it's hard on me, feeling like everybody is watching to see if I'm going to break down and fall to pieces. I feel smothered at times, but I don't want to seem ungrateful. It's a fine line to walk.

Finally, Mom leaves the sofa, comes over to the counter where I'm working, and perches herself on a stool to watch me. As I'm mixing the cream of mushroom soup into the beans, she exhales. It's the kind of exhale which tells me she's about to speak.

"So, tell me a little more about this Paul you're seeing."

I finish mixing the casserole, sprinkle the onion rings on top, and take my time finding room for it in the oven. Instead of turning around and answering her question, I walk over to the cabinet and bring down a couple of wine glasses.

"Red or white, Mom?"

I can tell she's a little uncomfortable asking me about Paul, but I also know she's dying for information. I'm not intentionally stalling, it's just I really don't know what to say.

"What are you having, Gemma?"

"I'm having Chardonnay Mom, but I have rosé and Merlot too. Which do you prefer?"

"I'll have what you're having." *I knew she'd say that.*

I pour two glasses of Chardonnay and place one in front of her on the counter and before I can put the candied yams in the oven, she asks a second question. "Is Paul from Wilmington?"

I take a long sip from my glass and slowly swallow. I've never been comfortable talking about my boyfriends with mom. She's not nosey, but I always feel she's mentally marrying me off to every guy I mention.

"He's not from Wilmington originally, but he's been living here since he was in college."

She's on the edge of her stool about to go into her rapid-fire mode so to spare her, I add, as casually as possible, "He's going to try and come by later for dessert. He's spending the day with family in Raleigh and if he gets back in time, he'll stop by and you can meet him."

Sitting up taller on the stool, Mom bubbles with anticipation. She swivels around and yells back to Dad and Aidan, "Did you hear that? Paul's coming for dessert."

I roll my eyes and let out a loud sigh, "I said he *may* come for dessert. It just depends on if he gets away from Raleigh in time to come over."

Fortunately, the guys are engrossed in the football game and only murmur their reply.

I was reluctant to have them meet Paul and now that Mom's making a big deal out of it, I wish I'd kept my mouth shut. Maybe my original instinct was right, maybe I shouldn't have invited him. I can feel my shoulders tensing up and I've got a knot in my stomach.

I have to change the subject so I engage Dad. "Hey Dad, will you come carve the turkey?"

He knows I can't stand cutting up a bird. Mom was out of commission one summer after shoulder surgery and I thought I could handle cooking a chicken for dinner one Sunday to help out. One incision with the butcher knife into said bird and I discovered I have a highly-developed gag reflex. Dad hops up and practically sprints to the kitchen. He must remember. I've successfully changed the subject, for now anyway.

❖

My phone rings around seven-thirty and we all look at it as if to say, *finally*. I walk over to where the phone is sitting on the coffee table and see it's Paul. I take the phone out onto the balcony, giving myself a little more privacy, before answering.

"Happy Thanksgiving."

"Happy Thanksgiving, Gemma. I'm so sorry I haven't called you sooner, it's just been so crazy here at my aunt's house, and I'm just hitting the road now. I won't be back in Wilmington until close to ten o'clock. Do you hate me?"

"No, I don't hate you. I said to come by if you got away early enough. It's no big deal."

"How can I make it up to you? How about we do lunch tomorrow? I really want to meet your folks"

I look at Mom and Dad sitting inside trying to act like they're not watching me on the balcony. "No, that won't work. They're driving down to see my older brother Peter and his family in Bluffton tomorrow."

"Oh, I feel terrible now."

I don't know what to say so I tell Paul, "Look, it's not that big a deal. They'll be back again soon. You can meet them next trip. Just drive carefully, okay."

"Okay, I'll call you tomorrow."

I hang up, walk back inside, and putting a smile on my face I announce, "Who's up for dessert? Paul is just leaving Raleigh so it looks like it's going to be the four of us."

Mom and Dad already have their concerned parent expressions on their faces. Hopefully, Paul hasn't made a bad first impression. He's not here to make an impression. I'm mad at myself for even mentioning he might stop by.

I walk into the kitchen before I'm hit with a barrage of questions. Aidan jumps up and asks, "Is the whipped cream in a can or a tub?"

I laugh and say, "You know I can't do the tub - I'll let you have the honors of spraying the whipped cream on the pumpkin pie."

Chapter 15

Handing Mom her Vera Bradley bag as she climbs into the passenger seat of the Buick, I smile at my brother in the back seat. It's funny seeing him riding with Mom and Dad like he did when we were little.

"It's gonna be a fun rest of the trip!" He grins and rolls his eyes at me. I know he's having a blast traveling alone with Mom and Dad, but I can tell he's ready to do some more age appropriate things for a young man in his early twenties.

Dad closes the trunk, walks over to me, and slips a fifty dollar bill in my hand. I know it's pointless, but I protest, "Dad, I actually have a job and pay my bills. You don't need to do this."

He waves off my protest and says, "We can all use a little extra from time to time." He leans in and gives me a fatherly kiss on the forehead. Pulling away, he looks at me and says in his most concerned father tone, "Take care of yourself and call if you need anything."

I know having his little girl living so far away must be hard on him so I smile and promise I will. "I'll see you in a couple weeks at Christmas. My flight is already booked."

My news puts a smile on his face and he climbs into the car. I stand waving as they drive off and let the tear welling up in my eye roll. It's always good seeing them and it's moments like this I ask myself why I refuse to move closer to home. I answer my own question with my next thought. So you don't become *poor Gemma.*

I turn and make my way upstairs to the condo, all the while reviewing my mental list of reasons for staying in North Carolina. It's cheaper, my friends are here, the ocean, I love my job, the weather is milder..... Now that Brad's gone, the biggest reason of all is gone, but it's still the best place for me at this time of my life.

I return to the kitchen and start scrubbing the roasting pan that's been soaking since I lifted the turkey out of it yesterday. It was an all-night soaker, but I'm making progress removing the drippings when I hear my phone in the other room.

I turn the water off and wipe my hands on the dish towel hanging on the oven door handle, but don't get there in time. I see the call was from Paul so I pick it up and call him right back.

"Well hello there, you're not screening your calls are you?" I hear the smile in his tone.

"Nope, just not fast enough getting across the room. What's up?"

"I feel terrible I didn't make it back in time to meet your parents last night so I want to make it up to you today if you'll let me."

"You don't have to make it up. Besides, it really wasn't meant to be a formal meeting of the parents, it was just dessert." I don't know why, but I'm emphatic, it wasn't about meeting my parents.

"Well, I still would like to see you if you don't have plans already."

I look out the balcony door and see it's cloudy outside, "What do you have in mind? I was thinking of taking my camera and heading to the beach."

"Wow, what a coincidence! I was going to ask if you wanted to go to the beach."

My mouth curls into a smile, "Sure you were."

"How about I come by around noon? We can bring lunch with us and have a picnic. Wear a sweater, it's a little chilly."

"I hope you don't mind, I stopped and got chicken and biscuits. I know yesterday was all about turkey - can you handle more poultry?" Paul gestures to the box of chicken in the back seat as I get in the car.

"No, I'm not overly concerned about my poultry intake. I'm sure I can beef things up next week." We both start laughing as I roll my eyes at my own corny joke.

The beach is practically empty. I suppose the cloudy day and Black Friday shopping is keeping folks elsewhere, but I'm glad. I love the beach in the off-season. It's peaceful and I can relax and enjoy taking pictures without worrying about people photo-bombing my shots.

Paul spreads out an old wool blanket he brought along and we tear into the box of chicken. He picks out a breast for himself and one for me and puts it on a paper plate as I pour sweet tea into two paper cups.

"I love picnics on the beach, don't you?" He looks at me as he tugs a large chunk of meat from the chicken breast, making eating chicken from the bone look almost graceful.

"It's one of my favorite things to do. Brad and I used to come down here all the time when he had time off." I can't believe I just did that without thinking. It's got to be bad form to speak of my dead fiancé while on a date, but I don't know the etiquette.

Paul finishes eating a piece of chicken, wipes his fingers on a paper napkin and puts it down before putting his hand on my knee. "Gemma, don't admonish yourself like that."

"What do you mean?" I try to be coy, but I know my poker face is awful.

"I mean it's okay if you mention Brad. He was important to you."

I look down at the blanket and begin tugging a loose thread, "I guess I worry about mentioning him too often."

"I'll let you know if that happens, but really Gemma, it would be unnatural for you *not* to speak about him from time to time."

Changing my focus, I look down at the heavy Aran sweater I'm wearing and begin flicking chicken and biscuit crumbs away when Paul reaches over and takes my hand. "Gemma, I know we've been moving slowly and I want you to know, it's not because I'm not crazy about you - it's because I *am* crazy about you."

I look into his hazel eyes which are fixed on mine. My chest tightens, but I don't know if it's because I'm terrified or happy. My silence must tell Paul I'm happy because before I speak, his lips are on mine.

First his kiss is gentle and soft. I don't kiss back, but his tenderness reminds me how lovely it feels to kiss a man. Sure, we had our moment after Sue's Halloween party, but we really haven't spent any time alone since then.

Paul's kiss becomes stronger, less tender and more desirous. I'm falling into him and kissing back. It's different, but familiar. I enjoy his embrace, his touch, and his urgency.

Paul's a good kisser and my kisses begin to match the passion of his. I'm kissing with new purpose, kissing myself back into life. These aren't the kisses of a sad, lonely, almost-widow. My kisses are the kisses of a twenty-six-year-old woman with healthy desires.

Paul's kiss pulls me in, his hands are in my hair as he puts his hand behind my head, holding me tight his tongue explores my mouth. I reach up and stroke his cheek and he kisses me harder. Inside, I'm coming alive, trembling and quivering. My thoughts run from wanting more to *thank goodness we're at the beach; if we were at my place, it would be all over. No turning back.*

With one, final soft kiss, Paul pulls away and tenderly brushes his index finger across my lower lip. Short of breath, he murmurs, "Let's go take some pictures, Gemma or I'm afraid..."

"Afraid of what?" I ask.

Standing up and brushing crumbs from his pants, Paul takes a deep breath and looks out at the ocean before releasing a long sigh, turning back to me and answering.

"Afraid I want more than you're ready to give me." His voice cracking slightly, "I don't want to be a bad decision."

He reaches down and pulls me to my feet, but I just stand and stare at him. I search his face, trying to understand what's going through his mind. He appears to be punishing himself, but I don't know why. He's waging some kind of inner-civil war. After a few seconds, I say the only thing that comes to mind. "Thank you, Paul."

Chapter 16

The photography club meets after school on the last Monday of the month. Our small group is huddled over pages of proofs when Sue saunters through the door. She immediately spies the fragrant addition to the classroom and gushes, "Gemma! Where did those gorgeous roses come from?"

We all look up at Sue as she tips her head in a gesture towards my desk. Now, there are seven sets of eyes fixed on the vase of pink roses on the corner of my desk.

Heat surges to my face as I casually reply, "Oh, Paul sent them."

Ashley Joyner, a star volleyball player looks at me and asks, "Miss O'Connor are you dating someone?"

I want to crawl under the desk. Sue can't feel the daggers my eyes are throwing her way and continues talking. "Oh wow, they're from Fallows! And pink roses are so beautiful! Now, what's the significance of pink? I forget."

"They're just pink, Sue. Pink. No secret code, it's a color." I turn back to the proofs on the table.

"No, I'm pretty sure each color has a meaning, Miss O'Connor," chimes in Olivia Madden, a petite red head.

"She's right." Ashley confirms with a nod.

"What? You're kidding, right?" Cooper Sanderson, the senior class president, Honor Society member, baseball player, and all around big man on campus looks at me and back at Olivia. He rolls his eyes letting us know he's never heard of anything so silly in his life.

"They're right." Sue adds in a matter of fact tone. Walking over to my computer, she sits at my desk and begins searching online for the meaning of rose colors.

"My mother got dark red roses from her boyfriend and the next thing I know, I have a step-father." Olivia proudly smiles at me.

"Ah ha! Here it is." Sue pulls her reading glasses from the top of her head and puts them on.

"What color pink does that look like to you guys? Is it light pink, pink, or dark pink?" Sue looks away from the screen and back at the flowers.

"Don't ask me, I'm practically color blind," Cooper says, holding both hands in the air in mock surrender.

"I'd say those are light pink," Ashley turns to me and smiles.

"No, they're plain pink. Look again," Daniel Newton says, adding his thoughts to the conversation.

"I agree, they look like regular pink to me too." Olivia says nodding.

"Let's see... pink. Pink symbolizes grace and elegance, admiration for beauty and refinement, sweetness. Hmm, so I wonder what Paul's trying to tell you?"

"Sue, please." I throw another harsh look, but she persists.

"Did it come with a note?" Sue begins rooting through the stems with her long slender fingers, in search of a card. Not having success, she stops, stares at the bouquet, and crosses her arms over her chest before turning her eyes back to the computer.

Placing emphasis on each word, I say, "Yes, Sue, but I removed it. You see the note is to me and for me so I put it away."

I love Sue dearly, but she can be a little slow on the uptake. I try hard to keep my personal life away from work, and here Sue is dragging it out in front of the entire photography club.

Finally catching on, Sue looks away from the computer screen, takes her glasses off, and puts them back on top of her head. "Well, they're lovely, aren't they?" She leans into the flowers and sniffs a pink petal. "Paul is such a gentleman. How kind of him to do something so considerate."

Now she sounds formal. However, the kids have already caught on to her attempt to make Paul sound like some kind of business associate.

"I think it's nice you have a friend who thinks you're refined, elegant and sweet, Miss O'Connor," Ashley says this as an announcement directed towards the rest of the group.

"Me too," adds Olivia as she picks up a loop and returns to the proofs in front of her.

I look at the clock and see it's getting close to four o'clock. "We should start putting these away if you all want to make the activity bus. Did we agree on our theme for next month? It's winter in Wilmington, right? Let's work on getting great shots we can add to our year-end display."

The kids pack up and as they're walking out the classroom door, Cooper turns to me and says, "Don't worry Miss O'Connor, we won't talk about your friend. That's kind of personal and I know you like to keep things on the down-low."

"Thanks, Cooper. You're pretty perceptive."

I pat Cooper on the shoulder as he walks out of the classroom and instantly turn around and glare at Sue. I pull the door shut, keeping my gaze on Sue. She's already got her hands up in the air, "I know, I know. I'm sorry Gemma, I got so excited for you when I saw the roses."

I can't stay mad so I point to the desk drawer where she's sitting, "The note's in there if you want to read it."

She slides the drawer open and pulls the tiny envelope out. Opening it, she slips the note card out, lifts it up as she pulls her glasses from her head with her free hand and begins reading, "Gemma, Thank You, I enjoyed the picnic very much. Fondly, Paul"

I see her processing the message and finally she says, "Fondly, hmm."

"It's quite benign, isn't it, Sue? Stop inflating it into more than it is. It's all very light and airy, as you like to say."

"Yes, but *fondly*? *Fondly* can mean all kinds of things. Things to come. Things he hopes will happen. *Fondly* isn't just *sincerely*."

"Oh for crying out loud Sue, give it a rest."

She takes her glasses off again, looks at me and smiles, "Well, I have news for you too on the man-front. Guess who is going for a drink with Richard after school Friday?"

Sue's grin is so broad she's about to burst so I playfully guess, "Mrs. Metzger from the cafeteria? He's finally professed his love for her tater-tots?"

Sue gives me a stern look, "Very funny, Gemma. No, he's going for a drink with *me*."

"So what brought this about?" I'm curious because until recently, Sue's interactions with Mr. Payne were awkward at best.

Sue's expression brightens, "I ran into him at the mall Saturday. He was doing a little Christmas shopping so we went to the food court for a cold drink. You know how hot the mall is during the holidays. Anyway, we sat at a table and had a lovely conversation." Inhaling, she leans in, exhales, and continues, "You know his family is one of the first North Carolina families? The Paynes are one of *the* oldest families in the state."

Sue's always impressed by family status so I grin, "Really? Very impressive!"

"Oh, yes, Gemma. He is very well-connected too."

She waves her hand, "Anyway, we had such a nice chat we agreed to go for a drink down at The Reel Friday after work. Isn't it wonderful?!"

"It's wonderful Sue, he's a nice man."

I mean this. Sue has a heart of gold and I'd love to see her happy and in love. She deserves to be happy. For all of her sometimes excessive enthusiasm, she's sincere and it comes from a genuine place in her heart. That's why she's such a good friend. She really wants her friends to be happy.

"Who knows, Gemma? Maybe you and Paul and Richard and I can double date sometime."

Lowering her voice, Sue takes a softer, more serious tone, "Do you think it will go anywhere with Paul? He sent you flowers and all, but do you have feelings for him?"

Ah, the ten-thousand-dollar question.

I stop and think for a few seconds before I reply, "I don't know Sue, I'm not sure. He's good looking, smart, and very nice. I'm just not certain how I feel about having feelings - if that makes sense." I never thought of romance in terms of whether or not I want to have feelings. Feelings are things that happen all on their own, whether I want them to or not. Why so pragmatic, Gem?

"I think you're taking the right approach, Gemma. It makes absolute sense to me. You don't want to rush, but you also don't want to turn into Queen Victoria either. Take your time, you'll know if and when it's right."

The momentary vision of me dressed in black like Queen Victoria puts a smile on my face. *No,* I don't want to turn into Queen Victoria, wallowing in grief.

Pushing the image of Queen Gemma-Victoria clad in black crepe out of my mind, I notice the time. "I promised I'd get home in time to talk online with my cousin. I'd better hustle before I miss my chance and she goes to bed."

Sue stands and walks from behind my desk as I move in to pack up for the night. She walks to the door, turns back, and asks, "Will you be taking Paul's flowers home or keeping them here?"

I glance over at the regular medium pink petals and smile, "Oh, what the heck? I'll keep them here."

"Good choice, Gemma. It would be a shame for them to die a lonely death in your condo when you could have them here to cheer you all day at work."

"See you tomorrow, Sue." I call to her as she walks out of the room.

Without looking back she waves, “Tomorrow!"

Chapter 17

I want to call Sorcha before it's too late, but I really need to thank Paul for the flowers. I plop my laptop bag down in the chair at my desk, dig my cell phone out, and dial his number. After two rings, it goes to voice mail so I leave a message.

"Hi, it's Gemma. Just wanted to thank you for the gorgeous roses. You really shouldn't have, but I love them. Sorry I missed you, hope you're not swamped at work. Talk to you later, and thanks again!"

Oh well, not the best voice message, but not terrible.

I look at the clock on my desk and see it's close to five. That means it's almost ten in Galway. Hopefully Sorcha didn't go to bed early. I pull my laptop out and while it boots, I go to the kitchen and pour myself a glass of what's left of the chardonnay from Thanksgiving.

I take a small sip. Not bad, considering it's been open since Thursday. I return to my desk and log onto the Internet. *Yes,* Sorcha is online so I send an instant message. "You free to talk?"

Within seconds, I hear the familiar incoming tone telling me she's calling. I click the green *answer* box and Sorcha bellows, "Hello, America!"

She's already wearing her pajamas so I tease, "Well, aren't you sexy in flannel?"

"Obviously, Liam isn't here tonight," she laughs, looking down at her pajamas. "Otherwise, I'd be wearing a lacy teddy. Ha!" She laughs again. "So, how's my favorite cousin? Did your folks get to meet Paul?"

"No, the timing didn't work out. Paul was at his aunt's house in Raleigh for Thanksgiving and didn't get back until late. Mom, Dad, and Aidan left early Friday morning to go down to Peter's so it just didn't happen."

Sorcha slumps a bit in her chair and tilts her head to the side, "Aw, that's too bad. I know Aunt Nora must have been dying to meet him."

"Yeah, she was. I felt badly I even mentioned there was a *chance* of meeting him. She seemed pretty disappointed when he called to say he wasn't going to make it for dessert."

"Well, maybe next time. If it's meant to be, they'll meet him soon enough."

"Meant to be? It's just the first guy I've been dating, I wouldn't start talking in terms of 'meant to be' yet."

"Oh, come on, now. You have to admit, it's more than coincidental he recognized you from school and that you ran into each other at a pub in Galway. Come on Gem, things like that don't just happen by accident."

"Okay, I'll give you that."

"Right, so. What's up? Why'd ya want to talk tonight?

I take another sip of wine, place the glass on the coaster beside the lamp, and say, "I heard from the tourism director in Boyle. He'd like me to take pictures of next year's arts festival. They want to use them to promote the festival from a participant's perspective. I guess they liked the pictures I entered in the last festival *or* Grandma has been working behind the scenes. Either way, I'm thinking of spending the summer again and want to let you know first."

Clapping her hands together and squealing, "Oh that's grand! This is huge, Gemma! I'm sure Da will let you have the cottage again and you can come spend a week in Galway with me if you like."

"That would be great. I enjoyed the solitude of the cottage. Thank goodness your dad doesn't use it much anymore."

Still grinning, Sorcha doesn't acknowledge my last comment but continues, "Hey, Gemma, I meant to tell ya; Declan said he's going to be in America for work, but I forget when."

I raise my eyebrows, "Oh wow, he should give me a call if he's going to be nearby. America is awfully large, can you narrow it down to which city he's going to?"

"Of course." She rolls her eyes and exhales before continuing, "He said he'll be in New York, but I forget when. You should get in touch with him and find out."

"Look on a map, Sorcha. New York and North Carolina aren't exactly close enough to go grab a cup of coffee."

"Well, I was just passing along the news." She pauses a second, looks up, then back at the camera, and modulates to a more serious tone, "He's sort of been seeing someone he met down the pub. But I can't figure him out."

"Oh," I reply in a steady voice. Declan's seeing someone?! I'm curious, but I have to play it cool. Play it cool, Gemma. Play it cool.

"What do you mean, you can't figure him out?"

"Declan is funny. Ever since Sheila, it's like he goes through long spells of not dating anybody and then out of nowhere, he'll mention so-and-so he's been seeing. It's like he doesn't want us to know he's been looking for a girlfriend. I can't figure him out."

"Maybe he's just dating for the company. You know, nothing serious."

Sorcha considers what I've said, "Maybe. He's so busy with his work, I guess he does feel lonely. Anyway, I'd better get going. I promised Liam I'd call before I go to bed and I'm fecking exhausted."

"Hey, will you ask your Dad if I can stay in the cottage or at least let him know I'll be spending the summer in Boyle? I'll send him an email and ask him officially."

"Sure, yeah. Not a problem, Gem. I'll be talking with him tomorrow. Ring me this weekend and we'll chat more."

"I will. Goodnight, Sorcha."

After we hang up, I return to the kitchen and make a hot turkey sandwich with the last of the Thanksgiving leftovers. One of my favorite things about Thanksgiving is the leftovers. Piling pieces of turkey on a slice of bread, I heat the gravy and pour it over the entire sandwich. I add a tiny bit of cranberry sauce to the plate and sit on a stool at the counter to eat.

I'm lost in thought, enjoying my sandwich when I hear my cell phone in the other room buzzing away on my desk. I retrieve it and see the number. It's Paul so I pick up.

"Hi, Paul"

"Hi, Gemma. I got your message. Sorry I missed your call, I was in a staff meeting."

I walk back to my dinner and climb up on the stool, shifting the phone from my left ear to the right, "I wanted to thank you for the flowers. They're beautiful."

Paul replies, "I had a lot of fun the other day and I wanted to say thanks."

I detect uncertainty in his voice so I say, "I did too Paul.... is everything okay?"

"Oh yeah, I've been busy at work. A lot going on and....."

He trails off distracted by something, so I wait for him to finish speaking.

"I hope you didn't think I was inappropriate in any way."

Inappropriate? What's he talking about?

"No, not at all." Confused, I add, "What did you think I might have felt was inappropriate?"

He sounds relieved, "Nothing, I just didn't want you to think I moved too quickly or did anything you weren't... weren't ready for."

"No, Paul, you were a gentleman the entire time. You're also a pretty good kisser."

His deep voice is much more light-hearted, "Oh, thank heavens. I was really worried about that." He laughs and adds, "Would you like to go to dinner this Friday?"

I stop to think if I have anything going on, "I'm free Friday, sure."

"Friday it is then, I'll call you later on to confirm. I've got to go now, but Gemma in all sincerity, the other day was great. You're great."

"Thanks, Paul."

We hang up and I look at the food on my plate. Half-eaten and cold again, I've lost what was left of my appetite so I take the plate, cover it in plastic wrap, put it back in the refrigerator.

There, it's tomorrow's dinner too.

My thoughts return to the call from Paul. I can't put my finger on it, but the call was awkward and brief. He wasn't very talkative, was he? He seemed different, but how?

I shake my head as I walk into the bedroom and dismiss my over-thinking.

I put on a pair of pajama pants and a t-shirt, pull my hair into a bun on top of my head, put on my reading glasses, and climb into bed with my laptop to begin sorting and editing the pictures from the trip to the beach.

Some people don't like when it gets dark early in the fall and winter, but I don't mind. I come home and get comfortable and begin to nest. I've propped myself up with the half-dozen pillows I keep on my bed. My computer sits upon a laptop desk with built-in speakers so I log onto Shannon Side to listen to Irish radio while I work.

I love my bed. One of the best things I did after Brad died, was buy all new bed linens. I was so exhausted and distraught, I decided my bedroom would be my sanctuary. I already loved my bedroom furniture, but I'd never splurged on beautiful bedding so I made it my mission to create the most comfortable and stylish bedroom possible.

I got the idea late one night when I was flipping through the channels and landed on one of the shopping networks. They were selling comforter sets and sheets made of the finest Egyptian cotton. The host was going on and on about luxurious blankets, sheets, comforters, down mattress toppers - I was inspired.

Being the consummate organizer, I started collecting magazine pictures and searching the Internet until I decided exactly what I wanted my room to look like. Before long, I had goose down pillow-toppers, a plethora of pillows, soft sheets and a comforter set that would make Laura Ashley *and* Martha Stewart envious.

Now that I've created my little sanctuary, I love coming home and climbing into bed for the evening. I'll spend hours on the weekend grading papers or working on lesson plans in bed. Tonight - it's photo editing in the comfort of my boudoir.

As I'm cropping a tight shot of a seagull, the instant message icon at the bottom of my screen lights up.

I wonder what Sorcha is still doing up this late.

I click the button and see, it's not Sorcha, but Declan. His message reads, "You free to video chat?"

Self-consciously, I glance at myself and type back, "I'm in my pajamas if you can handle that?"

Declan doesn't message me back, instead he calls, and I answer. As the video image of him appears, I feel a familiar flutter in my stomach.

He's so handsome.

I can only see him from his chest up, but he's got on a heather gray t-shirt and a big smile. "Hope I'm not interrupting anything," he grins.

I instinctively look around at the pillows surrounding me and smile back, "No, I'm alone. You're up awfully late, aren't you?"

"Aye, I've been busy at work." He stops, looks right at me for a moment, and says, "So this is you in your pajamas? You look beautiful, but isn't it a little early in America to be in bed?"

"Thank you, and yes, it's only seven-thirty, but I love working in bed. It's the most comfortable place in the house and I always feel more inspired in bed."

As soon as the words leave my mouth, his lips curl into a huge smile so I add, "That's not what I meant. You know; in bed I feel very motivated."

He's laughing out loud now. "Hey, I didn't say it. You did."

"You know what I meant. Oh, never mind," I say, shaking my head as he laughs.

"Ah, you're an angel. Really, you are Gemma. I love how easily you get flustered."

His smile is kind and there's a twinkle in his eyes. His playful side is charming. I can't imagine ever being angry with him.

"I don't fluster easily, just around you."

"I know, that's what makes it so darn cute. I fluster you for some reason."

A surge of warmth rushes to my face, "Consider it an honor that only you get to see this side of me."

His expression grows serious and his tone is staid, "I do."

"So what's up?" I say abruptly.

"Sorcha called and said she told you I'll be coming to America."

"Yeah, we spoke earlier and she mentioned it. She also told me you're seeing someone you met down at the pub."

Declan gives me a sheepish look, "Aye, did she now?"

"I think it's great. Is she special?"

I'm being nosey, but hey, it seems like the kind of conversation where I can be a little bold.

"She's nice enough."

Not exactly a resounding endorsement of the poor girl.

He obviously doesn't want to discuss his lady friend so he moves on, "I'm going to be in New York in late December and the first week of January. My company's got some meetings coming up; a big New Year kick-off sort of thing. Sorcha said you usually go to your parents' home for the holidays, so I thought before I book my flight, I'd see when you'd be up that way. Maybe you can come into the city one day, we can *hang out,* as you Americans say."

"I'm going up right after school gets out for the holiday. My flight up is December 22nd and I come back on January 3rd. Will you have any free time then?"

"I will. I'm probably going to fly in on the thirtieth and I'll return home on January 7th."

"Oh, that's too bad. You'll have to spend New Year's Eve in New York City," I tease.

"The company has a corporate apartment too, so how sad is that? A paid for apartment in New York City on New Year's Eve. Really quite dreadful when one thinks about it," he plays along.

"Are you kidding me?"

"No, I'm not. The only thing that would make it bearable would be if I were to have a wisecracking Yank to spend it with. Can you come into the city on the thirty-first? It's a two bedroom apartment; you'll have your own space for the night. We'll have good craic."

I hesitate a moment, looking down, thoughts of Brad flash through my mind. Next, I think a second about Paul. Am I *seeing* Paul? Then back to Brad......

"Hey, Gemma?" I look back up and see Declan's caring expression.

"Yeah?"

"Stop over-thinking. Just come into the city, we'll have fun. You'll have fun. That's all I want - to see you having fun. Do you understand me?"

I look at Declan, he's so certain of himself without being arrogant. His confidence is an attractive quality. I feel he knows me and I can't pretend or hide anything from him, so I don't even try. "Okay, I'll come into the city and have fun."

"Good girl. You need to start having fun again. Quit hiding away in your bedroom."

"Hiding away?" Slightly mocking him, "I never thought of it that way before. You're so perceptive, Declan. You could be a psychologist." I giggle.

"Aye, indeed. I've seen through you from the moment we met. Sweet Mary Gemma O'Connor acts all pulled-together in public, but when she's alone, she hides herself away in a bed full of pillows as her barrier from the cold cruel world."

We're both laughing now. "Okay, okay. New Year's Eve in New York City, it is. You tell me the time and place and I'll be there. *Sans* pillows."

"Grand! I'll be in touch. Now, I'm off to bed. It's nearly one in the morning here. Goodnight, Miss O'Connor."

"Goodnight, Mr. Gallagher." Without thinking, I kiss my fingers and place them on the computer screen.

I used to do this when I'd say good bye to Brad.

Declan tilts his head to the right and does the same thing. "I'll find you soon."

And we disconnect.

Chapter 18

When seventh period arrives Friday, my Major British Writers class is deeply involved in reading sonnets. My favorite is today's subject matter, Shakespeare's 116th. One of my more studious pupils, Todd Hammond, is reading with the most dramatic flair I've ever heard from a seventeen year old.

"Let me not to the marriage of true minds admit impediments.

Love is not love which alters when it alteration finds, or bends with the remover to remove: Oh no; it is an ever- fixed mark"

Sigh. Well put William, well put.

As the class is analyzing what to me is perhaps the most perfect writing of all time, my mind drifts to Brad.

"That looks on tempests, and is never shaken; it is a star to every wandering bark,"

Time has gone by and even though he's gone, I still love him. If he walked through that door right now, I'd run to him.

"Who's worth's unknown, although his heights be taken.

Love's not Time's fool, though rosy lips and cheeks

Within his bending sickle's compass come;"

The first time I read this sonnet, I was in high school. I was moved by it because of my teacher's enthusiasm. She explained what Shakespeare was saying and it made me wonder if I'd ever feel that kind of deep emotion for another person *or* if another person would feel such love for me.

Not that I didn't think I was capable of loving or being loved, but I couldn't conceive of such raw emotion and passion. At sixteen that kind of love seemed the stuff of romance novels or fantasies - not real life.

"Love alters not with his brief hours and weeks,
But bears it out even to the edge of doom.
If this be error and upon me proved,
I never writ, nor no man ever loved."

Sigh, again. Truly magnificent.

Remembering back to what seems ages ago, but in reality was just eight years, the corners of my mouth curl up into a grin as I look at the class. Maybe someone sitting here today is thinking those exact thoughts.

The bell rings and in response the students rise in unison. Chairs moving, book bags zipping closed, and farewells are exchanged as the class exits the room. When the last one leaves, I look at the clock on the wall.

Two-thirty; another week finished and tonight I have a date with Paul. I gather my books and computer, placing them in my bag, and think about the sonnet again. That kind of love is awfully special, I wonder if I'll ever feel that way again?

With Brad it was instantaneous - I knew it the moment his hand touched the small of my back to guide me through the room. I felt it. Sure, I didn't know the when or where, but I knew we were meant to be together.

I stand at my desk for a moment and think - is that kind of love only once in a life time? If it is, then what?

Catching myself before I go down the rabbit hole of over analyzing, I shake my head from side to side to clear the thoughts as if erasing an Etch-A-Sketch. I pick up my bag, place it on my shoulder and walk to the door. Flipping the light switch, another grin comes to my face, but I don't know why.

❖

"Is the Bridge House okay with you?" Paul smiles at me as I sit down in the passenger seat of his car.

"I love the Bridge House." I really do, it's one of my favorite restaurants. It's by the bridge that leads to Wrightsville Beach. It's got large bay windows overlooking the water and they serve wonderful seafood.

"Oh, good, I like it too."

As we drive, I glance over at Paul. He's a nice looking guy and he seems to like me, but sometimes I can't help wondering what *this* is. He's always a gentleman and he hasn't tried too hard or done anything to make me unhappy with him, but I don't know exactly where this relationship is going.

Perceiving my pensive mood as he pulls into the parking space he asks, "Is everything okay? You're lost in thought tonight. Not your usual self."

Snapping out of relationship thoughts, I smile at Paul, "I'm fine. It's been a busy week and the next few weeks are going to be hectic at school."

"You'll tell me if something is troubling you, won't you?"

I watch him take the key from the ignition and smile back at him, "Yes, I promise."

The hostess's blonde hair swishes back and forth across her shoulders as she guides us through the restaurant towards a back booth, away from the windows. The sun disappeared long ago and the sky is dark, and dotted with stars, but the water isn't visible so I'm not disappointed by our lack of a view. Across the dining room is a large group - obviously an office Christmas party or similar gathering. I suppose the hostess is trying to keep us away from the noise by giving us this out-of-the-way table.

Paul stands until I'm seated in the booth and then slides in across from me. The moisture from the ocean air has curled his hair leaving one piece dipping down on his forehead.

I reach across and twist the brown lock of hair around my finger, "Clark? Clark Kent? I knew there was something mysterious about you."

Softening his expression, we both are laughing as the waitress approaches and interrupts, "Hi, I'm Tessa, I'll be taking care of you tonight."

Grinning, I order a glass of cabernet and Paul does the same. Tessa flashes a smile, closes the folder with our drink order inside, slips it into the pocket of her apron then turns and walks to the bar. Once she's left us Paul turns to me and says, "Now, that's the smile I've come to love. Your entire face lights up when you smile, Gemma."

He reaches across the table, takes my hand, and begins gently stroking the back of it with his index finger. His fingers are rough and calloused, probably from his profession, but his touch is soothing. Lowering my shoulders, I relax and ask, "Are you ready for the holidays? Do you have big plans?"

Am I curious or am I filling dead air?

Before he can answer my question, Tessa returns with our wine. After she takes our dinner orders and disappears again, he lifts his wine glass, looks at me and says, "A toast?"

"Sure. You go, I can't think of anything." Truthfully, I'm terrible at giving toasts. I panic. I can't think of a thing to say, and when I finally come up with something, I choke on my words and absolutely nothing profound or intelligible comes out of my mouth. Really, it's quite dreadful.

"To us." He tips his glass and it touches mine.

Hmm, not much better than my toasts.

"To us," I repeat before taking a delicate sip of the silky, red wine. *What does he mean by "us?" Is there an "us?" Are we an "us?"*

Dinner is delicious and we chat away like old friends, laughing and joking. The wine lessons my tension - the dim lighting and ambiance has created an amorous mood and we're lost in each other, unaware of the other patrons celebrating nearby. When Tessa brings the bill and Paul sends her off with his credit card I ask, "Do you want to come back to my place for coffee?"

I hope he doesn't think coffee is a euphemism for..... Well, a euphemism.

Paul reaches over the table, takes both my hands in his, and says, "If that's what you want. I'd love to come over for coffee."

As we walk to the car he takes my hand, lacing his fingers between mine, he guides me to the passenger door. Helping me in, Paul leans inside and gives me a gentle kiss on the lips. The scent of his cologne paired with his tender kiss sends electricity through me. I have goose bumps as a shiver travels from my head to my toes. Now I'm not certain he thinks coffee means *just* coffee.

I'm quiet the entire ride home. When we get to my place, we climb the stairs in silence. Finally, as we walk inside, Paul breaks the silence. "May I use your bathroom?"

Phew! That's an easy question to answer.

"Sure, it's down that hall - first door."

I hang my coat in the closet and call to him, "Do you want coffee, beer, soda, or wine, or I think I may have some Jameson in the pantry?"

"A shot of Jameson would be perfect. I haven't had that since the summer."

I get a couple of glasses down from the cabinet and pour him a shot. I don't want him to drink alone, but I can't take whiskey straight so I add a little water to mine.

He returns to the room and removes his blazer and drapes it across the back of one of the bar stools. I join him in the living room and hand him his Jameson. He eyes my drink and asks, "You water down your whiskey?"

"I'm afraid so. I know it's practically a sin in Ireland, but that golden liquid is an acquired taste I've not acquired yet."

He sits down on the sofa and pats the seat next to him. I dutifully follow and begin slowly sipping the whiskey. The warm burn as it slides down my throat is uncomfortable, and I try not to let him see me wincing at the stinging fire heating my core.

Paul takes a draw from his drink and places it on the coffee table. Smiling at me, he shakes his head *no*, and takes the glass from my hand. "You're sweet to try Gemma, but I can see you *really* don't care for that."

He puts the glass on the table then turns back to me, lifts his hand to stroke my hair, and pulls me in close. He leans closer and his eyes search mine for a second. His breath is warm on my cheek as his lips touch mine and he kisses me. This time, I don't hesitate. I need to be kissed and I oblige and kiss back, passionately. More passionately than I thought I could kiss someone who isn't Brad.

Soon, our bodies are pressing together. Paul's strength envelopes me as his mouth explores mine. His hands guide my hips closer to his. Secure in his embrace, his lips surge forcefully upon mine as he takes control. I lie back slightly. He's above me now, and I'm beneath, still giving and taking kisses; kisses that send shivers coursing through me. As he presses into me, I feel his hardness and quiver with the knowledge *he wants me*. He reaches down, gently sliding his hand under my skirt. Exploring, his hand brushes between my legs, his fingertips dancing over the satin of my panties. At this, I tremble. I'm consumed with desire; desire to feel sexual again, desire to make love, and plain old desire to shag.

My longing is overpowering my better judgment and I'm ready to let go. No longer shy and afraid; I'm willing and ready to let Paul take me, but he halts abruptly. Pushing off of me, he retreats to the opposite end of the sofa.

I can't tell if I've done something wrong, but the look of agony or disgust, I can't tell which, on his face is shattering.

Hurt, confused and disappointed I gasp, "Is everything okay, Paul?"

"Yes," he breathlessly snaps. "It's fine. I ..." He trails off.

I feel crimson rising in my face. *Is he rejecting me? Did I do something he didn't like?*

I'm wounded and my face shows it. Seeing this, Paul reaches over and cups my face in his hands. "Oh, no. No, Gemma. You've done nothing wrong. Just the opposite, you're amazing. I guess that's why I ...." He trails off again.

Pools are welling in my eyes and my throat burns, but not from the whiskey - it's tears that are about to spill.

"I'm sorry, Paul. I don't understand. You sent pink roses, you invite me places, and you kiss me. But I don't get it." I angrily spit out the words as I wipe the tears escaping from my eyes with the back of my hand.

"Gemma, please don't misunderstand me. I'm crazy about you. It's just, I have to tell you something."

Recoiling from Paul in anticipation, I blurt, "Oh, God. What is it?"

Looking up at the ceiling to collect his thoughts, he grabs my left hand, bracing me for whatever this horrible revelation is. His hand is hot, and he squeezes tightly before finding the courage to hit me with this thing that's keeping us from consummating the relationship.

Barely audible, he begins, "I'm going back to Ireland next semester. They asked me to come back and teach, so I'm taking a sabbatical from UNCW and going to Cork." Inhaling deeply and letting out the air, he finishes, "Right after Christmas."

At first, his words don't register. I've gone from the bliss of anticipating a long overdue shag, to Coitus interruptus, to the shock of, "I've got something to tell you," in the span of fifteen seconds. My head's spinning and I'm waiting for the blood that was rushing to my nether regions to return to my brain. Wiping another tear from the corner of my eye with the tip of my index finger, I squeak out a high pitched, "Oh. I see."

After a moment of collecting myself, my voice is a little stronger, "That's great news for you, isn't it? A wonderful career move."

"Yeah, it's actually fantastic. But, well... I guess I was afraid of this."

He begins pointing back and forth between the two of us, "I really want this to happen, but I can't. Not without letting you know I'm leaving. Not permanently, but at least six months. Maybe longer."

I look down and adjust my skirt which is still hiked up exposing the lacy tops of my thigh-high stockings. "I appreciate that Paul. You could have convinced me to... you know, and then hit me with your news tomorrow, but you didn't. Thank you."

My tone is business-like, curt, but I don't mean to be short with him. The iciness in my voice is directed at me. I almost cheated on Brad's memory by sleeping with a man I'm not sure about. Had it not been for Paul's guilty conscience, I would have.

"I've upset you, Gemma. God, that's the last thing I want to do."

His finger is pointing back and forth between us again, "I know this is special and I would have felt awful doing this without being honest with you first. I still want this, and I'm willing to wait."

I let out a sigh and look up into Paul's eyes. "I think that's a good idea, Paul. Let's wait."

Paul's disappointment is written on his face, but he agrees. "Okay, good idea. But I want to keep in touch while I'm away. You know, video chat, telephone, email. Gemma, you're special to me."

I think Paul's special too, but I've begun doubting my instincts so I say the first thing that comes to me, "You're special too Paul and I promise, we'll keep in touch. I'll even be back in Ireland next summer, who knows?" I'm smiling, but it's only on the outside, I'm not smiling inside.

Paul leans in and kisses my forehead. "Thanks for being so understanding. I think the world of you, you know that, *don't you*?" I nod and smile up at him. His eyes are beautiful and warm. I'm not upset with him, not at all. It's me I'm upset with.

"I do Paul."

Eyeing his watch, he stands and says, "It's getting late. I've got a busy day tomorrow. I'd better say goodnight."

I stand too, help with his jacket, and walk to the door with him. "Thanks Paul, dinner was lovely."

"Thank you, Gemma. You're incredible."

I don't feel incredible.

Paul pulls me close and gives me a long, hard kiss. I kiss him back, but I'm not sure what the point of the kiss is. Is he trying to reassure me? Is he trying to assuage his guilt? Is he trying to say he wants me? Is he asking me to wait for him?

I have no idea. Maybe it just means *goodnight*.

Paul opens the door, walks into the hall, and turns back to face me. Tucking a stray strand of hair behind my ear, he smiles, "You're beautiful, Gemma. Sleep tight."

"Goodnight, Paul."

I close the door behind him, turn out the light, walk into the bedroom, sit on the edge of my bed and sob.

Chapter 19

I'm restless, waking up several times during the night. Tossing and turning, I'm miserable.

Perhaps the food was too rich. Maybe I shouldn't have had coffee with dessert. Or wait, maybe it was the whole Paul thing. Yes. Yes, that must be what's keeping me awake.

Finally, at five-thirty I concede. I fling my legs outside the covers, put my feet on the floor, and get out of bed. Convinced sleep is over for me, I drag myself into the kitchen and turn on the kettle. If there's anything I've learned from my Irish relatives, it's tea will always help.

When the kettle boils, I pour the hot water into the teapot. I watch the steaming liquid splashing over the tea and think of Grandma O'Connor. She gave me this teapot when I left for college. She bought it at Taylor's Shop in Boyle and I'm pretty sure it cost more for her to ship it to me than to buy it.

I pick up the pot and take small, carefully measured steps to my desk and slowly place it beside my computer.

No spills – huzzah!

Since I'm up anyway, I may as well get some work done on my website so I turn on the computer and pour myself a cuppa. The room is still dark, so I turn on the desk lamp and take a sip of hot tea. My head's muddled; groggy from lack of sleep, exhausted from tears, confused and reliving events from last night.

I think Paul cares about me. I think I care about him. So why am I confused?

Am I sad he's going to be leaving or am I kind of relieved?

The computer is barely on when I see Sorcha calling me online.

I must look like the wraith, but I don't care. *Oh well, here it goes.*

"Feck! Gemma, what's wrong?"

"Good morning to you too, Sorcha."

"Sorry, good morning. Now, feck! What's wrong?"

Chuckling I say, "Nothing's wrong. It's five-thirty in the morning, that's all. What's up with you?"

"I just talked to Declan and he tells me you two are getting together while he's in America."

I know she thinks I've been withholding this information, so I reply casually, "Oh yeah, we talked a few days ago. I think I'll meet him in the city one day."

"He tells me you're going to spend New Year's together." Her voice betrays her thoughts – she sounds like she thinks it's more than a *casual* meeting.

I take a sip of tea and say, "He gets into town the day before so we figured, hey, why not? New Years in New York- should be pretty fun."

I cut her off before she can continue her interrogation, "So what's up? Why are you calling me so early this Saturday?"

She pauses and clears her throat before forging onto the new topic, "I want to tell you, you're all set with the cottage. Spoke with Da

Thursday and he's thrilled you'll be back. He's not letting the cottage out at all this summer so basically, it's yours for the summer if you want it."

"Thanks, Sorcha. I'm excited to be coming back. I was a bit of a zombie last summer; maybe I'll be more fun this year." I smile and take another sip from my mug.

"My mum dropped by the taxi shop to see Grandma yesterday. She's thrilled you'll be back. She was bragging you up to poor Deidre in the office; saying how grand it will be having ye back for the summer." Sorcha giggles and reaches for her cup of tea, "Oh look Gem, we're having tea together. Just like when we were little girls and we'd have tea parties."

She holds her cup up as if to say, "Cheers," and takes a sip.

After a dramatic pause to swallow, she continues, "Gemma, what's going on with you and that Paul you've been seeing?"

Darn it. I thought I'd gotten away without having to talk about him.

Stalling, I lift the tea pot and pour myself another cup. As I pick up the cup to drink I say, very matter of fact, "Oh, you know. He's a great guy. He buys me flowers, takes me to dinner, and all. But it's fairly informal. He's about to go back to Cork for a teaching sabbatical."

There, I played it cool. Very cool. You're cool Gemma.

"Does that bother you?"

"Does what bother me?"

"Does it bother you that you've been seeing each other and now he's going away?"

I take a sip before answering, "You know, Sorcha, I really don't know how I feel. I like going out with him, and he's nice, but he's pursuing his career, which I really respect. Am I sad he'll be so far away? I guess, but since we're not what I'd call serious, I'm not all broken up over his leaving. Is that what you mean?"

Sorcha looks behind her, then back at the camera, lowers her voice and says, "You didn't sleep with him, did you?"

Sorcha always cuts to the chase. A wonderful, yet occasionally irritating quality.

"No, Sorcha, and even if I had, I'm pretty sure I'd be just fine with things the way they are. I'm perfectly content to wait and see where things go, if they go anywhere at all."

If she only knew how close I came to it though - that's another story.

Sorcha's quiet for a second, processing what I've said. Rather than push the topic, she moves on, "Anyway, do you think when you come this summer you'd like to have company for a week during the Boyle Arts Festival?"

Her change of subject is almost dizzying, but I'm grateful to be past the subject of Paul so I perk up and answer, "Yeah! What are you thinking?"

"I'm not sure yet, but Liam and I may take a couple weeks holiday in July. Ya know, maybe spend some time in Boyle and then travel around. Nothing confirmed yet, but I wanted to toss that out there in case."

"In case of what? I'll be around for the festival, remember? I'm going to be taking pictures."

"Sure, yeah right. Of course. I thought I'd book your time well in advance, that's all."

I shake my head and take another sip of tea, "You're nuts, Sorcha, but I love ya."

"Hey, Gem? Promise me one thing, will ya?"

She's serious so I shift closer into the computer and reply, "What Sorcha?"

"Be gentle on yourself, will ya? I don't know what's eating ya this morning, but snap out of it, okay? You've come a long way this year and I want you to enjoy the holidays. Okay?"

"I promise. I will."

"Oh, and one more thing, Gem."

I roll my eyes and say, "What now?"

"When Declan's in America, will ye try and find out about this Maeve he's been seeing? He won't bring her around us, but I know he's been seeing her. Even Liam is curious. We only want to know if she's good for him, that's all."

"Have you asked Declan about her?" I say, sarcasm dripping from my words.

"Of course we have. He dismisses us, like it's no big thing."

"Well, there's your answer. It's no big thing."

"Or, he's mad about her and doesn't want us to know."

"Oh good grief, Sorcha. Give it a rest." I can see her mind working and add, "You're a dear friend and I love how much you care and want the best for the people you love, but don't stress yourself worrying. Declan's a grown man and he'll do what's best for himself. Trust him."

"I do. I just want to make sure he picks the right girl." She smiles into the camera and adds, "Well, I'm off now. Liam and I are heading to a holiday luncheon a buddy from work is throwing."

"Have fun and say hi to Liam for me."

"Would you like me to say hello to Declan as well? We're going over his place for brunch in the morning."

"Yes, say hi to Declan for me too." The corners of my mouth curve upward into a thin smile.

Sorcha notices, "That's my girl. I like ya smiling a lot better. Bye, bye now."

"Bye, bye," I say, but she's already disconnected. That's Sorcha, always off and running.

I shake my head with a smile and log into my email account. Scanning the new messages in the inbox, I see a notification telling me someone has left a message on my website. I'm always excited to see if somebody's interested in purchasing a picture so I open it immediately.

I read the message out loud, "You never really know a person without learning their past, do you?"

That's it. Nothing else, no questions about photography? It makes no sense. Very strange.

I look at the email address, but it tells me nothing.
"xoxo@bigmail.com"

I decide it's probably just some spam bot or trash so I delete the message.

I look out the window and see the sun creeping up in the sky painting it an amazing pinkish-red hue. No longer in the mood to work, I put on a pair of yoga pants and my tennis shoes to go for a walk. I need to clear my head and get a little exercise to shake this mood.

I put on my heaviest fleece jacket, a knit cap and my mittens with the removable fingers. They're my favorite mittens because I can wear them and still take pictures. As I walk out, I grab my camera from the table by the door, put the strap around my neck, and tuck my phone in the jacket pocket. Picking up the keys that are hanging by the door, I venture outside into the chill to capture sunrise down by the river.

Mornings in Wilmington are beautiful. The city's still sleepy at six-fifteen, few people are stirring, yet there's so much going on. Seagulls are happily going about their morning routine, looking for food and calling out to one and other.

I begin snapping away when I see one standing on a fence post close to the water. Birds are fun to photograph. They don't mind posing, but only for a moment. They'll put up with me for just so long before they have to move along.

After my *subject* takes off, I notice another bird approaching the water poised to dive and grab a fish. I position the camera in anticipation and just as his talons touch the surface, I snap the shutter once, twice, three times in rapid succession then put the camera down and watch him fly away with his breakfast.

The late fall sky is breathtaking as the sun rises above the old historic city. Streaks of vivid pinks, deep ambers, purples, and radiant reds color the sky providing a stunning background for my pictures. The brisk morning air is invigorating. My breath is visible, but I pay no attention to the temperature. With each press of the shutter, I lose myself in what I'm doing.

Taking pictures lets me escape to another place. That other place is where I feel at peace, it's where I find healing. It's where I permit myself to heal. I know this because whenever I'm taking pictures, a calmness overtakes me and I'm swept away in my subject matter. I'm able to leave real life behind for a few minutes as I dive deeper into seeing things through the camera lens.

I notice a brightly colored maple leaf lying on the boardwalk, one of the last of the season. The brilliant reddish-orange hue is a stark contrast to the veins running within. I stand over it with a foot on each side, adjust my lens, take the picture, and smile. I let go of the camera hanging around my neck and look up at the sky. Tears begin filling my eyes. I'm having one of *those* moments.

From time to time, I feel with every fiber of my being that Brad's close by. I used to think people who said those kinds of things were foolish or indulging in wishful thinking. But I don't think that anymore. I can't explain it, but there are times when a certain energy surrounds me, my skin tingles, and I feel a wave of electricity. It's reassuring; nothing frightening or uneasy.

This is one of those moments. He's near me. I stand still in front of the beautiful maple leaf, look down at my feet, and whisper, "I miss you."

After a few seconds, I glance around, dab the tears away and move on. I can feel Brad nearby, I just wish I could ask him what to do. He knew me better than anyone else in the world, and now when I could really use his advice, he isn't here to talk to.

These are the loneliest times of all.

I keep walking towards Front Street and find an open coffee shop. If there's one thing I love about Wilmington, there's no shortage of coffee houses.

The barista is busy behind the counter brewing coffee when he hears the door and acknowledges me as I enter. Turning he says, "Good morning." He looks as though he just woke up and doesn't really mean what he's saying, but I smile back and greet him.

"Good morning. Could I have a cup of tea and a scone, please?"

I dig a wrinkled ten dollar bill from my pocket as he rings it up on the cash register. I find a table by the front window, remove my hat and mittens, and gently place my camera on the chair beside me. I wonder how bad I look if Sorcha thought I look like *feck*?

I giggle at her propensity to use the word *feck* in all forms of conversation, as I peer into the glass trying to catch a glimpse of my reflection in the shop window. I think the combination of puffy crying eyes, hat hair, and pale lips is a stunning look for this hour on a Saturday.

I turn away from the window and see the barista coming with my order, "Oh, thanks. I could have come and gotten it."

"No problem, I need to move around to wake up. I'm recovering from a late night."

He smiles as he puts the tea and scone down in front of me. I smile back and see he isn't kidding. He looks a little rough. I'm not even sure he's brushed his hair this morning. I study his piercings that look like two small saucers have been embedded into his earlobes. Fortunately, he walks away and doesn't catch me staring.

Lifting the string on the tea bag, I dip it up and down into the hot water until it changes from clear to a light brown. As I'm squeezing the liquid from the bag, I feel the phone in my pocket vibrating. I pull it out and see it's Paul calling.

I hesitate to answer because the shop is empty and quiet, and I don't know how private this conversation will be. I look across the tables to the counter, the barista is busy washing something so I shrug my shoulders.

"Hello?"

"Gemma, Good morning," Paul says in a soft, timid tone before continuing, "I'm sorry to call so early. I just, I just."

He's struggling to speak so I jump in, "That's okay, and I've been up a while. I'm down on the waterfront taking pictures already."

Don't overdo it, why so extra chipper?

"Oh, good." Sounding relieved, he adds, "I was afraid I'd upset you last night so I wanted to check on you this morning."

His concern is endearing, it's hard not to feel sorry for him. He must have had a rough night, thinking he hurt my feelings.

"No, I'm fine Paul. I was surprised, and the timing of your announcement was a bit awkward." *A bit awkward? Talk about an understatement.* "But I think it's good news for you and I'm happy."

Happy? Really? Confused, perplexed, uncertain, but happy? Okay, go with it, Gemma. Happy it is.

"I know. I felt terrible about how I interrupted our," he pauses, "date."

"No Paul, I appreciate you telling me when you did. You're very thoughtful and you didn't want to complicate things or hurt me. That's really a respectable thing to do. You shouldn't feel badly at all."

Wow, where is this coming from?

"You're incredible, Gemma. Thanks for being so understanding."

I take a sip of tea and respond, "Besides, it's not like we won't be in touch. Right? We'll talk on the phone or online."

Enthusiastically he adds, "Exactly. Well, I've got to go. I'm swamped with work, finals are coming up, and I've got a lot of catching up to do, and loose ends before the end of the semester."

"Go, have fun. I'll talk with you later," I say as I break off a corner of my scone.

"Thanks again, Gemma. Find ya soon."

Okay, that was a quick call, wasn't it? A tad clumsy, but nice of him.

I hit the *end* button, pop the piece of scone into my mouth, and think of Brad again. I look out the window and chew the orange cranberry scone. It's a little dry so I take a sip of tea to wash it down. I fix my eyes on a jogger trotting past the window, continuing to stare after he passes, I softly say, "What am I doing Brad? What am I doing?"

Chapter 20

It's the Saturday before school lets out for winter break and Sue and I are busy putting up decorations for the staff holiday party. There's so much I need to do today. I need to finish grading papers, I need to start packing for my trip to my parents, I need to get a dress to wear for New Year's Eve, but instead, I'm plastering the school cafeteria with snowmen for a politically correct holiday party which is beginning to look like it's dedicated to snowman worship.

If Sue weren't completely nuts about Rich, there's no way I'd be doing this. She's been such a good friend and I think she and Mr. Payne are kind of cute together so I grin and continue working.

"Tell me again why we're having a holiday party in the school where there will be no alcohol?"

"Oh, I know Gemma, it seems crazy. But you know, liability yada, yada, yada. So, it is what it is." Sue's standing on a step ladder, hanging a snowflake from the ceiling with a piece of fishing line.

"I wouldn't go to too much trouble if I were you. Don't you think most people are going to put in an appearance and then go somewhere else? Maybe somewhere they can get a drink or something to eat besides chips and dips?"

"You're probably right, but Rich was kind of given this assignment against his will so I want to help make it as nice as possible." She steps off the ladder and stands back to admire the array of snowflakes dangling over what's to be the DJ's table.

I smile at her and say, "Ah, snowflake perfection!"

We both start laughing.

"Hey, I have an idea, Sue. Since we're supposed to be all politically correct, you and I should have a contest to see who can go the entire night without mentioning the C- word. You know - *Christmas*."

"I love it! And the first one who mentions the C-word, has to buy the other a drink when we blow this popcorn stand and hit the bars downtown." Sue walks over to a large plastic light up snowman and puts her arm around him. "You're the new politically correct party theme, Frosty. That must put a lot of pressure on you, but hey this is public school."

Heading back to the table with the rest of the glittery snowflakes waiting to be hung, she asks, "Is Paul coming to the party tonight?"

"Yep." I pick up a snowflake and tape it to the wall.

"I guess he's about to go to Ireland too. How's that going to work for you two?" I detect Sue trying to send a message with her line of questioning so I return for another snowflake and casually remark, "Oh, you know. It is what it is, as you like to say. I leave for New Jersey right after school on the twenty-second, so tonight is probably the last chance we'll have to see each other before he goes."

Sue stops what she's doing and comes over to me. Her eyebrows are knitted, forming tiny worry lines on her forehead. She tilts her head and sighs, "Oh, Gemma. I'm so, so sorry."

"Why?"

"I wanted you to have a nice, steady relationship for a while. You know, someone there for you. You know."

"Not really. I like Paul, he's nice and very kind, but I don't know." I shrug my shoulders before continuing, "Maybe I'm not sure how I feel."

Sue seizes on my remark and says, "That's my point, Gem. What on earth are you two doing? If you're interested in him, then stop being so....so...."

Taken aback by Sue's candor, I reply defensively, "So, *what*, Sue?"

Noting my defensiveness, Sue bites back, "So fucking undecided. Either you like the guy or you don't. Stop stewing in whatever this is." She extends a hand and runs it up and down scanning me to make her point.

I look down at myself searching for what she's talking about as she continues, "Look, Gemma it's driving me nuts. This isn't like you."

My emotions begin to match Sue's, "Isn't *like* me? What are you saying?"

"I'm saying, from where I'm standing it looks like you're either leading Paul on, you're using him or he's using you. Whatever it is, it's not normal and I want you to have normal again. Shit or get off the pot, Gemma."

My jaw drops and there's heat rising inside as I spit back, "Shit or get off the pot? You've got to be kidding me. Did you ever stop to think maybe I'm a little confused? Why do you just assume it's all me and my issues?"

Sue lowers her voice and says, "I thought since you two are so on-again-off-again that it's *you* pushing *him* away."

"No, Sue. I admit; I'm holding back, but Paul's unlike any guy I've ever met. One day he's all *into* me and then I don't hear from him for a week or two. Just as I start getting closer, he backs up which only makes me more determined to be cautious."

I curl up a piece of tape and defiantly stick another flake to the wall, "I *had* the perfect guy and now I've been thrust back out into the dating world and I'm scared to death." I step back and study the snow flake I've just added to the wall. "Besides, if we're meant to be it will happen, right?"

Sue twists her mouth indicating she's thinking about what I've said, "You're right. I just like knowing you have someone to depend on. You know, a man in your life again."

I smile at Sue because she means well and is such a good friend. "I know what you mean, Sue. But, right now, Paul's perfect for me."

"I suppose, but I can't understand why on earth a guy who has one of the prettiest, smartest, kindest ladies in Wilmington would leave her to go thousands of miles away to dig around searching for bones of ancient bog men. Girls like you aren't easy to come by. He shouldn't blow his chance."

"First of all, Paul doesn't *have* me. Second, you're sweet, but you know... it is what it is."

Sue steps in closer and puts her arm around my shoulder. "Okay, Gemma. I get it. You hate when I say that so now you're using it on me. I can take a hint, but please know, I care about you and I want you to be happy."

The cafeteria is full of teachers by seven-thirty and the DJ is playing dance music with a mix of holiday songs. As Mariah Carey is belting out *All I want for Christmas*, Paul walks in the door. He looks amazing standing in the doorway wearing his leather jacket over a white button down shirt and a crisp pair of jeans. I study him for a moment.

He's a great guy, isn't he? Perfect for right now. I wonder if he'll be perfect for later too.

Paul sees me walking towards him and his face brightens with a smile, "Wow, you look beautiful, Gemma."

I love how he makes me feel pretty when I'm just wearing a simple red blouse and a pair of black jeans. "You look pretty handsome yourself, Mr. Blair."

He takes my hand, pulls me in and whispers in my ear, "Truly beautiful," as he gives me a soft kiss on the cheek. A happy thrill goes through me and a smile comes across my face.

"Thanks for coming"

"I wouldn't miss it for the world. It's important to you so it's important to me."

He does say all the right things, doesn't he?

"Let me hang up your coat."

Paul slips off his jacket and we walk to the coat rack where Sue's chatting with one of the P.E. teachers, Mr. Hutson. As soon as she sees us, I hear her say to Mr. Hutson, "Oh, you'll have to excuse me a minute."

Leaving Mr. Hutson in mid-sentence, she sails over and in her most chipper voice says, "Oh, Paul, it's lovely to see you again!" As she gets closer, she lowers her voice and leans in, "You saved me from having to listen to Mr. Hutson yammering on about not having enough funding for his balls."

If I didn't know better, I'd think she'd been drinking more than the soda and non-alcoholic holiday punch. I turn to Paul quickly to clarify, "Mr. Hutson coaches the soccer team."

Paul nods his head in understanding and says, "Ah."

Turning back to Sue, I give her a hug and comment, "You've done it Sue, it's a fantastic Chr- I mean *Holiday* Party."

She lifts her index finger and wags it while admonishing, "Ah, ah, ah. I almost won the bet."

"I was just testing you. But seriously, Sue, everyone showed up, it looks like they're having fun, and the decorations are out of this world."

"Well, yes. I had some help from a gorgeous, talented English teacher." She smiles and looks at Paul, "Isn't Gemma a peach?"

A Peach? Okay, now I'm pretty certain she's got a flask hidden somewhere.

"She's an absolute peach," Paul agrees.

Turning to point at the room, Sue directs us, "The DJ is playing until nine-thirty, so dance away. The refreshment table is over on that wall, and I see you've found the coat rack."

"Yes, Sue. Thanks. Remember? I helped you set up earlier today?"

Laughing, Sue smiles and says, "Of course, you know. What am I thinking? You know what? I think I better go mingle. I see Rich and he looks like he's bored to tears talking to that biology teacher. Have fun you two."

Sue flits away. She's giddy so I know our little tiff earlier in the day hasn't left any hard feelings. I turn back to Paul who's smiling back at me. "Wow, she's full of energy tonight, isn't she?"

"That's Sue. If I didn't know her better, I'd swear she's had a couple of drinks, but nope. She's just excited."

I hardly finish speaking, when the DJ changes tempo with a slow song. The crowd on the dance floor thins, and there are some awkward pairings like Ms. Sanders the guidance counselor and Mr. Vargas the science teacher. She's maybe four-foot-eleven and he's got to be close to six-foot-seven.

Paul sees me studying the odd couple and asks, "Will you dance with me?"

I've never been asked *will* I dance, it's always been a *do you want to* question. I smile, thinking of how Paul has taken a simple question and made it much more personal. *Will you dance with me?* Really loads the question and sets him up for a much more painful rejection, if I say no. *No, I won't dance with you* is much harsher than *No, thank you, I don't feel like dancing.*

He doesn't let me answer, but simply takes my hand and leads me to the dance floor. All eyes in the room are upon us, but I'm not concerned. If they're looking, it's probably because they're curious to see who I'm with or that I'm starting to move on.

Paul pulls me nearer and whispers in my ear, "God, I love the way you feel in my arms."

I don't say anything. I'm too caught up in being held closely. It feels wonderful so I relax and melt into him as he leads me. I rest my head on his shoulder and for a couple of minutes I'm lost in him.

The song ends, and Paul gently kisses my forehead then motions towards the refreshment table, "Shall we get something to drink?"

"Sure, let's go." I take Paul's hand and lead him to the refreshments.

He confuses me. Now he wants a soda. Okay, then. Let's get a soda.

❖

I fumble for the keys in my purse. "Here hold this," I say, handing Paul the snowman center piece Sue insisted I take home with me.

"Finally!"

I pull the key chain out, open the door, and walk inside. Turning to Paul behind me, "Care for a glass of wine?"

Paul places the snowman on the table in the hallway and helps me with my coat, "I can stay for one glass, but I really should be going."

"So soon? It's not even eleven o'clock."

After our last date, I'm not thinking of jumping the guy, but we never seem to get much time to sit and talk. We're not going to see each other for a while, it would be nice to have a better idea of what this thing is, wouldn't it?

"Oh, I've got some last minute Christmas shopping to do and packing."

"All very lame excuses." I smile and walk into the kitchen and reach for two wine glasses, "Red or white?"

"Red."

His eyes sparkle as I look at him so I ask, "What?"

"You. You're just so - I don't know. Sweet."

"Sweet?"

I pour the wine and hand him his glass, as we walk into the living room. I put my glass down on the coffee table, kick off my shoes, and have a seat. Paul sits down beside me and takes a sip of his wine before placing the glass next to mine.

"You're one of the sweetest people I've ever met. I knew from the time I noticed you on campus that I'd adore you."

I question skeptically, "How could you have known I was sweet just by looking at me?"

"It's written all over your face. You can't hide who you are for a minute. I guess that's why I'm so intimidated."

I take a sip of wine and think about what he's said before repeating, "Intimidated."

"Yes, do you know how intimidating it is to admire you from afar, and then see you half way around the world? At first I thought you were an apparition. How on earth could the girl I'd admired in Wilmington be sitting in the same pub I was sitting in, all the way across the Atlantic Ocean, in Galway? It was surreal."

"You're joking, right?"

"No. Only, you looked much sadder that night. Tonight, you're smiling, and I love to see you smile."

"That night was supposed to have been my wedding night, so I had good reason to look sad."

He's stricken for a moment with the knowledge he's reminded me of Brad, but then nods his head in agreement.

I quickly shake off the thought of what was to have been my wedding night, and continue, "But you still haven't told me why I intimidate you."

He picks up the pillow beside him and begins fidgeting with the tassels. I can't tell if he's stalling or searching for words. Finally he looks up, "You intimidate me because you're the kind of girl who can break my heart."

I sit looking at him for a few seconds. His expression is sincere, and he seems so vulnerable. I lift my hand and sweep his hair across his forehead, "You're wonderful, Paul, and I'd never want to break your heart."

"I know that. That's part of what intimidates me. You're genuinely good, and kind, and I'm afraid of falling in love with you before you're ready *or* able to fall in love."

A light comes on in my head. This entire time I've thought he's aloof when really, he's only trying to protect his heart. I thought he's keeping things casual because he's busy with work and life, but it's been to keep from getting hurt.

The moisture of tears fills my eyes, "Oh, Paul. I had no idea."

Paul gently puts his lips on mine and gives a sweet, soft kiss, then says, "I know. You're too sweet to even think of hurting someone. That's what makes you so attractive. You don't know how attractive you are."

Paul reaches for his wine glass, and changes the conversation, "Do you leave right after work on the twenty-second?"

I pick up my glass as well and say, "Yes, I'm driving to Raleigh and catching a late flight out."

"Oh, will you be parking your car at the airport the entire time?"

"I'm afraid so, I was hoping to catch a ride with Sue. She has family there, but she's not going home until the twenty-fourth, and then she's flying to Cancun on the twenty-sixth, and coming back to Wilmington on the second, so our dates didn't match up."

I'm babbling and I know he probably doesn't care, but oh well, he asked.

Paul adds, "I leave on the third. I'm flying into Dublin and driving to Cork."

Oh good, we're all caught up in flight arrangements now.

"Oh, that's a pretty drive. When do you start the semester?"

I take another sip of wine, but Paul reaches, takes my glass, and sits it back on the table, "What are we doing?"

"I honestly don't know, Paul."

"Look, I'm crazy about you, Gemma, but I'm also realistic. You're everything I could ever want, but I know you're not ready for what I'm afraid I would want with you."

Yikes, this just got heavy. I don't know what to say so I wait for him.

"Will you promise me one thing while I'm gone?"

"What's that, Paul?"

"Just be careful, and that you'll keep in touch with me."

Technically, that's two things.

"Of course I will."

He looks bereft so I do what feels right, I kiss him. Paul kisses me back, and it's the most passionate kiss he's ever given me. I'm weak inside and wanting more, we both begin kissing like there's no tomorrow. Without thought, I start unbuttoning his shirt. As my fingers deftly undo the first button, he firmly grabs my hand and pulls it away, stopping me.

He shoots up from the sofa, "No. I have to go."

Leaving me sitting with my mouth hanging open, he walks over and picks up his coat, "I don't want to leave you like this Gemma, but I'd feel horrible leaving you after just one night of...."

He walks back to me and I stare up at him. Paul lifts my hand and kisses it, "I want you and me to be together for the right reasons. And when we are, I want it to be perfect. No regrets, no wondering if it was too soon, no leaving you alone afterwards, no long distances between us."

Paul kisses my hand and then says, "I'm going to miss you."

Finally, finding my voice I croak out a reply, "I'll miss you too, Paul."

"Come on, walk me to the door before I forget everything I've just said and take advantage of you." He's smiling down at me and I see the familiar twinkle in his eye, so I oblige and stand up.

When we get to the door, he puts his jacket on and turns back to me, "Look, I know we said no Christmas presents, but I saw this and had to get it for you." He reaches into his pocket and pulls out a velvet jewelry case.

I take the case from him and open it slowly. Inside, is a dainty, silver necklace with a Claddagh pendant. In the center of the crown is a tiny amethyst.

"Oh, Paul! You shouldn't have. It's beautiful."

"I remember you said your birthday's in February, so when I saw it, I had to. Hope you're not mad."

"How can I be mad?"

"Will you wear it and think of me?"

I smile and nod, yes. Paul pulls me close and hugs me tightly before giving me one more kiss. Letting go he says, "I'll call you tomorrow. Thanks again, Gemma."

I say goodnight and close the door. Frozen by the events that just played out in my living room, I stand in the hallway before finally wandering back to my bedroom and placing the necklace on my dresser beside the Christmas card from Brad's parents that arrived earlier today.

Chapter 21

As I climb the stairs, the overnight bag hanging on my shoulder starts to feel like it's filled with bricks. I keep my purse close to my body and grasp the strap tightly - I'm in my New York mindset.

Ever since I was a kid, whenever we'd come into the city, my mother put the fear of God into me that nothing good happens in the city, so I'd better spend my time looking over my shoulder for muggers and thieves. I guess her version of New York was more akin to an asphalt jungle than the exciting metropolis I always saw.

I enjoy coming into the city. Perhaps I've just been lucky. Besides, I've usually come to New York for fun things, like going to the theater or school field trips to the museum. Mom used to take the train into work before she had us; maybe she saw the city from a slightly different perspective. I grin thinking of her admonitions to us as we'd take to the streets.

I reach the top of the steps and remember one of her admonitions - "Keep walking. Only tourists stop when they get to the top of the steps at the train station. The pick-pockets will be waiting, just looking for you."

Casually, I keep walking. I wonder what she would say about the people who stop because they're simply out of breath. I know what she'd say, "Easy marks!" No wonder my brother Aidan hates coming into the city; Mom's been terrifying him since childhood.

I start walking slowly, gazing around for Declan. He said he'd meet me near the doors, but the station is getting busy with New Year's Eve revelers arriving early to claim their space in Times Square.

We decided I should arrive before noon to avoid most of the crowds, but it's still New York City on December 31st so it's busy. Finally, I see Declan smiling as he approaches. *He looks incredible.*

He's wearing a navy blue overcoat with what appears to be a Burberry scarf. He's naturally casual and unpretentious wearing the designer scarf, and I'm pretty sure it's not a knock off from a street vendor either.

"Hello, Miss O'Connor!" His smile is amazing. His warm expression says he's happy to see me.

"Hello, Mr. Gallagher!" I sense a few butterflies in my stomach as he gets closer and gives me a small hello kiss on the cheek.

Instinctively, he reaches for the overnight bag on my shoulder and says, "Here, I'll get that."

"Oh, thanks. Hope it's not too heavy."

Not too heavy? He's over six-feet tall and plays rugby, I think he can handle carrying a girl's bag.

Playfully dipping his right shoulder towards the ground, "Good grief, Mary Gemma, what in the world have you got in here? Weights?"

"Toughen up. You're lucky I didn't bring the big suitcase." Patting his arm, I smile up at him and he smiles back.

"Gosh, ye look fantastic Gemma. So good to see you smiling." He holds my gaze a few seconds before continuing, "How about we catch a cab to Murray Hill, get you settled in and we go for a cuppa and do some exploring? You brought your camera, didn't ye?"

"Sounds perfect, and yes, I've got it in my bag." Again, per Mom's instructions, it's packed in my overnight bag. *Wearing a camera around my neck screams 'tourist' and makes me easy prey.*

Declan places his hand on the small of my back and leads me out of the train station to hail a taxi.

The clean, oaky aroma of the hardwood floors welcomes me, as Declan opens the door to the apartment and I walk inside. It's modern and spacious by New York City standards so I remark, "Wow, this is great."

"Yep, it's not bad for a company apartment, is it?" He takes my bag and walks down the hall. I follow like a puppy as he walks into what's to be my room for the night.

"I hope you'll be comfortable in here. You haven't got an *en suite*, but the loo is right across the hall," he says, placing my bag on the overstuffed chair in the corner.

I look around the room. There's a queen-sized bed with a white down comforter, a night stand, and a small dresser with a TV above it mounted to the wall.

"No, this is perfect. I'll be very comfortable." I walk to the window to check out the view and pull back the curtain, "Oh wow, I can see the water tower on the roof next door."

Declan comments dryly, "I wanted you to see the finest water tower in New York so, naturally, I took the larger room which overlooks the park across the street so you can see *that* water tower." I look back at him over my shoulder and he winks.

Just when I didn't think he could get more adorable, he winks at me.

"If you want to trade for the night I'll be happy to swap rooms." Declan's standing in the doorway smiling. He has such an affable demeanor, but I notice something else in his expression.

I hesitate for a second because it surprises me. It's as if he's watching in admiration. I can't quite put my finger on it, but it's a look of admiration bordering on being slightly protective. It's sweet.

"Don't be silly, I love this." Removing my coat and throwing it down on the bed, I walk to where he's standing, go up on my toes and give him a small peck on the cheek. "Thanks, Declan. Thank you for inviting me here."

I give his hand a gentle squeeze out of gratitude. I know Declan understands how hard all of the firsts are and especially the first New Year's. Christmas was tough enough, but there's something profoundly solitary about spending New Year's alone.

"Right, so, I'll leave you to unpack, freshen up, and then we can hit the town if you like." He pulls the scarf from around his neck and departs down the hall.

After I hang my dress in the closet, I go across the hall to the bathroom and touch up my face, and brush my hair before returning to the living room where I find Declan seated at the desk in front of his computer. He looks up and gives a boyish grin that tells me he's as honest as the day is long. I really am lucky to have made such a wonderful friend who understands what I've been through.

"Just catching up on a few emails. Hope you don't mind."

"No, go right ahead. I fully expect you to be busy; the young, successful, overachiever that you are." I joke.

He looks back at the computer screen and says, "I'll only be a minute longer."

I walk into the kitchen and start nosing around. It's a galley-style that's obviously been renovated in recent years. Tall cherry cabinets, granite counters, stainless steel appliances, travertine tile backsplash - very high-end stuff.

I open the fridge and see a carton of milk, orange juice and a box of Chinese take away - typical bachelor fare. I know he only got into town yesterday, but this won't do. I may have to take him grocery shopping while I'm here.

Moving on, I open a cabinet to find it fully stocked with glasses, dishes and coffee mugs. There's a Keurig machine sitting on the counter with a small basket of coffee and tea k-cups beside it. At least he can fix himself a warm drink.

I call to Declan in the other room, “I can see why you like staying here when you come to town. It's a great place."

"Oh, yes. I sometimes have to pinch myself to remind me it's not a dream, I really *do* get to stay here. I feel like I'm in a movie ya know. When I was a kid, I'd go to cinema and see films about New York City and wonder what it was like. Now, here I am. That kid from Galway."

I walk back into the living room as he's getting up from the desk. Looking directly into his piercing blue eyes I say, "You've worked hard to get where you are. You should feel proud of yourself."

His face betrays him, turning ever-so-slightly red. *Is he blushing? Did I make big, strong, confident Declan blush?*

"It's almost half-one, are ye hungry? There's a great diner down the block. We can get something light and a cuppa then go exploring, if you like." His sudden change of subject is the mechanism he uses to force his blush to fade. He's back to all business as he continues, "I don't want you to get too filled up. I've made a reservation for dinner at half-eight at an incredible Italian restaurant. I hope you like Italian."

I stand grinning at him for a moment before replying, "I love Italian food."

"Ah, grand." Declan walks to the coat closet and looks back at me, "Get your coat and let's go then, shall we?"

Chapter 22

We return a little before five o'clock and I'm chilled to the bone. After a full afternoon of walking the streets of New York, making our way to Central Park and back, all I want to do is put on my sweat pants and curl up on the sofa. Hopefully, I'll get my second wind before we go out to dinner.

Declan and I are bumping into each other in the kitchen, as we put away the food I insisted he buy at the small grocery store on the corner. I open the refrigerator and we bump bums as he bends to put a box of cereal in a bottom cabinet.

"Arse hole to belly button in here," he jokes, turning around and smiling at me he adds, "My apologies."

"Oh, no that was all my fault. I really shouldn't open the fridge with such aggressive dance moves," I kid.

Clever, Gemma. Awkwardly clever.

So as not to let him see me flustered, I walk to the coffee maker, "Hey, I think I saw some hot chocolate cups for the coffee maker, how about I make hot chocolate?"

Before Declan can answer, I'm picking through the basket of K-cups. One, two... "Ah ha! Two hot chocolates, coming up."

"Sounds grand, shall I turn on the telly in the other room so you can catch up on your American football scores?"

I turn towards him, touched by his thoughtfulness, "That would be great. I've missed so many of the bowl games this year. I usually spend the week between Christmas and New Years with my father and brothers, glued to the TV watching football. Drives my Mom crazy."

"I'll turn on the ESPN for you," he says as he turns to leave the kitchen.

"It's just ESPN, don't say *the*. That's kind of like saying *The Facebook* or *The Twitter*. It's just not done." I smile at him as he lifts his hand in dismissal and leaves the room.

I cautiously carry two mugs of cocoa into the living room where Declan's stretched out on the leather sofa with a knitted quilt thrown over his legs. He's got the remote in hand. "I think I've found the.... I mean ESPN," he nods at the television on the wall.

"Perfect." I sit his cocoa on top of a magazine on the end of the coffee table closest to Declan. I turn to take my mug and sit in the recliner, when Declan moves his feet, slides over, and pats the seat next to him.

Looking up at me with those swimming pool-blue eyes, he softly says, "Join me?"

It's not possible to say no to those gorgeous eyes, now is it, Gem?

I place my cocoa beside his on the magazine, and slide my bum back on the brown leather cushion next to him. Declan picks up the quilt and spreads it across both our laps, "There, that should warm you." He leans forward, takes a slow sip of his drink before adding, "Just how long were you willing to suffer in the cold, before you'd admit you were freezing?"

I don't answer. I take a sip from my mug, and after a dramatic pause, turn my head, and look at him.

He has a twinkle in his eye as he forges on, "You're really not such a great big enigma, Mary Gemma. Your tough-girl act is useless with me. Just concede to that."

He's smiling, yet it still feels as if he's scolding me. I study him for a while and finally answer, though I don't think he expects a response, "Declan, you're more astute than most, that's all. But, if I'm being honest, I think I'm not an enigma to you because when I'm with you, I drop all pretenses. From the time we met, I've felt like you see inside me. You seem to know me so well already, why bother trying to put up a front? Right?"

I'm pretty sure my penetrating comment has left him speechless, but instead, he casually lifts his mug, looks straight ahead at the television, takes a draw of cocoa, and says, "Well, I'm glad we've settled that then. Now drink your cocoa."

At that, I turn and slap his arm playfully and we both start laughing.

❖

I step into the hallway and run smack into Declan, as he's coming out of his room. "Oh, excuse me Gem." He stops in the middle of saying my name, “Gemma. You look absolutely gorgeous."

Self-consciously, I glimpse down and back up at him, "Thanks."

"You'll be the most beautiful woman at Roselli’s tonight."

My face is warming. I hate how easily I get flustered when he compliments me. Say something brilliant, Gemma.

"You look wonderful too."

I'm not just saying that to change the subject, he looks hot. He's wearing a navy blue suit with a white shirt, and a burgundy-striped tie. He's just showered and shaved, and the fresh, woodsy scent of his soap or cologne, or whatever it is, smells phenomenal.

I love the aroma of a freshly-showered man.

He takes my hand, lifts my arm out to the side, tilts his head, and says, "Red is a great color for you."

Oh, God. Am I still blushing?

He tips his head towards me, "Your dress. I like the color."

Declan looks at me as if I don't understand a word he's saying. If he only knew the truth - I'm lost in thoughts of being turned on by his clean, manly scent.

"Oh, this. Yeah. Thanks. I got it on sale the day after Christmas at Macy's." I look down at the crimson dress with the sweetheart neckline and delicate lace overlay.

Pretty sure my face is as red as this dress right now.

He gently lowers my hand, letting his fingers linger slightly as he lets go, "It's lovely. You're lovely."

Blushing, blushing again. I know it. Maybe the heat's set too high. Is it me, or is it hot in here? Stupid New York City apartment heat.

Declan walks to the hall closet and takes out his overcoat, "You ready?"

Snapped back from my thoughts, I stammer, "Oh, let me grab my coat and purse." I walk back in my room, lift my coat from the bed, and grab the small evening bag I brought and pop my cell phone, a lipstick and my license inside. Just as Declan and I are about to walk out the door, I hear my phone ringing inside my purse.

I open the purse and see it's Sorcha calling.

"It's Sorcha, should I answer?"

"She's probably calling to wish you Happy New Year, it's past midnight in Galway," Declan says while fastening the final button on his coat.

"That means she could be drunk," I laugh as I press talk. Before I can say hello, Sorcha shouts, "Happy New Year, Gem! Guess what? I'm engaged!"

"Liam proposed? Are you serious? What did you say?" I'm being sarcastic, but she thinks I'm serious.

"I said yes." She sounds confused I would even question what her answer was.

Declan's phone begins sounding off inside his overcoat pocket. "Let me guess." He pulls the phone from his pocket, "It's Liam." He smiles and walks to the other side of the room to answer.

I return my full attention to Sorcha who's bubbling with excitement, "He asked me at midnight. There's a blue moon ya know, and he said to me, 'Once in a blue moon, the right girl comes along. Will ye marry me, Sorcha?' Isn't that the most romantic thing ye ever heard?"

"Yes, that's incredibly romantic. I'm so happy for you Sorcha. This is fantastic news. Have you called your Mum and Dad yet?"

"Aye, they were in bed already. Who the feck goes to bed before midnight on New Year's Eve?" She pauses and I hear her taking a sip of something, "Anyway, I woke em up about fifteen minutes ago with the news. Mum's already mentally planning the wedding."

"I know she must be excited. Will you get married in Boyle or Galway?"

Sorcha snorts, "Holy feck Gem, I'm still letting it sink in. He just slipped the ring on me finger, I haven't thought that far ahead." She takes another sip, swallows, and says," I do know one thing, though. You've just got to be my maid of honor. You can't say no!"

"It will be an honor. I knew you were going to make me wear a sherbet-colored dress the minute I met Liam."

Declan and Liam's conversation is much shorter, and he's returned to me, and is pointing at his watch.

"Oh, Sorcha, this is wonderful. How about I give you a call tomorrow and we can talk more then? Declan and I have dinner reservations and we're about to be late."

"Oh feck. Silly me, I forgot. How's things with Declan?"

"Things are good, but he's giving me a look and pointing at his watch, which means I better hang up, now. I'll talk to you later. Say hello and congrats to Liam for me. I love ya!"

Roselli's is filling up as we arrive and the hostess seats us. There's definitely a festive feeling in the air. I giggle when I see the paper hats and noise makers waiting for us on our table. Somehow the thought of Declan wearing that shiny silver party hat is hilarious to me.

"What's so funny?" He says as we slide into the booth.

"Nothing."

He throws a doubting look at me, "I don't know why, but I don't buy that. You're laughing at something."

I pick up the New Year's specials listed on a thick piece of parchment paper in front of me, and begin scanning it, "It's just the thought of *Mr. Serious*, Declan Gallagher, wearing that hat and blowing a party horn, makes me laugh."

"*Mr. Serious*? Why, Mary Gemma, that almost sounds like a pejorative."

Looking over the top of the specials, I see he's still being playful and not offended, so I continue, "Not a pejorative at all, quite the opposite, in fact. Obviously, you're quite serious, when appropriate, but I know there's another side to Declan Gallagher he only shares with friends."

"Oh, and do tell me about this *other side*. You've clearly got some insights I'm unaware of."

He's smiling broadly at me, as the waiter approaches to take our drink order.

"Hold that thought Gem. What will you have? Would you like some wine?"

"I'd love some Chianti"

"Ah, sounds perfect." Declan looks up at the waiter, "We'll have a bottle of Ruffino Chianti. *Classico Riserva*, please."

Declan's seems even more worldly and sophisticated than I thought he was when we first met in Galway.

"What?" He sees me smiling at him, as the waiter glides away with our order.

"Nothing. You didn't hesitate on the wine order and that impressed me. That's all."

"You forget, Gemma, my parents are chefs. Do you know how many of my childhood holidays were spent tagging along with parents who thought a fun way to spend their downtime, away from the restaurant, was taking cooking classes in Tuscany or Paris?"

In my most sarcastic tone I say, "My, how tragic for you."

"Well, yes, really it was tragic spending holidays in exotic places, eating haute cuisine, while all I really wanted to do was rent a caravan and holiday at Renvyle Beach in Connemara, like normal people." He says this in his best *poor little rich boy* voice.

"Oh my gosh, we did that one summer." I'm laughing at the memory. "Our family and Sorcha's entire family; packed like sardines in a musty caravan. We were little, so we thought it was great, but I think my mother almost flipped out over that *holiday*. From then on, if we dare leave Boyle for a night, it's spent in a Great Southern Hotel or Mom won't go."

"My point exactly, I've none of those horrid childhood stories to share."

The waiter returns, pours two glasses of Chianti, and asks if we're ready to order. I've hardly even looked at the menu, but Declan speaks up. "If you don't mind Gemma." He looks at me then turns back to the waiter, "I think we'll go with *insalata di spinachi, Gamberi alla Rossini, Filetto di Manzo alla Rossini* and we'll start with *Calamari Fritti.*"

The waiter bows slightly and says, "Very good sir, thank you," and departs.

"Wow, not sure what you just ordered, but it sounds wonderful."

"I hope you don't mind. I guess it was a bit presumptuous of me. I ordered entrees I thought we might like sharing," he says, looking concerned.

"Not at all. I enjoyed listening to you order. You do it with such authority. Very attractive," I remark, patting his hand.

We both look down at my hand touching his. There's an awkward moment, as I quickly yank my hand back and place it on my lap, before Declan clears his throat, "Now, back to *Mr. Serious*."

"Oh, I thought we'd moved on from that, but if you insist."

I take a sip of Chianti, before continuing. "Like I said before, Declan, from the moment I met you, I've felt like you know my every thought, so there's no point in trying to pretend, right?" I ask rhetorically. "I think it has to do with the fact, well, with the fact we've experienced similar emotions of love and loss in our lives, and while you're further along in the healing process than I am, I can still see some of your defense mechanisms that perhaps others can't."

"Oh, really? Do tell *Dr*. O'Connor."

"Okay, I hear your sarcasm, which in fact, is one of those defense mechanisms." I take another sip of wine and forge ahead. "Your naturally stoic nature has served you well, but you also have a softer side, and you've decided to keep it hidden under your bravado, *all business* persona so you don't have to let others know just how much you feel things."

The man lost his wife, of course he's guarding his emotions.

Declan drinks some wine, as he considers what I've said, then gestures with his hand, "Go on. Go on."

I feel I'm flailing, but I persevere, "You're extremely proficient at compartmentalizing. It's a quality I admire. I *wish* I could do what you do."

"Do what I do? What, exactly, is it I do?" His eyes are penetrating as he searches my expression for clues to what I'm trying to say.

"You have this way of keeping your emotions neatly in-check." I shrug my shoulders, "You're very controlled with expressing your feelings, but not in a *Gee he's really stuffing his emotions deep inside, he's gonna blow up one day* kind of way. It's more of a calmness and clarity of thought; you let things glide off of you. You're unflappable."

Mercifully, the waiter arrives bearing insalada and interrupts us with his dramatic offer of fresh pepper.

Declan places his napkin on his lap and gives me another penetrating gaze, then lifts his fork to begin eating. "Okay, but you still haven't told me anything about the emotions you feel I hold back."

This one I have an immediate answer for. "You feel things much deeper than you let the world see, and those feelings are reserved for the most special people in your life. That's why you're successful. You don't let the personal interfere with the professional. Personal is an entirely different compartment. I'm telling you, it's a great quality, and I really wish I could be more like you." I lift my fork and stuff a piece of salad into my mouth, mostly to collect my thoughts. I'm afraid I'm not doing a good job of conveying what I'm trying to say to him. His look is hard to decipher.

Finally, he speaks, "And what about *love*?" Declan lays down the fork with a wounded expression on his face.

"What do you mean, *love*? How are you when you're *in* love or how are you at *expressing* love?"

With a touch of anger in his voice, he replies, "Both. You've got me fascinated, so I want to hear how you view me when it comes to what you think I'm like when I love."

I stop eating and look up to the corner of the ceiling, as if searching for the words up there. As I find the words, I look back at Declan and say, "You're amazing when you're in love. That's the best compartment of all your emotional compartments. When you really let yourself *be* Declan. You know, the Declan that only a handful of people ever see - *that* Declan."

I pick up my fork and begin chasing a tomato across the plate before looking up at his piercing eyes, "I could be wrong, but I think when you decide you're in love, there's no equivocation, you're in all the way - no holding back. You don't know how to love less; once you're in love, you only know how to love more."

I tilt my head and lift my eye brow in an expression that implores, *am I right?*

We go back to eating in relative silence, with the exception of the occasional comment on the salad or the wine and finally I ask, "Well aren't you going to respond to what I said?"

"Yes" Declan says dryly. "But I thought I'd save that for another time. My response is in another compartment that I'm not yet ready to share."

I lift my napkin and dab my mouth, "Touché, Declan. Touché"

After my deep analysis of Declan's emotions, we keep the dinner topic light, discussing an array of subjects like Sorcha and Liam and their engagement, my plans for next summer, previous New Year's Eves, U2 and food. From time to time, I delve into the personal with questions about Declan's family and his childhood.

I've gotten to where I know if I'm asking anything too personal, or if he isn't ready to tell me about a subject. He's fun to talk with and the wine is making me chatty. I feel myself becoming silly. I also note Declan is amused by my relaxed state.

Marco, our waiter, who feels like an old friend now, returns with a huge cannoli and two flutes of champagne. "It's almost midnight. You stay for toast, *si*?"

"It's almost midnight? Wow, Declan we've been talking so much, I lost all track of time."

Declan turns to Marco, "*Si*, we'll stay to toast the New Year."

"*Meraviglioso!*" Marco is pleased with Delcan's response as he charges off to distribute champagne to other customers.

"So, now that I've gotten ye all chatty with Chianti..." Declan's wearing a smile that tells me he's got an ulterior motive.

"*Yes*, what is it, Declan?" There's caution in my tone.

"I can't go back to Galway without talking to you about Paul." Declan puts his hands up in a defensive position before finishing, "I promised Sorcha. She'll have me head if I come home with no news of this Paul you've been seeing, so I need to ask."

I let out a dramatic sigh, "I see how uncomfortable you are bringing this up. Tell Sorcha, if she wants to know, she should ask me herself. It's not fair of her to make you do her dirty work."

Hello? Where's this anger coming from?

Declan sees he's touched a nerve, "I'm not just asking for Sorcha. I consider you a friend, and as a friend, I'd like to know as well. Is he a decent fella? Is he treating you well or is he messing about with ye?

A flash of anger overtakes me and I spit back, "*Messing about*? Does that mean something more in Ireland than it does here?"

"Calm down Mary Gemma, that's not an inuendo for anything. I just want to make sure he's not going to break your heart."

I take a deep breath, sigh, and look into Declan's caring eyes, "Sorry, I guess I'm a little sensitive. It's been tough going through the whole grieving thing with a bunch of worried faces watching my every move.

I always feel like they think I'm this fragile bird about to get sucked under the blade of a lawn mower."

Declan laughs out loud at my remark. "Gosh, you're fun when you've had a couple glasses of wine. A little violent in thought, but fun nonetheless."

He reaches with his fork for a bite of the canoli in the middle of the table and says, "But I know what you mean. You feel like you're in a fish bowl and people are staring to see what you do next. They do it because they love ya, they're just concerned."

I reach for a bite too, "I know, but after a while it gets old. I want to stop living my life under the microscope."

He nods in agreement, "Amen to that."

We share a moment of silence that punctuates the fact we both understand. I finally say, "Just tell Sorcha I still don't know what the deal is with Paul and that's fine with me."

Declan reaches for another bite of canoli. "What's he like?"

"You saw him in Galway, do you remember? He's good looking, very career oriented, nice. He's always a gentleman to me, and he's going back to Cork in a week for work, so that's that."

Declan keeps eating as he studies my expression. "You know, like it or not, Miss O'Connor, I think you compartmentalize your emotions as well."

Shaking my head back and forth to say, *Where did that come from?* I crinkle my nose and ask, "What?"

"And your little secret, about the entire Paul thing, is that you're not sure if you're sad he's going to Cork, or relieved."

I shake my head back and forth in protest, "That isn't it at all. Besides, what makes you the authority?" I feel the sting in my words as they leave my mouth.

"Yep, I hit a nerve." Declan smiles and adds, "You know, the stoic ones are also quiet observers. We see a great deal others miss while they're busy talking."

"I'm not exactly an enigma. You don't need a Rosetta's stone to decipher me." I stab at the cannoli for one last bite.

Declan puts his fork down on his plate. "I didn't mean it as a bad thing. I love how you compartmentalize your emotions. It's a very admirable characteristic. I'm being sincere."

I can't tell if he's mocking me with my own words or if he's being serious.

"I also care about you, and I don't want to see you get hurt or do anything you're not ready to do. I guess I'm one of those people who is worried about ye."

Declan tips his head to the right and back to the left, like he's looking at a painting on a wall to see if it's hung straight. "Mary Gemma, what can I say? You've sucked me into your world and now, well, now I want all the best things for ye too. Sorry, hate to break it to you, but I care."

I feel guilty now. "Thanks for your concern. I mean it, it's really sweet of you to care." Exhaling before I proceed, "Paul's a very nice guy and

I'm being careful to take things slowly, and if it will make Sorcha feel better, tell her I haven't shagged him."

Declan laughs and slams his hands down on the table, "Priceless! Gemma, you are indeed priceless! And I'll be sure to tell Sorcha the news."

As if on cue, the manager announces it's almost midnight and begins counting down. "Ten, nine, eight..." Declan picks up my glass and hands it to me. As the countdown hits midnight, the restaurant is filled with the sounds of glasses clinking, horns blowing and shouts of 'Happy New Year!'

Declan and I touch glasses and take a sip. I swallow my champagne when I hear the musicians strike up *Auld Lang Syne.* The melancholy tone of the music sweeps over me and in an instant, I'm struck with the thought of Brad. I feel the familiar burn as my eyes fill with tears. The tears are about to spill down my cheeks.

Without hesitation, Declan jumps from his side of the booth and in a flash, he's right beside me, wrapping his arm around, pulling me close. His arm is strong, and I rest my head on his comforting shoulder.

I breathe in, trying to suck the tears back and make them go away. I don't want to ruin the night with crying. He looks down at me, sees me trying not to let the tears flow, and squeezes me tighter then leans down, and kisses my forehead. "Ah, gosh you're an Angel, Gemma."

I can't say anything. I'm afraid if I talk I'll start sobbing, so I simply put my hand on Declan's knee and give a slight squeeze to let him know, I'm okay. He smiles down at me and says, "Happy New Year, Baby Girl," and softly brushes my lips with his.

Declan raises his hand to get Marco's attention, "I'll get the check so we can get out of here."

Chapter 23

I peel one eye open, then the other, and survey the room as I peer over the covers and remember, I'm in New York City and today is January 1st. The early morning colors of light gray and white peek through the curtains so I surmise it must be close to sunrise. I turn my head to see the large red numbers on the clock by the bed that reads, 6:14.

I sit up, lean against the pillows at the headboard, and think about last night. New Year's was fun, thanks to Declan. I probably had more wine than I should have, but I don't remember saying or doing anything out of line.

It's early, I should stay in bed, but my mouth is dry after last night's Chianti and bubbly. I need a cup of coffee. Sitting on the edge of the bed, I stretch before putting my feet on the ground and standing. I dig through my bag and find my fleece pajama pants and slip them on. They don't exactly match Brad's t-shirt I slept in, but it's probably poor form to roam the apartment in nothing but a baggy t-shirt.

I tip-toe across the hall to the bathroom, brush my teeth and hair, and walk as quietly as I can to the kitchen, only to discover Declan on the sofa with his computer open. I hear soft music playing.

"Is that Van Morrison?"

Declan looks up from his computer, "Oh, sorry, did I wake you?"

He's wearing sweat pants with a white t-shirt. The t-shirt clings to his chest, accentuating his muscular build. His feet are propped on the coffee table. My eyes fix on his chest. *Nice pecs, very nice pecs.*

"No, I automatically wake up about this time. You're fine. Is that Van Morrison you're listening to?"

"Aye. My parents turned me on to him. They had his greatest hits CD. I listened to it all the time as a kid. Can I get ye a cup of tea or coffee?"

His Irish lilt sounds thicker this morning for some reason, but it's charming. "No, stay put. I'll fix it."

I walk into the kitchen to begin the task of brewing with the Keurig. As I dig through the basket of K-cups, Declan calls from the other room, "I guess I'm still on Galway-time. I've been up for an hour. You'd think after such a wild night, I'd still be passed out."

"Ha! Yes. It was *wild,* wasn't it?" I compete to be heard over the gurgling and hissing sound of the coffee brewing. "It's a coffee morning for me, I'm afraid. You really shouldn't have let me have both glasses of Chianti." I joke.

When the coffee's ready, I pour a little milk in and stir, then return to the living room and plop down beside Declan on the sofa with my big cup of coffee. I prop my feet up on the coffee table and notice him checking out my fuzzy, striped socks. "They were a Christmas present from a student. You should see some of the *nice* things I got for Christmas."

"I'll bet you're the favorite teacher." His smile warms me inside.

"I try. What ya working on at this hour on a holiday?"

"Just checking emails. How'd ye sleep?" He picks up his coffee sitting in front of him and takes a drink.

"I slept just fine. Hey, thanks again for last night. I really had fun. I mean it. Despite my momentary emotional hiccup." I blow across the top of my mug and take my first sip.

Declan watches me as I sit the mug down on the table. "What?"

"How do you know I have a question? Can't I just admire your morning beauty?" There's a hint of sarcasm in his smooth tone.

"Oh, yeah, this is morning beauty - a baggy t-shirt, flannel pajama pants and fuzzy socks."

"You make it look effortless."

I laugh at the thought of me making anything look *effortless.* I pivot towards the window and see the sky's a heavy grayish-white color and remark, "Is it supposed to snow today? It looks like it could."

"Aye, weather man says it's supposed to. Don't ye worry, you can always stay another day if ye get stuck. I like having the company." He takes another sip of coffee then asks, "Hey, did ye hear from your fella back in North Carolina? Did he call to wish ye Happy New Year yet?"

His question surprises me, but I answer, "No. Why?"

He's staring at the computer screen. "Oh, I was just curious."

Being deliberately obtuse, I question, "Should I have heard from him?"

"It's just... Ah, nothing."

Now I'm curious, "It's just *what*?"

"It's just, if I had a girl like ye, I'd be calling you to wish you a Happy New Year."

I quietly drink my coffee, thinking about what he's said. *It is strange I've not heard from Paul. He was so sad before I left for Christmas, but we've only spoken one time since I've been in New Jersey.*

"He called on Christmas." I hear defensiveness in my words so I know Declan does too.

"Well, like ye said. You're taking it slow, right?"

I look at Declan who's involved in reading an email, but I can tell he's silently making a point.

Is his point that Paul should be doing more if he's interested in me? Is his point that he thinks Paul isn't being good to me? Maybe he's trying to make me think about what I'm doing with Paul.

Declan has me befuddled so I do the only thing I know how to do when I feel I'm on the defensive. I'm not proud of this trait, but I can't stop myself.

"So, what's going on with you and Maeve? Her name *is* Maeve, isn't it?"

The corners of Declan's mouth move up into a small grin. "I was waiting for this."

"Waiting for what?" I snip back.

"Think about it, Gemma. If Sorcha made me promise to find out about your friend Paul, I'd be stupid not to think she's put you up to finding out about Maeve."

"Sorcha may have mentioned something...." I trail off because I know how pointless it is for me to try and play coy with Declan.

"You can tell Sorcha, if she wants to know she can ask me herself. I believe that's an exact quote, isn't it, Gem?" Declan looks away from his computer and turns his piercing blue eyes my direction. "Now, if you're asking for yourself, that's different. Maeve is a lovely girl I met down the pub, and it's nice having female company from time to time, but there's nothing beyond that."

I feel like a guilty child who has been caught, misbehaving. I don't like this feeling at all. Declan's always fair and even tempered with me. Why on earth did I feel I had to lash out like that? I hate myself right now. Besides Brad, Declan's the one person who's understood me, without having to press for answers. He's so steady and calm, and I unfairly snapped at him.

"Declan, I'm sorry. I had no right to sound so..... To sound so bitchy."

He puts his computer down on the table, turns to me, and takes my right hand. I see him eyeing my engagement ring. I started wearing it on my right hand in September, when I decided to try moving forward. I haven't had the heart to put it away. Besides, it's too pretty to shut in a drawer. It would be like putting Brad in the drawer with the ring, and I'm not ready to relegate him to my past entirely.

Declan gives a sympathetic look and continues, "I'm not mad at ye, Gemma. Honestly, you're kind of cute when you get riled up. I'm not mad, and I think I'd have a hard time getting upset with ye. You're a friend who's concerned about me and I appreciate ye caring. Now, let's go in the kitchen and make some breakfast. I can't send you back to your folks hungry now, can I?"

Declan pulls me up from the sofa and into his arms for a bear hug. "You're too good a friend to do anything to upset me. Oh, but if Sorcha has to know about Maeve, tell her I haven't shagged her."

I look up and see the twinkle in his eyes and in a flash it's gone again, and he leads me by the hand into the kitchen.

❖

Heavy, wet flakes are falling as we get out of the cab. The skies are gray, and the entire city is cold and moving slowly after a night of partying. Declan carries my overnight bag and guides me inside, out of the snow, and downstairs to the train platform. He spots a man in a railroad uniform and walks over to him to double-check and make sure I'm on the platform heading to the New Jersey side of the city. He returns to where I'm standing and with a smile says, "Okay, Miss O'Connor, the gentleman over there assures me, this is the platform for the train you're taking back to Ma and Da."

"My hero!" I reach for my bag, which is still on his shoulder.

"I've got it. I'll hold it till the train comes. No need for you to burden ye self."

"Thanks again for everything, Declan. This was really fun. We'll have to do it again if you're in town and I'm around too." I look down the platform in anticipation of an oncoming train that's not coming yet, before continuing, "I didn't know how the holidays would be without.... I didn't think I'd...." I'm struggling to find the right words.

Declan wraps his free arm around my shoulder and finishes my thought for me. "You didn't think you'd smile, or laugh, because the person you thought you'd be spending your holidays with isn't here anymore."

I smile up at him and see the warmth and understanding in his expression, "Exactly."

"I've got a secret for ye, Mary Gemma. I didn't think I'd have this much fun either. You're really good for the craic."

"And you have no idea how much I enjoy listening to your *aye* and *ye* and *craic* and all the other Irish expressions. It's soothing for me to hear. I'm glad I'm coming back to Ireland for the summer."

He adds, "Only five months away!"

Hmm, is he counting the days?

With my best Irish brogue I say, "Aye! Whatever ye do, please save a dance at Liam and Sorcha's wedding for me."

"That's a promise. Oh, and not to go getting all serious on ye, but promise me something, will ye?"

He looks somber, so I ask with concern, "What, Declan?"

He swallows hard, looks down the track to see if the train is coming, then turns back to me. "If Paul doesn't know what he's got, he's a fool. Don't be that girl some dick only comes around for when he has time on his calendar. You don't ever want to be sitting out on the periphery waiting. Don't be someone's bad habit."

I hear the train in the distance, and feel the air in my mouth, which is hanging open, as my mind spins contemplating Declan's words.

"That's all. I'll say no more, just be careful, and please take care of yourself."

I'm still reeling from his advice, and by his uncharacteristic use of the word *dick*, but I see the train pulling into the station, and people crowding the platform. My voice cracks as I shout above the din, "I will, I promise."

Declan leans in, gives me his strongest bear hug, and I feel the familiar burning of tears welling in my eyes, as it dawns on me - I'm going to miss him. I'm going to miss Declan Gallagher.

Our embrace ends and Declan gently places the bag on my shoulder. I'm about to turn around towards the opening train door when he adds, "Oh, and you were right last night. Your assessment of how I love. You were right."

I turn to board the train, but look back and see Declan. He waves, so I wave back and call to him, "I know. I know!"

Part III

Back in Boyle

Chapter 24

Tippy sits on his bed beside the fireplace as I stoke the turf and add another brick. The flame kicks up, and the peat coals below begin to catch fire, glowing and emitting heat into the chilly cottage. Once he sees the fire is growing, he turns twice in his bed, plunks down, and lets out a sigh before resting his chin on his front paws and closing his eyes.

I smile down at him, "So, it looks like we're picking up where we left off last summer, aren't we, fella?"

If he understands me, he isn't acknowledging it. He keeps his eyes shut as I go to the sink and pour water into the kettle to make a cup of tea. Aunt Francie has the place spotless. The stainless steel sink is sparkling, as are the windows. She's put a small carton of milk, some butter, and a bottle of Chardonnay in the fridge, as well as brown bread and Lyon's tea in the cupboard. She's even added new lace curtains over the kitchen sink, and a beautiful burgundy duvet on the bed.

I see Uncle Tom's hand in the preparations for my arrival as well. There's a new shower head in the bath, the Internet connection is turned back on, and there's a full basket of turf on the hearth.

I'm thankful for the turf tonight. Yes, it's June, but the weather is cool and rainy. I'm chilled through after carrying loads of groceries and suitcases in from the trunk of the car Grandpa's lending me while I'm here.

The sky is still bright at nine-thirty, which is typical for Ireland this time of year, but I'm tired. I lost a night on the flight over and Grandma insisted I stay for tea before Tippy and I could settle in the cottage. It's hard to say no to Grandma, but I won't complain because she made a plate of left over pot roast and potatoes to take with me.

While I wait for the kettle to come to a boil, I make one last dash to the car. I grab the bag of food from the back seat, slam the car door shut with my foot, then run back inside. Tippy picks his head up as I shut the door behind me, but when he sees me put his bag of food in the cabinet he drops his chin back down on his paws, no longer interested.

"Thanks for the help, Tippy."

I move the suitcases into the bedroom and put my computer bag down at the desk. *I'll leave the unpacking for tomorrow.*

I dig a pair of sweat pants and a sweatshirt from the small suitcase, and finally change my clothes. I've changed my mind about the tea too, that might keep me awake, so I find the romance novel I was reading on the plane in my tote bag and go back to the other room to sip wine and read.

I open the fridge and grin at the thought of Aunt Francie buying a bottle of wine. I remember her telling me about a woman who lived out by Cavetown Lake who would drive all the way to Strokestown to buy a bottle of whiskey. She wouldn't buy her booze anywhere near Boyle.

Aunt Francie lowered her voice as not to utter words too scandalous to speak at full volume, "We're Irish, we drink at the pub and go home. Now, if ye buy a bottle to take home, what will folks think?"

I uncork the *scandalous* bottle of Chardonnay and open the cabinet above the counter in search of a glass. To my astonishment, there are four brand-new crystal glasses with a note taped to one. I pull down the glass, and remove the note which reads, "Four Galway Crystal wine glasses, mouth-blown personally by Liam Tully for Gemma O'Connor."

Ha! If I weren't too tired to get involved in a long phone conversation, I'd call Sorcha right now and thank her. Besides, she's coming to Boyle tomorrow, I'll thank her then. Instead, I take my wine and climb into the recliner, pull the afghan over my legs, and open my book.

I meet Sorcha and Aunt Francie at Maryanne's Boutique on Bridge Street in town. They're already seated in the fitting area when I walk inside. "Holy, feck Gemma, you look fantastic!" Sorcha jumps from her chair, throws her arms around me, and gives a giant hug. Feeling left out of the moment, Aunt Francie taps her on the arm to say, *It's my turn.*

"You'll have to forgive *Lady Sorcha* for her un-ladylike language. How are ye dear?" Aunt Francie gives a warm embrace then steps back to look at me. "I'm not sure you're eating enough, but your eyes are brighter, and your smile is happier than last time we saw ye. That's grand."

"Yes, Aunt Francie. I'm doing much better than I was last summer. I guess time really does heal all wounds. I still miss Brad, but I feel more like my old self again."

"Aye, it will never be the same, but the good Lord is holding ye in the palm of His hand and you're surrounded by His angels protecting ye."

I see Sorcha over Aunt Francie's left shoulder rolling her eyes. She finally pulls her mum away and says, "And yay though I walk in the shadow of the valley of death - enough already Saint Francie, we're here for Gemma to try on a bridesmaid dress for feck's sake."

"Just remember Sorcha, I'm only ignoring that blasphemous remark because I don't want to upset Gemma on her first full day home." Aunt Francie plays like she's just been mortally wounded by Sorcha's chiding, but I see the twinkle in her eye as she sits down in the over-stuffed chair in the corner. "Right, so. Let's get this dress for our Gemma now."

Breda Murphy joins us from behind the counter and unzips a garment bag revealing the strapless royal blue gown and holds it up for me to see. The rich crepe fabric flows to the ground, there's a delicate jeweled detailing just under the bosom of the gown and a georgette fabric train flowing from the waist in the back. It's a stunning gown so I comment, "Oh, Sorcha it's even more beautiful in person than in the picture. I love it!"

"Go on now, try it on for us. I've got to see it on ye and Breda needs to fit it to ye."

From inside the fitting room, I hear Sorcha and Aunt Francie making idle chitchat with Breda as I slip into the gown. I stand back and look in the mirror and decide it will show better if I pull my hair up. I hunt for the clip inside my purse and sweep my hair into a make-shift up-do before opening the curtain.

"Oh, Jesus, Mary, and Joseph, Gem! You look amazing!" Sorcha's smiling with approval.

"Honestly dear, you look like a model or Duchess Kate," Aunt Francie adds.

Breda charges in with her pin cushion diving like a stage-hand for U2, she ducks down and begins pinning the hem and cinching the waistline. She steps back to study me in the dress before moving back in to nip the bust.

"Thanks, Breda, I was afraid if you didn't take it in there, the whole thing might fall down at the altar." I smile at Breda and she smiles back.

"You've got cute, perky breasts. Just a little tuck is all ye need."

I look back at Sorcha who is mouthing to me, *Perky*!

I struggle to hold in my giggles. "Yes, that's me. Perky American breasts."

Breda stands with her hands on her hips and announces, "Well, there ye have it, a maid of honor ready to be crowned the Rose of Tralee."

"That's a great idea, Gem. See, I told you I'd find a dress you can wear again. You can wear it to try out for the Rose of Tralee." Sorcha and Aunt Francie laugh along with Breda who walks towards the phone to answer a call.

"So, do you really like the dress, Gemma, or are ya just being polite?"

"Are you kidding? I love this. I seriously love the style and the color. You've chosen wisely." I do a small turn and look over my shoulder so I can see the back of the dress.

"Your tight little American bum looks pretty good as well as those perky breasts." Sorcha snorts with laughter at her own comment.

I do another full turn causing the georgette fabric of the train to float through the air. "Well, you know, I've been doing Pilates ever since you bestowed me with the honor of being your maid-of-honor." I finish my twirl and curtsey before asking, "Will I get to see your dress, or is that a surprise?"

"So far, only Mum's seen it, but I guess I can show you. Breda's got it in the back for alterations, but I can show the sample to ye." Sorcha makes her way to the rack of dresses and pulls out a flowing white silk gown and says, "It's called the Sable Sophisticate," as she dramatically holds the dress up to her chin.

"Oh, Sorcha. It's beautiful, truly beautiful." I'm sincere. "It's a classically beautiful dress. It's timeless."

"Aye, that's what I said. As soon as she came out of the fitting room I told her, 'That's it Love, that's the dress'." Aunt Francie proudly sits taller in the chair to emphasize her words.

"You're right, Aunt Francie. She's going to be an absolutely beautiful bride, isn't she?" We all admire the gown in Sorcha's hands as she gently moves it causing the light to make the crystals on the bodice sparkle.

Breaking the silence of our dress-admiration, I say, "Why don't I go change and we can go to Sergio's for lunch. My treat."

"Now, now, Gemma I insist on buying us lunch today. After all, I made ye my maid-of- honor, it's the least I can do."

"No, let me." Aunt Francie chimes in, as I'm closing the curtain of the fitting room. "I want to do this for my daughter and niece. I'm firm on this one, so don't argue."

As I step out of the dress, I hear Aunt Francie and Sorcha going back and forth over who'll pay for lunch. I honestly don't care. I just want to eat, it's been a while since tea at Grandma's yesterday, and I didn't eat breakfast.

Sergio's is located on The Crescent and serves the most phenomenal Italian food in all of Ireland. Well, at least that's what I think as I order the penne pasta with smoked salmon. "Aunt Francie are you sure there's no Italian blood in our family? I eat more Italian food than Irish by far." I'm joking, but Aunt Francie looks like she's thinking this one over.

"Oh, feck mum, she's kidding. Aren't you, Gem?" Before I can answer, Sorcha jumps in and asks, "So, Gemma, when are you going to see Paul? It's been since Christmas, right?"

"Hold on, who's Paul? Is he a Boyle boy?" Aunt Francie looks puzzled, but I find it hard to believe nobody's mentioned Paul to her.

"No, he's an American I met last year in Galway. He's from Wilmington and we ran into each other there, but he's here now on a teaching sabbatical in Cork. It's a long story, Aunt Francie. But in answer to your question Sorcha, I think I may go down to Cork next weekend.

Sorcha twists her mouth and pauses before saying, "He's not coming here to see you?"

"No, why would he? I don't mind going to Cork. I haven't been there in years, it will be fun."

Okay, that didn't sound the least bit defensive, did it? Ugh...

"I guess... I just thought he'd be mad to see ye, and that he'd come to Boyle straight away. I mean it's been what? Five months?"

I'm pretty certain Declan said something to her. Her words sound oddly similar to his admonition on the train platform. Giving my best try at modulating my tone, I respond, "Well, that's not how Paul and I operate. It's all quite casual."

I just failed miserably at playing it cool. My curt tone tells Sorcha, *I'm done talking about Paul.* I think Aunt Francie understands as well, because she changes the subject. "The weather is supposed to be much sunnier this summer so that bodes well for the wedding day."

"Aye, I only hope it's warm enough, now that we'll all be wearing bloody strapless gowns." Sorcha tips her wine glass and takes a swig then continues, "At least we'll have a heated marquee."

"Marquee sounds so much nicer than what we call it in America. A tent just sounds so, well, so like it's meant for camping. What made you decide to have a marquee at Lough Key?"

Aunt Francie dramatically rolls her eyes and says, "It was a compromise."

"That's right, it was Mum, and let's not rehash the entire thing for Gemma." Turning back towards me she continues, "If it were up to me the whole fecking thing would be out at the Lough, but Mum was hell-bent on us having a Mass at Saint Joseph's and a reception in town." She closes her eyes to emphasize her frustration before finishing. "So, we agreed; a Mass at St. Joe's, the reception under a marquee at Lough Key, a band and dancing, a buffet, and a fecking ice sculpture."

"The ice sculpture is my idea." Aunt Francie smiles proudly. Obviously, the ice sculpture was a victory for which she must have fought hard to win.

"A fecking swan. Three hundred quid for a bleeding bird made of ice." Sorcha acts like it's the most ridiculous thing in the world, but deep down I think she likes the idea.

"An ice sculpture adds a classy touch to the event, don't you agree, Gemma?"

"It sounds lovely, and yes, very classy Aunt Francie. Brad and I talked about an ice sculpture for our wedding. They're so festive."

We talked about one, didn't say we were going to have one.

Aunt Francie nods her head at Sorcha in a *See I told you so* gesture.

"I hope you don't mind that we scheduled the wedding right on the tail of the Boyle Arts Festival, Gemma." Sorcha is serious now, she's done sparring with her mother for the time being.

"Oh, I'll be busy taking pictures, but won't it be nice to follow-up the festival with your celebration? I think the timing is perfect. The town will still be wearing its finest for the festival."

"That's our Gemma, always able to see the silver lining."

The waitress returns with our entrees and a basket of bread. Sorcha passes the bread to her mother and says, "Here you have some, I've got to fit into a wedding gown at the end of next month."

Just as I stick the fork into my pasta, Sorcha comments, "Ya know, Declan really had good craic when he was with ye in America on New Year's."

I see Aunt Francie from the corner of my eye perk up to listen.

Play it cool, Gemma. Play it cool.

"Oh? I had fun too." I reply casually then take another bite of pasta.

"I don't know why, but he's awfully protective of you. He'd not tell me hardly a thing about your visit with him. If you hadn't told me about your night out, I'd know nothing of it at all." Sorcha is twirling a fork full of angel hair pasta and acting coy.

"We had a lovely time, but I've not spoken to him since April when I called to wish him a happy birthday. How is Declan?"

"He's well. Still seeing Maeve." Sorcha emphasizes Maeve's name and rolls her eyes, indicating her annoyance with the situation.

"Oh, is he bringing Maeve to the wedding?" I ask.

Please say no. Please say no.

"Yes. We felt like we had to include her on the invite, but we've never met her. Just seems odd he won't bring her around me or Liam. I don't get it."

I take a sip from my glass and thankfully, Aunt Francie steps in, "I guess we'll get the chance to meet her at the wedding. Won't we?"

"Hey, Gemma, you don't mind that I included Paul on your invite, do you?" Sorcha is looking at me squarely.

"No. You didn't *need* to include him, but I appreciate you inviting him. His work schedule is a bit hectic. They're on some kind of archaeological dig right now, but he should know if he can come or not in a week or two."

I feel I'm making excuses for Paul and I don't know why.

"I'm looking forward to meeting your new friend." Aunt Francie says, patting my arm. I look down at my penne and keep eating. I'm no longer in a celebratory mood, but am eager to go back to the cottage.

I wonder if I'm the only one with doubts about me and Paul. Well-meaning friends and relations are starting to ask questions. Paul and I have been having a fantastic Skype-relationship for the past five months. I've gotten to know him much better, but I guess in their eyes, it's going to take a lot of convincing before they'll be satisfied with anybody who tries to fill Brad's shoes.

Chapter 25

When I initially made the offer to drive Deidre to Cork, it had been more of a rhetorical gesture. We were both heading the same direction, but I assumed she had her travel plans arranged already. Now, here she sits beside me in a Cork pub, waiting for her friends to meet her to go see a show.

I had stopped to see Grandma at the taxi office earlier in the week to let her know I'd be taking the car to Cork for the weekend. I know Grandma and Grandpa said it's mine to use for the summer, but driving to Cork isn't exactly the same thing as driving around Boyle, so as a courtesy I stopped in to tell her.

"Oh, Gemma, won't the petrol be terribly dear for a trip like that?" Grandma peered over her reading glasses from behind her desk, a concerned expression on her face. I couldn't tell if she was really concerned about the cost of gas, or the fact I'd be going to see a boy.

"Cork is quite far. Couldn't your friend meet you halfway?"

It was at that moment, Deidre, who was working dispatching the taxis, joined the conversation and said, "I'm going to Cork this weekend as well to meet some friends at a show - the Cork Summer Concert Series." She flipped her long blonde hair over her shoulder and smiled.

Grandma turned and looked at Deidre and then back at me. I could see the thought bubble above her head before the words were spoken. "Maybe Deidre could ride with you and keep you company!"

Being the people pleaser, I asked, "Deidre would you like a ride to Cork?"

How badly I'd miscalculated, thinking she'd have her travel plans confirmed in advance. Deidre perked up, practically jumping out of her chair and said, "Oh that would be grand! I was going to take the train, but I'd much prefer riding in a car. I'll pitch in for the petrol, of course. I'm not due to come back till Monday, does that work for you?"

Still shocked at the prospect of a long car ride with Deidre, I had the presence of mind to remember I'd be coming back Sunday. "I'm coming back on Sunday."

"Oh, that's okay, I can get the train or a bus home, but we'll have good craic on the ride down, won't we? We'll leave Saturday morning, right? What time shall I be ready?" Clearly she was excited, far more excited than I. It's not that I don't like Deidre, it's just I never really know what to talk to her about so the prospect of a long car ride with her seemed daunting.

I smiled and said, "Is eight o'clock too early for you?"

"That's perfect!" Deidre was practically dancing as she skipped back to her desk to answer the phone. I turned to see Grandma was happy as well. She now had the satisfaction of knowing I wouldn't be traveling alone to the big bad city of Cork.

I glance over the tea cup as I sip and smile thinking of how Deidre, my unlikely traveling companion, and I have come to be sitting in a pub near Cork University, waiting for an American archaeologist and a group of potential hooligans she met at a concert last summer.

As I place my tea cup down on the saucer, the pub door opens, and it's Paul. He stands in the doorway searching to find me, so I wave my hand until he notices the motion. The moment of recognition is priceless to me. After only seeing him via computer for five months, seeing him in person reminds me how handsome a man Paul is. His smile is wide as he greets me with a big embrace, and a kiss on the cheek.

"Now, you are a sight for sore eyes. Gemma, it's wonderful to see you after all these months." He gives me another hug before turning towards Deidre, "And you must be Deidre." He extends his right hand and Deidre looks puzzled by the gesture for a moment before taking his hand and shaking it weakly.

"Aye, I'm Deidre. Nice to meet ye, Paul."

Paul's courteous and charming, "Thanks for keeping Gemma company on the ride down. I'm happy she had you along."

"We had a good trip, uneventful. Gemma's a good driver, for an American." Deidre smiles up at Paul and continues, "I've got some friends stopping by in a few minutes to collect me. We're going to the summer concert down at the Marquee."

"Yes, that's what Gemma tells me. It should be good craic." Paul laughs at himself, "I guess you can tell I've been here a while?" He turns to me and pats me on the shoulder.

"I'm having a cup of tea while we wait for Deidre's friends, care to join us?" I point to the extra chair at the table, and Paul sits down between me and Deidre. We get the waitress's attention, and Paul orders tea, and we chat and sip until Deidre's friends arrive.

Two girls and a guy in their early twenties clad in leather jackets arrive and Deidre jumps up, waving them over to our table. They seem nice enough, but I can't help wondering if her parents are okay with Deidre hanging out with this crowd. Deidre's a sweet girl - a tad innocent - but

I also sense, at twenty-one, she's got a wild-streak and enjoys a good party.

I'm just a few years older than Deidre, but my protective instincts take over and I begin questioning this motley crew about where they live and what they do for a living. I can see Deidre's eager to leave us, but I keep quizzing and instructing. "Now, you've got my mobile number, right? Promise you'll call me if you get into a situation you're not comfortable with or if you need a ride. Oh, and whatever you do, don't get into a car with a stranger or someone who's been drinking."

"Wow, Gemma, who did this to you?" Deidre's looking at me with her mouth hanging open.

Her look of surprise makes me self-conscious. *Note to self; have developed an as yet unseen, maternal instinct.* "Sorry, I got a little carried away. I just want to make sure you'll be okay."

The tall, leather clad young man pipes up, "Don't ye worry, Deidre's in good hands and my older brother is An Garda if we need help."

"Oh, well, in that case." I'm not sure this bloke is catching my sarcasm, but Deidre does. She grabs him by the sleeve, pulling him towards the door. She shouts back to me, "I'm fine Gemma, now *you* on the other hand. Mind yourself with that handsome Yank."

As they amble out the door to the street, I turn and see Paul, smiling at me as he drinks his tea, so I ask, "What's so funny?"

"You. That mother hen impersonation you just did was absolutely adorable. Judging by the little bit of time I've spent with Deidre, I'd say it was completely unnecessary, but sweet nonetheless."

I retort defensively, "Maybe I *was* a bit over-protective, but if anything were to happen to her, I just know my grandmother would somehow hold me responsible. I can hear her now, 'You're older than Deidre. You should have warned her.' "

"You don't give Deidre enough credit. I get the impression she's quite capable of taking care of herself. Her friends seem harmless. Not the sharpest tools in the shed, but harmless enough. Besides, the big guy's brother's a cop. What could go wrong?"

Releasing a sigh I concede, "You're probably right, but let's hope she doesn't need help from the police."

The saucer rattles as Paul puts his empty tea cup down and exclaims, "Let's get moving shall we? After your long ride this morning, you must be eager to freshen up. We'll stop by my flat, let you unpack, and we'll go explore Cork. Sound good?"

Feeling playful I ask, "Is it true there are twenty-nine bridges in Cork City alone that cross the River Lee? I'd really like to cross them all, if it's okay with you?"

"That sounds about right, and I'll be happy to show you a few bridges, but I thought I'd take you around University College Cork since that's where I spend so much time. After that, we can head to the Murphy's Brewery for a tour, roam around Oliver Plunkett Street a while, and then, if you're not too exhausted, we'll find a trad session down on Coburg Street."

"That's an ambitious schedule, but it sounds fun. I love traditional Irish music so I hope I make it to the last event." I stand up, put my purse over my shoulder, and Paul takes my left hand. Leading me out of the pub, he grins, "Oh, I didn't say that was the *last* event of the day."

I know he's joking, well, I think he's joking, but I feel a flutter in my stomach as the thought I've been pushing out of my mind for weeks bubbles to the surface. He's moved very slowly, but he *is* a guy, after all. What are his expectations of this weekend?

The bigger question is, what are *my* expectations of this weekend?

❖

We park my car at his flat, drop my overnight bag inside, and Paul gives me a few minutes to freshen up before exploring University College. His flat is a fully furnished two bedroom apartment. He shares the flat with another visiting professor; the same one he stayed with last summer.

From the other room I hear Paul call me as I pull a sweater out of my bag. "My bedroom is all yours tonight so make yourself comfortable."

I set my bag on the floor under the window, pick up my camera, and put the strap over my head, then turn to walk into the other room as I slip into my sweater.

"I hope I won't be putting you or your flatmate out." I smile when I see him standing by the door waiting for me. He's wearing a light-gray windbreaker jacket and he's got his sunglasses perched atop his head.

Paul takes my hand, and as he opens the door says, "You're not putting us out, and I don't even know what my flatmate's plans are tonight, anyway."

He turns, gives me a peck on the cheek before asking, "Shall we?"

❖

It's nearly eleven-thirty when we return to Paul's place. The full day, the fresh air, the food, the music - I feel giddy and exhausted all at once. It's been years since I've been to Cork, and even then, it was with my family, so what I remember best is arguing with my brothers over where to eat dinner.

Today, Paul showed me so much of the University and the City I'd never seen before, it feels like the first time I've seen the place. It's been a fun day, I'm happy I made the trip to see him.

"Do you mind if I get comfortable?" I say, as we reach the door and Paul lets me inside the flat.

"No, go ahead. Would you like something to drink? I think I'm going to have a beer."

"Maybe just a glass of water, thanks." I walk into his room, open my overnight bag, and find a pair of navy blue fleece pants and a loose fitting heather gray t-shirt to change into. When I return, Paul's in the kitchen opening a bottle of Harp, so I join him.

I see he's taken a glass down for me so I fill it with water and sit down at the dinette table and watch him pour his lager into a pint glass. He joins me at the table and lifts his glass, "Cheers, Gemma."

Lifting my glass, I tip it towards him, "Slainté, Paul."

Paul takes a sip of beer, puts the glass down, and grasps my hands in his. His hands are warm and he squeezes mine as he asks, "So, what did you think of your day in Cork?"

Paul's head is slightly cocked to the side, as he studies me. I can't figure out if he's admiring me, or if he's trying to figure something out as I answer evenly, "I had a lovely time."

"Gemma, are you comfortable with me?"

"Yes, why do you ask?" My voice cracks a little, betraying my unease.

"No reason. I only want to be sure you feel completely comfortable when you're with me, and there are times I'm not certain you do." He takes another sip of his beer as he stands and says, "Let's go sit on the sofa."

Paul continues talking as we sit down, "I think it's important for two people in a relationship to be able to completely let go." He leans in and caresses my cheek before tenderly brushing his lips across mine. His mouth is warm against mine and encouraging me to answer his kiss. He presses his lips harder against mine and slides his hand underneath my shirt, exploring.

I'm lost now. Feelings and emotions are rising inside. I know at this point, even if I want to stop what's about to happen, I'm powerless. I guess this is what he was talking about. I'm letting go. I let him lead me, guide me; each kiss more powerful, more probing. I kiss back.

I'm lying back now and he's on top of me. I feel how badly he wants me to let go as his hands gently make their way higher and higher beneath my shirt. He teases me with his fingers and I begin to tremble with desire and urgency.

Sensing my inability to stop, and that I want more, Paul forges on. At the moment he reaches to untie the string on my pants, I hear a key turning in the front door. Startled, I instinctively push Paul off of me, reassemble my clothes, and brush my hair down with my hands.

Paul, now on the other side of the sofa where I've basically thrown him, is much cooler than I, turns and says in an even, slightly breathless tone, "Oh, you're back. I wasn't sure you'd be home tonight."

"Obviously."

Standing in front of us is a tall, slender woman with long blonde hair cascading over her shoulders. Her full lips are curled into a Cheshire grin accentuated by her cherry red lipstick.

Dizzy from what's almost taken place, I'm flummoxed and can't speak. I look back and forth, between Paul and this beautiful creature. My mind's unable to compute who this Taylor Swift look-alike is.

Seeing my confusion, Paul turns and says, "Gemma, I'd like you to meet my flatmate, Ashlyn." He looks back at the leggy blonde, "Ashlyn Allen, this is Gemma O'Connor."

Ashlyn's eyes scan up and down as she takes me in. My embarrassment is rising. I detect her silent amusement with the situation she's just interrupted.

I'm mortified. My face is on fire. I want to slide under the sofa cushion. I want to run to my car and drive home, now. My face must be redder than Ashlyn's lipstick. Fortunately, Paul comes to my rescue and begins filling Ashlyn in on the details of our fun-filled day in Cork. I hear him explain to me that Ashlyn is from Belfast and teaching at University College as well, and for convenience sake, they've been sharing the cost of this cozy two bedroom flat.

I know he tells me this, but right now, all I hear is blah, blah, blah because there's no blood in my ears, it's all in my face. What little blood is left in my head, is devoted to thoughts of humiliation and berating.

He did tell me he had a flatmate.

Am I a sexist?

Is it sexist of me to assume his flatmate would be a guy?

He never mentioned a name.

Maybe he never told me her name because his flatmate looks like a super model.

Ashlyn's friendly enough, and we chat for what feels like an eternity, but is probably more like a few minutes. I'm completely off my moorings at this point. All I can focus on are her long slender pins, her golden tresses and the resounding question, *Why hasn't Paul mentioned her in all these months? Why, when we talk online at least once a week, has he never thought to say, 'Oh, by the way, my flatmate is a hot blonde.'??*

Ashlyn stays and talks with us for a few minutes, but as the blood is leaving my face and returning to the rest of my body, exhaustion sets in. It's been a long day; the drive from Boyle, dropping Deidre at the pub, touring Cork, almost shagging Paul, the blonde bombshell - I'm barely able to keep my eyes open any longer.

As Ashlyn gets up to go into the kitchen to get a drink, I decide it's my cue as well. "Paul, it's been a wonderful day, but I'm really tired. I'm going to excuse myself now and go to bed."

I manage to stand up without looking as off-balance as I feel. "I'll say goodnight, now."

Ashlyn gives a smirk and waves with her fingertips as she sips her water. From behind the glass she offers, "Goodnight, Gemma, nice meeting you."

Her eyes are dancing with delight, but I keep my composure and reply, "Such a nice treat meeting you as well, Ashlyn." I hear my words, noting I put emphasis on her name. *Ashlyn*. I turn to Paul who looks utterly pitiful, "Thanks again, Paul. I had fun. Goodnight."

He jumps up and walks with me to the bedroom door. He's perplexed at my sudden departure. I see he's unsure, half thinking the date may be over, and half wondering if he should follow me into the bedroom. I take the initiative, saving him the dilemma of what to do next. I put my hand on the door knob, turn back to him and gently kiss him on the lips. "Sweet dreams, Paul."

I leave him standing there and close the door behind me.

Did I handle the situation properly? I have no idea. What I do know is if we hadn't been interrupted, I would have fully let go and right now, I'm glad I didn't.

Chapter 26

There's nothing like a three-and-a-half-hour drive to help clear your head. I woke up early and had a cup of coffee and some cereal with Paul. He acted as always, calm and reassuring. Never once did he mention what happened or *almost* happened last night.

We made small talk about his work at the university. I filled him in on the arts festival and the latest plans for Sorcha and Liam's wedding. Paul acted interested and even a little excited about coming to Boyle. He said he can't make it to the festival, but he'll definitely be able to come for the wedding.

He was a little surprised when I told him I needed to get back to Boyle early. I feigned I have a lot of work to do to get ready for the arts festival. Honestly, I do have a lot to get done, but nothing that can't wait until tomorrow.

I told Grandma I'd stop and pick up Tippy before going to the cottage, but again, nothing that has to be done immediately. Paul was happy I'd come to Cork and about the date. The more naturally Paul acted, the more absurd I felt.

What exactly am I upset about? Am I upset? Am I jealous? I haven't a clue.

I've come to the critical part of the journey just outside Cork City where I must choose which road I take back to Boyle. If I bear right and take the M8 to the M6, it's about three hours and twenty minutes to my grandparents' house. If I keep left and take the N20, it's closer to three and a half hours.

I turn on the radio, find Cork 96fm, and crank up the volume. It's a Van Morrison song, "Brown Eyed Girl." Rolling down the window, I let the wind blow my hair back. Without another thought, I bear left towards the N20.

What's ten extra minutes? Right? Besides, the N20 leads to the M18 which goes directly to Galway.

I spot the mobile phone on the seat beside me and wonder if Sorcha's home. I pick it up and hit speed dial.

The phone rings several times. I look at the clock on the dashboard and wonder if she's gone to early Mass. I laugh out loud at my own silliness. Sorcha doesn't get up early for Mass - ever. She's lucky if she makes it to the eleven o'clock Mass. Never was there anyone more delighted when Father Mark at St. Joseph's started the five-thirty Sunday evening Mass.

I could have sworn she'd paid him money to add that service when we were teenagers. Back then, sleeping was practically a sport for Sorcha.

Her voice mail picks up, "Hey, it's Sorcha. You know the drill."

I hesitate to collect my thoughts before starting, "Hi there, Sorcha. I guess you're sleeping in. It's me and it's about nine-forty-five. I'm driving back to Boyle from Cork. I'm on the N20 so I'll be driving right through Galway and I thought if you're not busy maybe we could have lunch before I drive back to the cottage. So, if you get this message anytime in the next two hours, call me back. Otherwise, I may just go straight home. Or, I may stop at the cliffs first if I don't hear, but anyway..."

I'm rambling. My message is getting long, but I add, "Oh, and I've got to tell you about my date with Paul and the huge surprise I got last night. Call me. Bye."

I know Sorcha has a habit of screening calls so if she's there and plays back my message right away, that little nugget at the end will have my phone ringing in five, four, three, two....

The phone on the seat beside me jumps as it rings and vibrates on cue. "Hello, Sorcha."

"What huge surprise?" She's out of breath with excitement.

"Oh, I really don't want to talk about it on the phone while I'm driving."

"You've got to come over right now. Do not, I repeat, do not go to the cliffs. Do not go to Boyle. You've got to stop and fill me in on your date."

"Okay, I'll come Sorcha. But seriously, you're getting worked up and it really isn't a big deal."

She shouts into the phone, "You shagged him, didn't you? Oh my holy feck, Saint Gemma you shagged him, didn't you?" Not giving me time to reply she continues as if I'm no longer part of the conversation, "But you said you got a huge surprise...." She trails off in thought before gasping, "Oh feck. That's the surprise, he's got a huge wanker!"

"Oh, for the love of Pete! No, Sorcha! That's not it at all."

Fishing for an answer, she tries this time with a note of sadness, "It's a tiny wanker? Oh, gee I'm sorry, Gem. Well, they say it's not the size of the ship, but the motion in the..."

I cut her off before she completes her thought, "Will you please stop?"

Still searching, she tries again, "He's got a crooked langer. Oh, bless his heart, the poor lad. His willy is pointing south when he wants it up north."

"You kill me." I'm laughing as I speak. "No, Sorcha, I assure you, it has nothing to do with Paul's willy, langer or wanker. Now, be patient and I'll be there a little before noon."

"Oh, shite!" she blurts into the phone.

"What's wrong?"

"I promised Liam I'd meet him for noon Mass and lunch round at the pub in Salt Hill. He and Declan had a rugby get-together out there last night so we're meant to spend the afternoon there."

"Well, that's okay Sorcha, we can get together another time. I'll be seeing you in a couple weeks anyway." I say this, but I know she's busting to find out about the date.

"Just come get me, you don't have to come upstairs, just blow the horn and we can go together to Salt Hill."

"Are you sure Liam and Declan won't mind?"

"Crikie, you know Liam thinks you're fun, and Declan is always asking when you'll be coming to Galway. They'll be mad if you *don't* come." There's momentary silence on the other end of the phone, then she asks, "You don't need to go to confession before Mass, do ye?" She's giggling now.

I smile and say, "No Sorcha, my absolution from the last confession is still good."

"Well, okay. Grand, I guess that settles it, I'll see you soon, Gem. Drive carefully."

"I will. Bye, now."

I hang up the phone and place it back on the passenger seat. I'm feeling much better than I felt a few moments ago.

Chapter 27

Sorcha was restless throughout the entire Mass. She'd hit me with a barrage of questions about Paul on the ride to church, but once inside, she must have thought of a hundred follow-up questions she had to stifle until Mass ended.

She had reacted about as I'd expected her to react. "Why the feck wouldn't he tell you his flatmate is a girl?!"

"My question exactly. Granted, we're not exactly an exclusive couple." I gesture using air quotes. "But that's kind of a detail you'd think would come up in casual conversation, and we've been having nothing *but* casual conversations for months."

I'm grateful for the peace and quiet during Mass so I can clear my head and think. Liam keeps looking at us with a quizzical expression begging, *What is going on with you two*? I pleaded with Sorcha not to say anything to Liam and I think she's held up her end of the deal, but she looks like she's ready to burst.

Liam was already seated in the pew when we arrived. We barely made it inside before the priest started down the aisle, so Sorcha hasn't been able to say a word. We exit the church, proceed down the steps where Liam gives me a big *hello* hug, and finally says, "Okay, what's going on? I've not seen Sorcha look like this before. Did something happen I should know about?"

Sorcha cuts her eyes my direction, begging me to tell him, so I finally contribute, "Nothing really happened. I just got a surprise, that's all. I visited Paul in Cork yesterday, and it turns out his flatmate is a pretty blonde female. I had assumed when he mentioned his flatmate he meant it was a guy."

Liam's eyes widen with what I think is recognition, but could be surprise. I'm not certain. "Ah, well, that would explain my darling Sorcha being a complete fidget during Mass. That's a pretty big detail to not mention to the girl you're dating." He pronounces this as if it's *The Gospel according to Liam,* then points across the street and says, "We're going to The Capall Celtic Pub, across the street." Liam takes Sorcha by the hand and they step off the curb, but I remain behind, thinking over what he's said, before I scurry across to catch up with them.

The Capall Celtic, which means Celtic horse in Irish, has a large sign over the door with a Celtic-style drawing of a horse. As we're walking inside, Liam spots Declan already waiting at a table near the back. I see Declan's expression alter when he sees me walking a few steps behind Liam and Sorcha. It's apparent, he wasn't expecting me.

At first he smiles when he sees me, but then I detect an uneasiness wash across his face. I could be imagining it, but he's always so collected and that's why his change in expression is notable.

"Look who we found on her way from Cork." Liam's thundering voice fills the pub.

Declan stands as I approach. He pulls the chair beside him away from the table, permitting him to reach my side, and gives me a tiny peck on the cheek. “This is indeed a happy surprise, Gemma. I didn't think I'd be seeing you for a couple of weeks."

As I sit down, Declan pushes my chair into the table and the waitress appears. I look up and see a striking, raven-haired young woman slide past me and give Declan a kiss. "Hey, Sweet," she says.

I'm looking up. My eyes cut between Declan, who is turning a light shade of pink, and this blue-eyed waitress who now appears to be more than *just* our waitress for the day.

I pivot to my right, where Sorcha is seated. She gives me a wincing expression and mouths the word, "Sorry."

Oh, this must be Maeve. The Maeve she told me about from down the pub. The Capall Celtic is the pub and Maeve works here. It's fitting into place when Declan finally makes the introduction.

Clearing his throat, Declan starts, "Gemma, this is Maeve Monahan. Maeve, this is Gemma O'Connor."

Thankfully, Maeve speaks first. "Oh, *you're* Gemma!" She's genuinely pleased to meet me. "Declan goes on and on about his friend Gemma from America. I'm so excited to finally meet you."

"It's nice meeting you too, Maeve." *There, I managed to get the words out without sounding insincere.*

Turning to Declan, Maeve playfully pats his shoulder. "Silly, you never told me Gemma was coming today."

"I'm only just finding out myself." Declan's tone is a combination of surprise tinged with the tiniest hint of anger.

I come to Declan's rescue. "I was visiting my boyfriend in Cork yesterday, and on a whim called Sorcha on my ride back to Boyle this morning. My trip to Salt Hill has been very spur-of-the-moment."

I see Maeve is pleased with my answer. I also feel Sorcha's eyes fixed on the back of my head. Most likely because I just called Paul my boyfriend. Declan, on the other hand, looks bewildered as Maeve cheerfully replies, "Well, it's so nice meeting you and welcome to The Capall Celtic." Turning to the others at the table she adds, "What can I get everybody to drink?"

As Maeve takes our drink orders, I study her. She's dressed in a short black skirt and a tight burgundy t-shirt with the same Celtic horse that's on the pub sign embroidered on the pocket. She's about five feet five inches, I'm guessing, with a slight build, and perfect tits. Her jet-black hair is pulled back in a head band away from her face. Her blue eyes are almost violet and framed by impossibly long, thick lashes that flutter as she blinks.

As she strides away, I pay attention to her perfectly straight, silky hair swishing with each step and consider my own wavy brown hair. No amount of product in the world would keep my hair that smooth in this damp Irish climate.

Liam adds as we begin studying our menus, "You know, Gemma, Maeve is going to school to become a barrister. She's smart as a whip, she is."

And at that, I feel completely defeated. Pretty, smart, friendly, accomplished in her own right; she's perfect for Declan.

"Is that so? She seems lovely," I say turning to Declan. I mean it too.

We place our lunch orders and as soon as Maeve's out of ear-shot, Sorcha announces, "After all that *Peace be with you* hand shaking in Mass, I need to wash my hands. Come on Gem. Let's find the loo."

This is clearly a command, so I obediently follow her to the room with *Mná* or women written on the door. As soon as we're inside, Sorcha turns, "Holy, feck I'm so sorry, Gem. When Liam told me we were meeting Declan here, I didn't know *she'd* be here."

"Why are you apologizing? She's nice and seems perfect for Declan."

"I know, but I also know you and Declan are close and I wasn't sure what kind of close ye are so...." Sorcha stops, tilts her head downward, and gives me a look of pity. "We've only just met her for the first time yesterday at the rugby game," she adds then turns and pumps the soap dispenser.

"Evidently, he likes her enough to introduce her to his friends. Isn't this a *good* thing? I seem to recall *you* were the one complaining to me about how he never brings these girls around his friends. I would think you'd be happy about Maeve." I pump soap on my hands, turn on the water, and begin scrubbing. "Besides, you've invited her to the wedding. It's not like he was going to keep her a secret forever."

"I guess you're right, it's just I thought…" Sorcha pauses and tears off a piece of paper towel.

"You thought what?"

She finishes wiping her hands, crumbles the paper towel into a ball, and throws it away before finally answering me, "I thought you and Declan would get together. There, I said it."

She's wearing her disappointment on her face, so I softly say, "Look, Sorcha, Declan and I share a mutual experience of loss. Yes, we've developed a friendship." I throw the paper towel I'm still holding into the bin and as I place my hand on the door add, "But nothing more. You should be happy, we're both making progress."

Well, one of us is.

With this, I push the door open and walk back to the table a few steps ahead of Sorcha. Declan stands and pulls my chair out as I return. He's the consummate gentleman, as ever. Liam sees Declan's chivalrous gesture and feeling shamed into doing the same, rises and pulls out Sorcha's chair.

The four of us are silent for what seems like an eternity, but is really only about ten seconds. The silence and their expressions tell me Liam and Declan have been having a similar conversation.

Once our food arrives, it's Liam who brings up my trip to Cork, directing a question to Declan. "Dec, if you had a gorgeous blonde flatmate, and you were casually dating a girl for what say, six or seven months, would you mention to said girl you're casually dating that you have a gorgeous blonde flatmate?"

Declan lifts his head from his plate and directs his blue eyes towards Liam with an inquisitive look, "What? Is this some sort of hypothetical?"

"No, I'm asking for a friend." Liam's smiling and looking at me.

Declan sees this, looks at me, and back at Liam before wading in with his answer. "I guess it would depend on how serious said girl and guy are. I kind of think it would come up in conversation fairly early in said courtship."

He goes back to his food, breaking off a piece of boxty with his fork, but I catch the note of disapproval in his voice.

I take a long sip of water and another bite of the giant banger on my plate. Gathering my thoughts as I chew and swallow, I finally pipe up. "Look, Paul and I are *casually* dating. Yes, I was a bit taken aback when I met Ashlyn, but you know what? She's his flatmate, that's all. Now, can we *please* talk about something else?"

Sorcha quickly changes the subject and I return to my banger. Looking down at my plate, I spy Declan from the corner of my eye, wearing a wry grin of approval.

Why does he think it's funny when I get angry? The moment I feel ashamed of my behavior, he finds it funny.

Shaking my head, I stab at the banger with gusto as Liam and Sorcha banter on about their honeymoon plans in Spain. Between unexpectedly meeting Ashlyn and Maeve, it's been a weekend full of surprises. Paul's surprise caught me completely off guard. Not because he has a female roommate, but because he never told me.

Meeting Maeve wasn't on the agenda, but my feelings about her are unexpected. I feel ambivalent about meeting her, at best. I'm struggling to figure out what exactly I'm feeling. Am I sad, angry or happy?

I take another bite of food and swallow hard because I know precisely what I'm feeling and I don't want to admit it to myself. I feel, dare I think it? *Jealous.*

As soon as we're done eating, I make my excuses, and say goodbye. "I'll see you in a couple of weeks," I say to them, as I walk away from the table. I wave goodbye to Maeve who's behind the bar and I make my way out of the pub.

My eyes take a second to adjust to the sunlight, so I stand on the curb outside the pub digging through my purse searching for my sunglasses. I put them on and locate my car across the street in the church parking lot. I'm about to step off the curb when I feel a hand on my shoulder. It's Declan.

I look up into his eyes and feel like I'm going to cry at any second. He lifts his hand, "You forgot your jumper on the back of your chair."

I look down to see my black cardigan in his hand. I reach to take it from him and he puts his other hand on mine and says, "Mary Gemma, are you *really* okay?"

Staring at his hand on mine, I'm thankful to be wearing sunglasses so he can't see the tears about to spill from my eyes. Forcing a smile, I say, "We call a jumper a sweater in America."

He tries again, "Are you all right?"

I reluctantly acknowledge his question using the best tactic for answering a question I don't want to answer. I answer his question with another question. "What do you mean?"

"I mean, you obviously were surprised Paul hadn't told you about his flatmate. Are ye worried about what else he hasn't told you?"

Declan's squeezing my hand and all I can do is stare down at his large hand enveloping mine. I want to tell him, *No, I'm not okay. I don't know what I am, but I almost slept with the guy, and now I feel like I don't know him at all. After months of getting to know each other, it feels like I don't have a clue about who Paul Blair is.*

Instead, I look at Declan and say, "I'm fine Declan. I'm being cautious and taking things slowly because a very wise friend told me I should." I smile, and see his expression soften upon recognizing his own words.

He studies me for a minute before leaning in and gently kissing my cheek. He pulls away and looks down at me, "Grand. I don't want anybody messing about with ye. Now, go on so ye get home before the sun goes down. Will you give me a call to let me know you're safe home?"

I nod my head because there's a lump in my throat preventing me from speaking. Declan gives another gentle peck on my forehead as I let go and step off the curb. When my foot hits the pavement, I find the words and promise him I'll ring when I'm back to the cottage.

I drive out of the church parking lot and onto the road. I glance in the rear view mirror and see Declan going back inside the pub. Finally, I let go - the tears spill down my cheeks.

Back at the cottage, I throw my overnight bag on the floor as Tippy blows by me to get to his water dish. Thankfully, Grandma was at a meeting at church and Granddad was busy watching a re-run of *Keeping Up Appearances* so he hardly noticed me taking the dog and leaving.

My head's pounding and my eyes are so puffy, they're nothing more than tiny slits, so I climb directly into bed and gather up my laptop computer. I know I promised Declan I'd call on the phone to let him know I'm home, but tonight I don't feel like talking to anybody other than Tippy.

I pick up the mobile phone lying beside me, find Declan's number, and type a message, *I've made it back to the cottage. Tippy and I are in for the night*. I hit send, drop the phone beside me, take a deep breath, and look up at the ceiling.

I hear the familiar vibration of the phone as a text message comes across, so I glance down to see his reply, "Grand. Goodnight, Macushla."

"I'll give him the last word, Tippy." Tippy picks up his head, turns and looks back at me from his corner at the foot of the bed, holds his gaze on me for a moment before turning and putting his chin back on his paws.

Smiling at Tippy, I return to my computer and check email. I see several notes pertaining to the arts festival, a *hello* from my brother, Peter, who's preparing to travel to Ireland for Sorcha's wedding, and a couple from the photography website.

Wouldn't it be great if I sold a couple more pictures?!

I open these first. The first note is a comment from someone who saw a picture I'd taken of Moylurg Tower at sunrise and loved it and wanted to tell me.

The second one has a familiar email address. I don't know who it is, or why they'd send a personal note on my photography website, but I'm certain I recall the address, xoxo@Bigmail.com. I click and open it. I tilt my head trying to understand the brief note that reads, *Mind Yourself. Things aren't always as they seem.*

Chapter 28

"Aidan can stay with me at the cottage." I put my foot down on this point. Not just because I know he's dreading being stuck in the same house with Mom, Dad, Grandma, Grandpa, Peter, Peter's wife Cheryl, and the baby, but because I want the company.

Aidan looks at me. He says, *Thank You* with his eyes as Dad jumps in, "Well, it sounds like that's settled."

I haven't told anybody about the unnerving emails, but they've got me a little spooked. They aren't threatening, but they're creepy. There was another one last night and all it said was, *Dig deeper*.

Again, nothing threatening, but who's sending them and why? What do they mean?

The excitement of my family arriving for the festival and Sorcha's wedding is exactly what I need to take my mind off of the cryptic messages. I've decided if I get anymore, I'm going to say something. I just haven't decided whom I'm going to tell. I know the reaction I'll get. Or should I say the *over* reaction?

Mom turns and asks, "But what about your friend Paul? Where is he staying when he comes for the wedding?"

I take a bite of roast beef before answering, "I made a reservation for him at the Royal Hotel, Mom. He's coming by train so he won't have far to walk from the station."

"Well then, sounds like you've got it all under control." Mom leans across my father to speak with my brother, Peter, at the end of the dinner table. "Peter, will you and Cheryl be able to get to Gemma's exhibit before the end of the festival?" She's asking, but we all know, she's really telling them they need to get to my exhibit.

Peter has just placed a fork-full of carrots into his mouth so Cheryl jumps in to answer. "We're going to go by in the morning if we can find someone to keep Shane for a few hours." Cheryl turns to shovel another spoonful of mashed potatoes into eleven-month-old Shane's mouth.

"I'll keep Shane for you tomorrow." Mom's relishing spending time with her first grandchild and there was never any doubt Grandma Nora would keep Shane for a few hours. My mother begins using baby talk and leans further across my father to speak with the baby. "Won't we have fun Shaney Wayney?"

Aidan rolls his eyes and says, "Well played, Cheryl. Well played. You can take off for a week and Mom won't notice you're gone."

Peter turns to me and asks, "Have you sold any of your pictures this year? I know you sold a few last year."

"I did sell a few this year. I did a series of framed prints. My most popular was a photo collage called *The Pubs of Boyle*. It's a grouping of four pictures of pubs done in black and white. Very popular; I've sold four and taken orders for five more."

"Brilliant!" Peter's visibly pleased. "Let me guess, four of the ones you've sold went to the four pubs."

I smile and nod, "Yep. I'm not stupid. They were the first ones I approached with a deal."

"That's my girl." Dad lifts his water glass and tips it towards me. "Mary Gemma always had a head for business. If she hadn't become a teacher, I'm sure she'd be a high-powered business tycoon by now."

"And you've always been my biggest cheerleader, Dad."

We finish dinner and Dad helps Aidan load his bags in the back of my car and slips us both twenty Euro. "Get yourself a lemonade at the festival tomorrow."

"Geez, Dad. You never change. Thanks!" I give him a kiss on the cheek and get into the car. He waves as Aidan and I drive off through town towards Lough Key.

"Now the fun *really* begins." Aidan leans across and turns the volume up on the radio. "Do you have any beer at the cottage?"

I take my eyes off the road for a second and look at Aidan. "Have you ever known me to keep beer on-hand? Wine, maybe, but sorry, I don't have any beer."

I see Aidan's disappointment so I ask, "Do you want me to stop at an off-license?"

"Eyes on the road. Eyes on the road." Aidan dramatically slams his hand on the dash board.

"Relax. For crying out loud. You're not used to the left side of the road yet." I shake my head and drive on, "Do you want me to stop at the off-license and get some beer?"

"Nah. I'm good. We'll have plenty of opportunity for that sort of thing tomorrow night at the rehearsal dinner and at the wedding. We can have a glass of wine when we get to the cottage."

We arrive as the sun's setting on the lake. The sky is aflame with pinks, reds and gold. Ignoring my brother, I grab my camera from the back seat and walk closer to the water's edge.

"Don't mind me. I'll let myself in." Aidan shouts to me, but I'm lost in the sky and ignore his sarcasm.

I yell back, "I left the keys on the driver's seat. Let yourself in. I can't miss this sky."

I approach the lough like an animal sneaking up on its prey, trying not to disturb or startle it. The hot pink streaks in the sky are like fluffy cotton candy, or candy floss as the Irish call it, reflecting on the water. The lighting at this hour is magical so I snap picture after picture. Looking up, I see a bird soaring in front of a soft cloud pattern. I lie flat on my back and point the camera letting the shutter do the work capturing the breathtaking beauty of the evening, scarcely aware of my finger pressing each snap.

After several minutes, I put the camera down and gaze up at the heavens. The grass beneath me is soft and cool and I hear the water lapping delicately against the shore. It's peaceful so I draw in a deep breath and slowly let it go. I shut my eyes and envision Brad. He's a memory now, and though I see him in my mind's eye, his features are getting less clear.

I take another lung-filling breath and sigh out loud. I still feel him near me, but I'm having trouble holding his image in my mind. I don't want to forget him so I keep my eyes closed and try to picture his face. I squeeze my eyes tighter as if this will help sharpen the memory.

I hear movement and detect Aidan approaching with Tippy leading the way. Almost simultaneously with the realization I'm no longer alone, I feel Tippy's wet tongue on my cheek. "Bleh, bleh. Get off of me Tippy," I protest, sitting up.

Aidan's standing above me. His head's blocking what's left of the sunlight, "This was taped to the door for you." He looks puzzled as he hands me a folded piece of yellow note paper.

I reach for the note, take it from his hand and unfold the piece of paper. Written on the paper in black block letters is one sentence. *BACK OFF, OR ELSE.*

I stare at the words in front of me. At first, my mind is blank. I am at a loss to grasp its meaning. I read it again. The coldly written block letters are meant to be some sort of warning. Finally, I get it.

It was one thing when the messages were emails, it's entirely different when they're pinned to my door. A cold shudder travels through me. I try to shake it off, but the sudden change in my expression is obvious to Aidan who's still hovering above me.

"Do you want to tell me what this is?" Aidan extends his hand and helps me to my feet. "Is this some kind of joke or prank? Do you know who it's from?"

The crease between his eyebrows tells me his brotherly concern has him on heightened alert. He may be my younger brother, but his protective instincts are intense. I don't want to worry him, but at this point, I have to tell him.

"Let's go inside," I say, brushing my bum with my free hand as I stand. I'm stalling to think of how to explain these mysterious messages.

Once inside, I pull down two of the glasses Liam made and fill them with red wine. Handing him a glass I say, "This is the first one I've gotten here. I've gotten a couple of other notes, but they were anonymous emails. This is different, and I'll be honest, I'm a little freaked out by this one."

"What do you mean? Other notes? What kind of notes?"

I can see I've done nothing to put Aidan at ease so I explain, "Over the past several months, I've gotten two or three mystery messages. They aren't threatening, they're more like warnings. One said, *Things aren't always as they seem*. Another said, *Dig deeper*. Nothing threatening, but I don't know who's doing this and I don't know what they mean."

"Have you told Grandma or Grandpa? What about Uncle Tom or Aunt Francie?"

"No. I didn't tell anybody. I thought they were nothing, you know, spam, but now this." I hold the piece of yellow note paper up and Aidan looks at the message in my hand.

"Do you want to go to the police? Technically, this one constitutes trespassing. I think."

I pick up my wine glass, take a sip, and swallow before speaking. "Tomorrow. I'll talk to the Garda tomorrow. I know Bernard Mullany will be at King House working security at the exhibit, I'll mention it to him. He's a detective, he'll know what I should do, if anything at all."

"You sure you want to wait? I don't mind if we call someone now." He takes a sip of his wine and puts the glass down on the table in front of him.

"No. Let's not make a big deal out of this. I'll talk to Bernard tomorrow, see what he says. I'm sure it's nothing, and the last thing I want to do is upset Sorcha's wedding."

Aidan tilts his head considering my words momentarily, "I suppose it can wait. Besides, I'm here with you, and so is Tippy. It's all good." He says this to reassure me, but I detect a modicum of doubt in his voice.

Not wanting to bring things down further, I change the subject. "You know what goes really well with red wine?" I get up and walk to the cupboard and open the cabinet door. Reaching inside, I produce two Cadbury Flake bars I've been saving for just such an occasion.

Aidan's recognition is instant. "Flake! Sweet, yes. Flake and red wine, now that is refinement, Gemma."

He cracks open a bar and splits it with me. When the going gets tough, the O'Connor's pull out the Flake. Chocolate has always had a special place in my heart. It's ideal for cheering a blue mood. Tonight, I need this confection to lift my spirits and to calm my nerves.

Chapter 29

The final day of the arts festival is always busy. Many of the artists are eager to take down their exhibits and go home. I've learned it's actually a wonderful day to hang out with my pictures. It was on the final day of the festival last year I sold most of my pictures and took orders for several others.

I put on a lavender sundress and tie my hair back in a purple ribbon. I decide to go for comfort over style and slip into a pair of beige ballerina flats. I give myself a look in the mirror then walk to the kitchen where Aidan's crunching on a bowl of muesli.

"Did you let Tippy out?" He nods yes and I ask, "Are you coming with me into town?"

Aidan has a mouthful, so I walk to the refrigerator and pull out a yogurt, take a spoon from the drawer, and sit down to wait for his response.

"Yeah. I can ride to King House with you and walk to Uncle Tom's and Aunt Francie's." He takes another giant scoop of cereal. The milk drips from the spoon and as he's about to shovel it in he adds, "I'm going to hang out with Martin and Fergus. We might check out some of the bands playing at the festival."

I nod in acknowledgement and take a spoonful of yogurt before saying, "Please don't mention the note to Mom and Dad. It's no big deal and I really don't want it to cast a shadow on the wedding events. *Especially* tonight at the rehearsal dinner. You know if Mom has anything to worry about she gets that look on her face."

Aidan finishes chewing his muesli and gets up to wash the bowl. Standing at the sink he turns back and says, "Just promise me you'll talk to Bernard Mullany today."

"I will, I promise." I hand him my spoon to wash. "Besides, the notes haven't been threatening, so I'm sure it's nothing."

Aidan pats me on the shoulder and smiles, "If you say so."

"I do say so. Come on, I need to get down town." I glance down at Tippy who's looking up with his doleful, coffee-colored eyes. "Sorry fella, this is another one of those days, but I promise you'll get a long stroll around the lake when I get back."

Picking up my purse, I take the keys off the hook by the door and lock up behind us.

❖

I see Bernard Mullany sipping coffee from a Styrofoam cup near the doorway of the large exhibit hall. If I don't just walk up and talk to him I'll lose my nerve. I collect my thoughts and force my feet to move in his direction.

Bernard's a stout man, with wavy salt and pepper colored hair. His eyebrows are untrimmed and prominent. I attribute their unkempt state to him being single. I can't believe any woman would allow that to go on with her man. I know I wouldn't, but maybe I'm a bit of a control freak when it comes to male grooming issues.

As I approach him he lifts his bushy eyebrows and smiles, "Good morning, Gemma. Lovely day for the closing of the festival, isn't it?"

His eyes are cheerful and kind, but I imagine they can be fierce and determined when interrogating a criminal. I smile and answer, "Indeed, it is lovely, Bernard."

He's either a wonderful detective, or I'm an open book, because the next thing he says is, "What's it you're wanting to ask? Have ye some trouble?"

"Wow, Bernard, you're good." I smile, move closer, and tell him about the anonymous emails, and of the handwritten note that appeared at the cottage. His expression turns serious, but he makes me feel at ease as I answer his questions. Our families have known each other for years. The Mullanys are longtime citizens of Boyle, and though he's at least fifteen years older than I am, he's always treated me as an equal, never speaking to me in a condescending manner or treating me as if I were a child.

His questions are direct; Have you any enemies? Anyone who may be jealous of you? Anybody who might think you've wronged them? Are you involved with someone? Could there be a jealous lover?

His inquiries are thought-provoking, yet I can't think of anyone who would go to the trouble of what seems to be warning me of something, but what? What are they warning me of?

I answer all his questions and can see he's winding up to one final question. Crossing his arms over his barrel-chest, he takes in a deep breath and lets it out, then leans closer. The strong aroma of the coffee in his hand hits my nostrils as he asks, "Do you feel threatened, or have any of the notes threatened you or your physical safety?"

I look down at the floor and think for a second. I notice his black dress shoes are dusty and well-worn. I compare them to my own spotless flats, as I consider his question. Finally, I look up and say, "No. I don't feel threatened, but the note appearing at the cottage is unsettling."

"Well, I tell ye what, if you change your mind and if it will make you feel better, come down to the station and we'll fill out a report. If ye hear again or the notes become more frequent or threatening, call me. In the meantime, I'll send a car by the cottage from time to time just as a precaution."

"Thanks, Bernard. I'm probably worried about nothing, but I promised Aidan I'd ask you about it."

Bernard pats my right arm and smiles, "Not to worry, Gemma. Ye did the smart thing in letting me know. It's probably nothing at all, but t'is best to be safe."

I smile up at Bernard who is a good three inches taller than I am. "Well, I'd best get back over by my pictures in case anybody wants to buy one."

I start walking back towards the exhibit, relieved to know the Garda will be driving by the cottage to check on things. I'm happy I mentioned it to Bernard, but still perplexed by the entire situation. Lost in my thoughts, I don't notice there are people standing by my display until I'm almost there. It only takes a second to identify the couple examining the collection of photographs. It's Declan and Maeve.

Their backs are toward me so I have a moment to compose myself. Having just been interrogated by a detective, only to turn around and find Declan and his girlfriend, I need to switch gears abruptly. I stop, run my hands over my hair making sure all is in place, and then step beside Declan and say, "Hi there! I didn't know you'd be coming to the festival today."

There, that was pretty cool, wasn't it?

They turn simultaneously at my comment and Declan starts first, "Gemma, how are you?" His smile is beautiful and my stomach performs a small flip flop as he leans in to give me a hello kiss on the cheek.

Maeve comes closer and follows Declan's lead giving me a *girl kiss* hello on the cheek. I call it a *girl kiss* because it seems a little disingenuous. A little too rehearsed. Or perhaps I'm reading too much into her hello.

Declan's still smiling as he turns to point at my exhibit. "These are incredible Gem, even better than last year's pictures and those were wonderful."

I feel my face flushing, but manage a reply, "Thanks, Declan. And thanks for coming. I thought you might be arriving later."

Maeve wraps her arm inside Declan's and says, "Nope, Declan took the day off so we drove over late yesterday afternoon. We're staying at the Lough Key House. Have you been there? It's the most beautiful bed and breakfast I've ever stayed in."

Declan doesn't even seem to notice Maeve's wrapped her arm inside his. This makes me feel a little sad. Maybe it's the level of familiarity, or knowledge they spent last night together at a gorgeous inn, but I brush the uneasy feeling out of my mind and continue talking.

"I'm so happy you could make it to the festival."

Maeve lets go of Declan to turn and look at my pictures again. As she goes from one photograph to the next, Declan turns back to me and smiles, "I wouldn't have missed your exhibit for the world."

His deep voice and dark Irish features pull me in and I'm lost looking up at his handsome face when Maeve turns around and squeals, "Honey, look! This is the same picture you have hanging in your office! It's got a first-place ribbon too!"

We both turn to see what Maeve's talking about. She's standing directly in front of the picture I took of the Boyle Abbey. The black and white shot I entered in last year's festival.

I look to Declan who moves closer to Maeve and says, "Aye, yes. So it is."

"That's the picture that started it all. Someone bought that picture for 350 euros at last year's festival." I feel quite proud giving this piece of news to Maeve.

Clearly impressed, Maeve moves closer, "Wow, 350 euros for one picture, and your first sale too. Well done, you!"

I look at the picture and at Maeve studying it, then turn back to Declan. I'm certain his cheeks are turning pink as the words shoot out of my mouth, "But I never gave you a print of that picture." I'm speaking softly, more to myself than to Declan, but he sees I'm piecing it together. The person who bought the picture paid cash, didn't leave a name, and took it that day. Declan grins a sheepish grin that says, *I'm caught*.

Why would Declan buy one of my pictures for 350 euros, especially when all he had to do was ask for it if he likes it so much? I'd have given it to him for nothing.

Maeve's prattling on about some other pictures, but I'm lost in thought. Why did he keep it a secret from me? Did he buy it because he felt sorry for me? This is either the kindest gesture, or I should be angry with him. But why would I be angry he bought my picture? Is he the most awesome friend ever?

I'm a million miles away when Maeve, now finished examining my work, returns to me and Declan and says, "Dec, we'd better get going." She slips her arm in his and once again, I feel a slight pang. "We're going to listen to a band at The Moving Stairs before we get ready for the wedding rehearsal." Her smile is brilliant, and her impossibly long eyelashes flutter.

"Sounds fun. I'll be here a few more hours till the exhibit portion of the festival closes."

Declan, being the Boy Scout that he is asks, "Do you need help taking down your exhibit?"

"No, but thanks. My brothers are going to help me do that the day after tomorrow. Thankfully, I don't have to tear down today. We've got a grace period of a couple days. I'll go home, freshen up and head to St. Joe's for rehearsal."

Maeve seems pleased with my answer because she's excited to go see the band. "Come on Dec" she purrs, "let's get going." She pats his arm and turns to me, "Your pictures are beautiful, Gemma. See you later."

"See you later." I smile and watch them glide across the exhibit hall and out the door. They make a cute couple, I have to admit. She's very attractive and so is Declan. I decide to be happy for them.

Chapter 30

St. Joseph's is a fascinating church. The parish itself has been in Boyle for ages, but this particular church was built in the early 1980s and is *the* most unique church I've ever attended. The architecture is meant to resemble an ancient Cashel. The battered limestone exterior walls look like an old stone fort and the round domed roof sets it apart from ordinary Irish churches.

Inside, its open roof, windows and expansive space fill with light making it a peaceful place to pray and contemplate. As a little girl, I loved coming here to pray with my father. It's so different from our church at home.

I open the large glass door and enter the sanctuary. There's a group of people huddled together talking and laughing in front of the altar. I hear Liam's voice above all others.

I'm halfway down the aisle when I hear Sorcha, "Gemma! Oh grand, we're waiting for ye." She turns to Father Mark and says, "We can start rehearsal now, Gemma's here."

I feel heat rising in my face as I recognize it's me they've been waiting for. Addressing Sorcha I say, "Sorry, I'm late. I was waiting for Paul, but his train is late. I texted him to come directly here."

Taking me by the hand and leading me to the crowd in front of the altar, Sorcha gently pats my hand, "Not to worry dear, we've only just gotten here ourselves. Now, come, I'll introduce you to the entire crowd and expect ye to have all the names memorized right away."

She tilts her head back and laughs as though she's just made the funniest remark of her life. This tells me she's nervous. I know Sorcha, and despite being the life of the party, I can always tell when she's anxious. Her laughter takes on a pitch I've always described as half tea kettle whistle and half New Hampshire Red chicken.

Sorcha begins with Liam's family. His parents, his siblings, an auntie or two and a couple uncles, a grandma and granddad - I'd forgotten how big his family is so when all the introductions are finally made I say, "Welcome to Boyle. Where are you staying?"

One of Liam's brothers, I think his name is Rob, speaks up first, "Some of us are out at Glencarne House, a few others are at Forest Park House and then a couple more are at Cesh Coran." His voice is even louder than Liam's and is out of place in the church, but he barrels on, "We've quite a crowd so it wasn't easy finding rooms being that it's the final days of the arts festival and all."

Across the aisle, I spot Declan and Maeve talking with my brother Peter and Cheryl. I can't imagine how loud Liam's house was when they were growing up and think of Declan spending so much time there as a child. No wonder Declan's quiet in comparison, it was out of necessity. When would he have gotten a word in edgewise with all of these loud Tully kids?

I answer Rob, "Oh, yes. Sorcha started snapping up rooms all over the county the minute she and Liam set the date. She wanted to be sure her guests could find a place to stay."

Father Mark steps up on the altar to try and gain control of the jolly gathering. Clearing his throat, "Right, so. Shall we begin the rehearsal?" His attempt fails, so he tries again, "I know we're all excited, but mind ye, this is the House of the Lord."

Still nothing.

I nudge Sorcha, "I think Father Mark needs help calming the crowd." She walks over to Liam and whispers in his ear. Liam looks at the altar, sees Father Mark standing patiently, and turns to his family and shouts, "Oy! Jaysus, ye rowdy lot, shut it! Father wants to start."

The stunned gathering turns to look at Liam who's proud of the quiet he's created. I see my grandmother over his shoulder making a sign of the cross. Sorcha jabs an elbow into Liam's side. Confused by her angry expression, he says, "What? Ye said to shut em up."

"That ye did, Liam. Whopper of a job, my pet." Sorcha turns to Father Mark and smiles. "Right, so. Let's do this."

Father Mark begins organizing us. Josephine O'Neil, whose father heads up the arts festival, is beside him to act as the church wedding director. Josephine was in school with Sorcha and to say they don't like each other is putting it mildly.

Josephine is barley five feet tall, a little plump, and dowdy. She's one of those girls who's got what Sorcha calls, *a resting bitch face*. She's looked old her entire life. Sort of sad if you ask me, but Josephine was always mean to Sorcha. Aunt Francie once told me Josephine's jealous of Sorcha and since I'm Sorcha's cousin, she's jealous of me too. There's irony in the fact it's her job to assist with the weddings and Sorcha's of all weddings.

She assembles the bridesmaids and bride and we follow her like a gaggle of goslings to the back of the church so we can rehearse our procession. As we walk behind her, I hear her slacks making a swishing sound as her chubby thighs rub together. Sorcha notices too and digs her elbow in my side and whispers, "Bless her heart."

Suppressing giggles as we reach the back of the church, I see Paul seated in the last pew.

I'm surprised to see him and my smile grows as it's obvious he's happy to see me. He smiles and waves as he steps out of the pew to greet me. He looks amazing for a man who just got off a train. He's wearing gray slacks, a blue button down shirt and a navy jacket with nary a wrinkle!

He takes my hand and pulls me in to kiss hello. His kiss feels like magic and his touch, immediately relaxes me. "You made it."

"I'm so sorry, Gemma. That was the train ride from hell. It took so long, but gosh I'm glad to be here. You look so sexy. You do know the color red drives men wild?"

I flush at his compliment and glance down at my dress. It's the same red dress with the lace overlay I wore on New Year's Eve in New York. "I may have heard that somewhere before?" I say bashfully.

"Look, I wanted to see you to tell you I'm going to go to the hotel and check in. I need to freshen up. Can I meet you at the rehearsal dinner?"

I see Josephine out of the corner of my eye. She's shifting, leaning on one hip then the other, arms crossed over her expansive bosom, clearly growing impatient, so I answer Paul quickly, "Sure. You know how to get to the restaurant?"

"The Coach and Four? Right?" Paul squeezes my hand and I feel electricity surge through my body.

"Yep, reservation is for eight o'clock." I lean in and give a small peck on the cheek.

Paul whispers in my ear, "God, it's good to see you. I'll meet you there at eight." I let go of his hand and watch him walk out of the sanctuary. He's so handsome. I sigh and return to Josephine who is looking rather cross.

"How long have you been in Ireland?"

"Did it take you long to get here from Cork?"

"When will you return to the States?"

"Where did you and Gemma meet?"

My family peppers Paul with questions. I feel sorry for him. It's bad enough meeting the parents, but he's being hit with most of the family all at once in addition to Liam's family, friends and the odd distant relations. And this is just the rehearsal dinner. Tomorrow at the wedding will be worse.

Mercifully, due to the crowd size, Liam and Sorcha decided to go with a heavy hors d'oeuvres menu instead of a sit down dinner for tonight. We're free to move about the room and get away from overly inquisitive relatives, if need be.

Paul asks, "Can I get you a glass of white wine?" I look down at the small plate of food in my hand. I've got two bacon wrapped scallops, three stuffed snow peas and a couple cheese cubes so I tell him, "Make it a Chardonnay, please." He gives me a kiss, "Your wish is my command."

I watch Paul walk to the bar in the corner of the party room. I feel silly now for having been upset about his female flatmate. He's incredibly attentive and loving tonight. How could I have ever been concerned about something so minor?

"He seems smitten with you." The soft voice next to me is Maeve's. She's stunning in a burgundy halter dress that shows off her porcelain shoulders. Her poker straight raven tresses tumble over them, accentuating her delicate frame.

I've just popped a scallop into my mouth and it's hot. Waving my hand in front of my mouth to indicate just how hot this scallop is, I'm uncertain as to whether or not I'll spit it out on the floor. Maeve laughs at me. "I'm sorry, I caught you just as you're taking a bite."

I want to hate her, but she's nice. Who am I kidding? I manage to keep the scallop in and swallow. I could really use that glass of wine to wash it down, but I'm finally able to speak, "That's okay." I look at her and say, "You look beautiful tonight."

"Thanks. I was afraid I'd be a little overdressed, but I wanted to look good for Declan. It seems I'm the first girlfriend he's brought around since.... well, since Sheila."

I detect frustration in her tone. She's pensive, so I ask, "Is it hard living with the memory of Sheila? I mean, I know how much he loved her. Must be tough to come along behind someone he loved so dearly."

Maeve takes the olive from her drink, eats it from the plastic sword, then places the empty sword back in her martini, "That's the thing, Gemma, I don't know how much he loved her. He never talks about Sheila. It's strange. He *seems* to enjoy my company." Shrugging, she continues, "I mean, he brings me here. We're staying in an incredibly romantic inn. We've got a huge, king-sized bed in the Red Room, which is supposedly the honeymoon suite." She takes a small sip of her drink, swallows, and says softly, "But he never finishes the deal."

I see sadness in her eyes as Maeve tosses back a large sip of her drink, punctuating her words. I want to ask what she means, *he never finishes the deal,* but Declan's coming over and he's with Paul. Maeve sees them and immediately starts smiling. Clearly, our discussion is over.

Paul hands me a glass of wine, "Chardonnay for my lovely lady."

"Look who I found over at the bar?" Declan announces as he joins us.

"Maeve, have you met Paul yet?" I turn towards Maeve, who is now smiling from ear to ear.

"I haven't," she says, taking Declan's free hand in hers.

"Maeve, this is Paul Blair. Paul, this is Maeve Monahan."

We chat for a couple minutes and as Declan begins his interrogation of Paul, we're joined by one of Liam's brothers. I know Sorcha told me his name, but it escapes me at the moment. Fortunately, Declan steps up and does the introductions.

"Gemma O'Connor and Paul Blair, allow me to introduce you to Kevin Tully. Kevin is two years older than Liam and I, and I'd say from the volume level, he's also two to three pints ahead of us."

Kevin throws his head back wildly and laughs, "Aw, feck. Ya got me. I might be slightly pissed at the moment, but it's not every day my little brother gets married. Shite, we didn't think it would ever happen. He wraps an arm around Declan's neck and leans in feigning a whisper, but still loud, "We Tully men are like prized-bulls, t'is very unnatural for a Tully male to still be on the shelf at thirty years of age."

Kevin takes a draw of his stout, then looks at Paul. "Jaysus, Paul, ye say it is? Paul's confused, but replies, "Yes, it's Paul."

Kevin barrels on, "Ye look the spitting image of a fella we saw down at The Moorings last night. T'was that *ye*?"

I turn to Kevin and say, "Paul just came in on the train from Cork a little over an hour ago."

I don't have much patience for loud drunks, so I cut Declan a look to ask, *Is he pissed or is this his personality?*

Declan escapes Kevin's headlock, looks at him and back at me, then shrugs his shoulders to say, *sorry - he's pissed.*

Kevin continues, "Ah, then, sure as feck, there's a doppelganger out there looks just like ye. Only he was at The Moorings with some Sally."

Before Kevin can continue, Liam shouts above the din, "Can I have your attention for a minute?" Some of the talking ends, but Liam puts it all to rest with one earsplitting, two-fingered whistle.

Again, I catch a glimpse of my grandmother sitting in a chair across the room as she looks heavenwards and rolls her eyes. Inside I'm laughing, wondering what she must think of this crowd from Galway her eldest granddaughter is aligning herself with.

"I just want to thank ye all for coming tonight. Sorcha and I are very excited to be getting married tomorrow and it means a lot to have so many of ye with us to celebrate." One of his brothers begins to clap, but Liam interrupts, "Hold on ya eejit, I'm not finished."

Turning away from the embarrassed brother, he proceeds, "When I met Sorcha, I'd never seen a more beautiful girl in my life, and tomorrow, the beautiful Sorcha is doing me the honor of becoming my wife. In my wildest dreams, I never thought I'd be so blessed. So let's all raise a glass to Sorcha."

Liam raises his glass and we join him, "To Sorcha. In Irish, Sorcha means bright or radiant. To me, it means the light of my life. Today, tomorrow, and every day after; I love ye Sorcha, you're the light of my life."

"To Sorcha!"

The entire room echoes back. "To Sorcha!"

The rest of the evening sails by and before long, the room is clearing out. A group of Liam's family is making plans to go to the pub, but I'm tired and want to get a good night's sleep since tomorrow promises to be another busy day.

I ask Paul, "Do you mind terribly if we leave now?"

Paul's holding my hand, so he lifts it to his lips and presses a small kiss on the back of my hand, "No, I'm tired too."

We say our good nights to the family and find our way out to the street. The air on The Crescent feels cool and refreshing after being holed-up in a room full of people for a couple hours.

"Where's your car?" Paul asks.

"It's over there." I point to the top of The Crescent near the clock which is the opposite direction of the hotel where Paul is staying.

Paul looks to my car and back towards the hotel. "Tell you what, how about I walk you to your car and I'll walk back to the hotel. It's a nice night and I'll enjoy the fresh air."

He picks up my hand and leads me in the direction of the Ford Focus.

"I hope my family didn't overwhelm you tonight."

"Not at all. I'd expected them to grill me pretty hard."

"You did?"

"Heck, yeah. Gemma, you're beautiful and smart, and sweet. You're special, and it's obvious your family and friends adore you. I can't blame them for being protective."

I shrug my shoulders as I think about his words. "I guess they worry about me."

We arrive at my car and I pull the keys from my purse. As I'm putting the key in the lock I hear Declan calling to us. I look up and see him and Maeve getting into his car. He's just helped her into the passenger seat and is walking to the driver's side, "Goodnight. Nice meeting you, Paul. Safe home, Mary Gemma."

Paul looks over at Declan and gives a small wave. I call back, "Night Dec, see ya tomorrow."

Declan climbs inside and starts the car. Paul and I watch and wave as they drive off. Paul points with his head at Declan's car as they drive down the hill, "That one is really protective of you. How is he related again? Is he a cousin? "

"Who, Declan?" I'm surprised Paul noticed since we really hadn't spent much time talking with Declan.

"Yes, Declan. He keeps his eye on you. Really watches. Made me more nervous than either of your brothers." Paul says opening the door for me.

"Not a cousin, he's the best man. Liam's best friend." I sit down in the driver's seat and Paul leans on the open door.

"He sure watches your every move."

I look up at Paul and decide to tell him, "Declan was married, but his wife died of cancer. I think he's just looking out for me because he knows what it's like starting over."

I see understanding in Paul's eyes and it makes me adore him. He leans forward and kisses my forehead then says, "You're a beautiful person, Gemma." He leans further into the car and gives me a deep, passionate kiss and whispers in my ear, "I want you, Gemma. You better go now or I'll forget myself and invite you back to my hotel room."

He pulls back from me and I feel my insides turn to jelly. I want him too. Unable to speak, he finally says, "Goodnight, beautiful. I'll see you tomorrow." He shuts the car door and I drive away.

Chapter 31

Tippy's pretty miffed at me for shutting him in the house for yet another day of long hours home alone. I took him for a long walk when I woke up, but I still feel guilty when I see his nose poking through the curtains as I drive away.

One more day of this hectic schedule and I'm going to crash for two weeks. My last two weeks before returning to Wilmington will be complete rest and relaxation. Tippy and I will do nothing but take long walks around the lake, sip tea by the fire, and read books. Well, I'll sip tea and read books, Tippy will keep me company. I smile at my own thoughts as I flip on the wipers to clear the soft mist from the wind shield. I hope the weather improves by this afternoon. I think of Sorcha. Every bride wants the sun shining on her big day.

I made the mistake of checking my email before leaving the cottage. I've been getting orders on the website ever since the festival began. I've also been posting the pictures I've taken at the festival on line for festival goers to order. I get excited each time I see an email indicating another order for photographs has come in. It's also fun seeing the money landing in my PayPal account.

There were several new orders this morning and another note from xoxo@Bigmail. Today's offering said only, "Mind yourself."

What on earth does *that* mean?

I brush aside the thought as I drive into town. I'll worry about the mystery messages tomorrow. Right now, I'm meeting Sorcha and the others at Streaks-A-Head Salon. We're getting our nails, hair and makeup done. Following the hair salon, we're having a 'light lunch' at

Grandma's before going to Aunt Francie's and Uncle Tom's to get dressed.

The bell on the salon door tinkles and lets the others know I've arrived. Sorcha is already seated in the chair and Philippa is deftly working on her hair. She turns when she hears me enter the shop, "Ah, grand you're here. Maura is going to do your hair. Have a seat in the chair beside me. She'll get working on your hair first, then Sara over there will give you a manicure, and finally, Kate, in the blue smock over there, will do your make up."

"It's a regular assembly line of beauty." I smile at Sorcha who is without doubt enjoying being the star today. She's radiating happiness.

"Won't Gran's 'light lunch' muss our makeup?" I say as I sit down to let Maura begin work on me.

"Oh, yeah, that. Well, I told her nothing greasy or heavy. Nothing we have to tear at with our teeth, like giant sandwiches on hard rolls. And absolutely nothing that will make this bride fart." She turns in the chair and whispers loudly, "There's nothing worse than a big old rat bark in church."

She waits for my reaction which is a big laugh followed by a snort. I look in the mirror and see Maura behind me stifling a laugh. Finally, Sorcha adds, "My guess is it will be soup and crackers at most. Besides, your brother Aidan crashed on her sofa last night so who knows if he'll have moved from her front room by the time we get there."

I turn back and look in the mirror as Maura begins running the comb through my hair, "I got a text from Aidan last night telling me he wouldn't be coming back to the lake. I figured he was having good craic with Martin and Fergus."

"Craic, indeed! They were paralytic."

Maura leans in to tell me, "Sorcha wants you all to have an up-do. Are ye okay with that?"

I smile and answer, "Whatever Sorcha wants, Sorcha gets. Today is her day."

"That's right, Maura. Pile that chestnut brown hair high on her head." Sorcha laughs and twists in her chair to see me. "So, Gem, everybody likes your Paul. He's ever so handsome and certainly seems taken with you."

Philippa struggles to turn Sorcha's head back to a front facing position as she winds a lock of hair around the curling iron. "Do you love him?"

"It's too early to say, Sorcha. Besides, I'm not talking about me. This is your day. Today is all about you and Liam." I'm grinning because I know she won't pursue her line of questioning now that I've reminded her this day is all about her. Ever since we were kids she's talked about being the queen on her wedding day. Knowing Sorcha, she intends to be royalty until midnight.

"Fair enough, you're right. T'is about me and Liam." She stares into the mirror for a second as Philippa twists another curl. "But when I get back from my honeymoon in Spain, you're going to tell me every little detail. Ya got that?"

"Yes, Your Highness. I've got that."

The cab rolls up in front of St. Joe's at precisely five minutes until four o'clock. I know this because Derrick Beirne, one of Granddad's oldest drivers, has a digital clock mounted to the dashboard. Derrick gets out, walks around the cab and opens the door letting out Sorcha's bridesmaids. First Liam's sister, Mary Pat, and then Sorcha's flat mate from university, Caroline Day, next Christine McKenna, a childhood friend, and finally I step out, Sorcha's maid of honor.

I step onto the curb just as Sorcha and Uncle Tom arrive riding in Granddad's prized possession. His 1952 classic Mercedes 170V cab. The black cab with white roof and matching white wheels glistens in the sunlight that's finally peeking from behind gray clouds. Granddad acquired the cab from a friend who bought it in Berlin many years ago. He's had the cab as long as I can remember, but seldom drives it anywhere. He babies the old cab like it were a real child; polishing and buffing it gingerly each week. From time to time, he lets it out for weddings or drives it in the St. Patrick's Day parade, but today it's being used for the most special occasion of all - his eldest granddaughter's wedding.

Draped across the hood, or should I say bonnet, is a large white bow and ribbon. Inside I recognize Deidre's father is their driver. Sorcha and Uncle Tom are in the back seat and Sorcha is waving like the queen.

As if on cue, a ray of sun gleams down on Sorcha when she steps out of the cab onto the curb in front of the church. I look to the sky and see the gray clouds have disappeared, pushed away by quickly moving fluffy white ones on a brilliant blue canvas.

I step closer, joining Sorcha and point up, "Did you order this beautiful blue sky, Your Majesty?"

She smiles and says dryly, "Naturally."

Josephine O'Neil trots over to the cab to pull the back of Sorcha's train out of the car door. She shuts the door and huffs at me, "Here now, hold her train till ye get inside."

She turns on her heel and barks at the others, "Ladies, I need you inside and lined up, now. Father insists we start at four o'clock sharp so we're out of here before evening Mass."

The other bridesmaids jump at her command, I snicker to myself. I'm holding my flowers in one hand and Sorcha's train in the other watching Josephine take charge. Sorcha turns back to me and gives a small salute, mocking Josephine's little power trip.

The ceremony is mostly a blur. I glide down the aisle, smiling and noticing guests in the pews. I recognize faces I've seen around town my entire life. I see family and friends, Liam's family and friends, I spot Maeve sitting on an aisle midway, and I catch a glimpse of Paul seated beside Aidan.

Paul's wearing a dark navy double breasted suit that accentuates his broad shoulders. He mouths the word, *beautiful,* as I pass. Then I reach the altar where Liam is nervously rocking and Declan is standing beside him. Declan looks incredible in his dark charcoal tuxedo. The blue vest and bow tie coordinate with the bridesmaid's dresses, but all I notice is how the blue sets off his beautiful eyes.

I reach my place and look at Declan, he smiles and gives a wink. I smile back and feeling my cheeks flush, gaze down at the bouquet of yellow and white roses I'm clutching in front of me.

The music changes so I look to the back of the sanctuary where Sorcha and Uncle Tom are now positioned. The sun is beaming through the glass doors behind them making her dress and her an absolute ethereal vision. Josephine gives one last fluff of Sorcha's train then scoots over and gives Uncle Tom the signal. His hand trembles as he takes Sorcha's and they begin walking down the aisle.

I look to my left to see the expression on Liam's face. One glance and I know, Liam and Sorcha are forever. This man is in love. Over his shoulder I see Declan smiling too. Liam's like a brother to him and I think he's seeing the same thing I am.

As Uncle Tom kisses Sorcha and puts her hand in Liam's, I feel a catch in my throat and a puddle developing in my eye. She looks serene and happy as Uncle Tom chokes up and gives away his little girl. I blink my eyes in hopes I'll push the tears back and prevent messing my mascara, but to no avail. I feel a small wet bullet break free from the corner of my right eye and slide slowly down my cheek.

I'm caught up in the emotions of seeing my dearest friend and cousin marrying the man of her dreams when I have a momentary flash of Brad. Another tear makes its way down my left cheek.

Chapter 32

The band is playing under the marquee and out on the parquet dance floor Liam and Sorcha are leading a conga line. I think most of the line is Liam's immediate family, but I see Maeve and Declan trailing near the end so I wave.

All of the stress in the lead up to the ceremony is over, the reception is well into its third hour, and the guests are feeling no pain. Aunt Francie is finally kicking back and enjoying herself now that everyone has filed through the buffet and complimented her on the delicious roast beef and elegant ice sculpture.

I see Aidan and Peter huddled together with Martin and Fergus laughing raucously at what must be a hilarious story. Seated at the table beside them, my mother is bouncing my nephew Shane on her lap while Cheryl takes a moment to eat. Grandma is on the other side of Cheryl knocking back her second or third gin and tonic.

The sun is setting and the tiny fairy lights under the marquee are becoming necessary. The atmosphere is festive and the party goes on.

Paul's sitting next to me and we're watching the crowd. "Your family really know how to have fun," he yells above the music.

Leaning closer so he can hear me, "I think they're mostly Liam's family, but we do alright too." I place my hand on his knee which is pressed against mine. I'm thankful he came to the wedding and delighted he's fit in so naturally. He puts his hand on top of mine and smiles at me.

"I've got to head up to the activity center to use the restroom." He gives me a kiss on the cheek as he gets up. "I'll be right back."

I watch him navigate the crowd as he walks towards the path leading to the activity center. He's impeded momentarily by a short conversation with Liam's brother Kevin, but finally breaks free.

"May I join you?"

I turn away from my view of Paul to find Declan pulling out the chair beside me at the table. "Please do. Join me."

"It's a great wedding isn't it?" he says as he sits down on the white folding chair.

"It's been amazing. Sorcha is radiant. I've never seen her so happy. And everything turned out lovely. I'm happy for her - she deserves to be happy."

Declan smiles, amused by my comments. "You're beautiful, Gemma. I love how genuinely happy you are for other people. It's a dear quality and I'm not sure you're aware you have such a beautiful character trait."

I tilt my head and study his face, "How much have you had to drink?"

I've never seen him drunk, not even a little tipsy. I don't think he's pissed.

"Can't I make an observation without being accused of being in the pints?" He scoots in closer to emphasize his point. "But seriously, you're beautiful today. Prettiest bridesmaid by far."

I look down at my blue gown and back at Declan who is still smiling. "You do realize Sorcha has surreptitiously dressed a group of Galway boys in Roscommon blue and gold, don't you?"

Declan looks down at his blue vest and the yellow rose boutonniere with matching blue ribbon on his lapel, leans into my ear and whispers, "First thing I noticed when we pinned our flowers on, but I haven't said a word to the Tully crowd. They'll go ape shite when they figure out she's put them in Roscommon colors."

I begin laughing and lean closer to be heard above the noise, "You know what they say, you can take the girl out of Roscommon, but you can't take the Roscommon out of the girl."

"T'is true, indeed." He laughs and pats my bare shoulder.

Feeling his touch reminds me he's here with Maeve so I ask, "Where's Maeve?"

He points to the other side of the marquee, "She's over there next to me mum." I see Maeve seated next to his mother, but she's turned away from her, deeply engrossed in conversation with a red head in a teal dress. Declan adds, "She's discovered one of Liam's cousins is a barrister so she may be talking about the law all night."

I nod in acknowledgement, when over his shoulder Bernard Mullany appears and interrupts, "Pardon me, Gemma. Have you got a moment to speak with me?"

Declan sees the change in my expression, so he excuses himself, "I was just going to get a drink. If you'll excuse me." He stands, nods to Bernard, then leaves.

Bernard asks me if we can move to the back of the marquee where it's quieter, so I leave the table and follow him towards the rear. "What is it? Have you found out who's been sending the messages to me?"

We reach the back of the tent and the relative quiet when he turns and says to me, "I'm working on finding out who sent the emails, but I've learned some other news I think you should know. I wanted to wait till tomorrow, but seeing you here talking with him tonight..." he hesitates and lets out a sigh before finishing, "I thought I better tell you now."

I feel a cool chill and my heart pounding as I tense, "What is it?"

For the life of me I can't imagine what his next words will be, but by his expression I know I should brace for a blow. I pray this won't be a blow like the one I received the day I found out Brad had been killed. I don't have it in me to recover from another devastating blow like that.

Bernard draws in his breath and proceeds, "After we talked yesterday, I went back to my office and got on the computer. I ran all the names of the people close to you. You know, in police work we always start close and move out from the victim or in your case the person receiving the messages."

I nod my head in understanding, but I'm still breathless waiting for him to drop the proverbial bomb on me. "Right, right, makes sense." I agree.

"That's when I came across some information I'm fairly certain you're unaware of, or if you're aware of it, you didn't mention."

I feel my hand moving, motioning him to *go on, go on*.

Bernard sees this and continues, "Gemma, Paul Blair has a wife and child in America."

At first, I stare at Bernard, uncomprehending. After a few seconds, what he's said registers and I stagger back a step, taking his words like a body blow. Feeling a tent pole behind me, I lean against it before asking the questions forming in my mind, "He's married? Paul? My Paul Blair? Are you sure you have the right guy?"

Bernard sees I'm unsteady so he takes my arm at the elbow to lend support. "I'm afraid so. I discovered he married four years ago in Raleigh, North Carolina. His wife recorded separation papers at the court house there over a year ago, but the divorce hasn't been finalized. There's a minor child listed in the separation papers. From what I learned, the child is a boy not quite two years old."

My head's spinning and I feel wobbly, but I'm determined to keep my wits about me. I pull myself up, willing myself to stand up straight again. No longer propping my weight against the tent pole, I loosen from Bernard's grip and ask in my most businesslike tone, "And the emails? Were you able to determine who is sending them?"

Mirroring my tone, Bernard replies, "The email is coming from an IP address in Cork City. I can't say exactly who at this time, but we can piece that together if need be."

I take a deep breath and exhale as I consider what Detective Bernard Mullany has just told me. I regain my composure and say, "You're right Bernard. This *is* news to me. I wasn't aware of Mr. Blair's marital status, nor did I know he has a child." I nod a couple of times and continue in a softer modulation, "Thanks, Bernard. You've done me a great favor."

Bernard puts his hand back on my arm, "You're welcome, Gemma. You're a kind person and I know you've had it rough the past couple years. I hated to think you might get your heart broken again." His eyes are expressive and I see the sincerity behind his words. "Will you be alright or should I find one of your brothers to be with you while you consider what I've told you?"

"I'm a little stunned, but I'll be fine Bernard. I'm going to the ladies room, freshen up a bit, and finish the evening. I'll deal with Mr. Blair after Sorcha and Liam have left. I will not let this upset her big day."

Bernard gives my elbow a gentle squeeze and lets go, "Understood. You're a class-act, Gemma. Always have been." He turns to leave me but looks back, "I'll be in touch to let you know what I learn about the IP address those emails have come from."

I nod as he turns and walks back to the table where the rest of his family are seated. I'm close to the path that leads to the activity center, so I exit the marquee and begin walking. It's getting dark, so I look down at the path as I walk with purpose to the restroom.

At the activity center I notice two people standing in the grass to the right of the entrance. Their heads are together and they're giggling. I recognize the laughs, they're familiar to me. One of them must see me coming because I hear someone say, "Shush" as they step apart from each other.

I'm closer now and they're no longer silhouettes in the dusk, but faces I know. It's Paul and he's with Deidre. Deidre who helps in the taxi office. Deidre who rode to Cork with me a month and a half ago. The wheels in my head are turning when it dawns on me that the two of them are more than casual acquaintances.

I now understand. Nothing is as I thought it was, but everything I'm seeing *is* as it appears. I straighten my back, building my resolve I say, "Paul, there you are. I wondered what was taking you so long to return from the loo." I'm now standing between Paul and Deidre. "Good evening, Deidre."

She looks sheepish and murmurs, "Evening, Gemma."

Paul is sizing me up. I see he's trying to decide just how much I've witnessed. I turn away from him and face Deidre. "Deidre, darling. I see you and Paul are quite..." I pause to punctuate my next word, "friendly."

Her pale, blank expression betrays her nervousness and guilt at being caught so I ask, "Were you with Paul the other night at The Moorings? Were you? Because I've had several people swear to me they saw him with you."

Deidre looks around me to Paul as if she'll find the answer to my question there, but Paul is silently looking at the ground when I turn to him. I look back at her and she looks at the ground and whispers, "Yes. He got in late on the train so I picked him up in me father's car. We went to Knockvicar where we thought we'd go unrecognized."

Deidre is obviously ashamed, but my hunch has proven accurate so I'm not letting her off the hook. "I see. After my grandparents have been so good to you. You had no compunction about having clandestine meetings with the first person I've dated since my fiancé was killed. To say that's heartless is an understatement. I'm disappointed in you, Deidre. I thought you were better than that."

Her eyes are filling with tears as she makes an attempt to explain, "I ran into him back at the pub in Cork where you dropped me off that Sunday after you left. We got talking and..."

I cut her off, "Your story is irrelevant." I snap in a low tone, then turn to see Paul. He knows he's finished, but I keep going. I'm looking directly at him but speaking to Deidre, "Deidre, Paul is all yours. I only regret I didn't figure out earlier that he was too good to be true. But it's like they say, better late than never."

I look back at Deidre and finish, "Oh, and by the way Deidre, before you get too involved with Mr. Blair, you may want to ask him about his wife and child." At this she snaps her head up, with eyes as wide as saucers. She's gob smacked.

Paul finds his voice after I drop this truth-bomb, "Gemma, I wanted to tell you from the very start, but the time just never seemed right and you were so wounded and sweet. You're such a kind and good girl, the longer I was with you, the harder it was to bring it up. I really do care for you, I just didn't know how to tell you."

I see his eyes are filling with tears so I gently place my palm on his cheek, "Oh, Paul. Stop." My hand is still resting on his smooth skin, "I can accept forgetting to mention the leggy blonde you share your flat with. I can even think about getting past your dalliance with Deidre, but I'm sorry. Forgetting a wife you're still married to and a baby boy you've fathered; I'm afraid that's a bridge too far. It's not just a sin of omission, it's dishonest. It makes you a liar. I can't abide dishonesty."

I pat his cheek, then place both of my hands in fists at my side, "Now, if you both will leave. This is the biggest day of my cousin's life so I won't make a scene, but you will both leave and leave now. I'll have nothing to do with either one of you again."

I stand firmly planted in my spot as they take their leave. I watch as their figures become shadows and disappear into the dark. I decide to return to the reception and act as calmly and happy as possible, for Sorcha's sake. I turn to face the marquee, but instead I see Declan standing mere feet in front of me.

"How much did you hear?" There's anger in my voice, but it's not directed towards him. I'm angry with myself for having been so foolish not to see through Paul's lies.

"I heard most of it."

"I see. Well, don't I feel like a fool?" I let out a deep sigh which opens the flood gates. I begin trembling as the stream floods down my face. I'm aware of Declan rushing in and pulling me into his chest. He holds me tight as waves of sorrow splash down my face.

His words are gentle, "It's okay, Macushla, let it out. I've got ya. You've earned this cry."

My father called me Macushla whenever I cried as a child so his words sooth as he gently rocks me in his arms. His broad, muscular shoulder is like a sounding board for my pain; as I let it go, his chest absorbs my anguish. His lips kiss my forehead as he whispers, "I've got ya, and you're going to be alright."

I can't control my weeping and my body shivers in the cool night air. I feel his jacket as he drapes it over my bare shoulders. Still, he doesn't let go. His tight embrace tells me he won't let go, he's going to hold me for the duration. As long as I need to shed this acute distress, Declan Gallagher will be there for me. Declan is my rock.

The sobs begin to subside as he continues rocking me gently. I look up into his eyes. I'm searching for words, but none come. His eyes tell me he understands everything I'm feeling. He lifts a hand and wipes a tear with his thumb. "Aw, Mary Gemma, God I'm sorry he hurt you."

We both turn our heads at the same time. We hear voices. Walking up the path is Declan's mother and Maeve. Declan's mom keeps walking towards us, but Maeve stops abruptly. Time stands still until she says, "This! Holy feck, I finally understand." Tossing her hands up in the air, “This! This is why you never talk about Sheila!"

Declan calls to her, "Maeve!"

She turns away from him and calls over her shoulder as she storms off, "You don't talk about Sheila because all you can *think* about is Gemma!"

Declan hands me over to his mother who tells Declan, "Go, go talk to her. I'll take Gemma inside to freshen up."

With that, Declan's arms slip away from my shoulders and he's gone.

He's running after Maeve.

One Year Later

Chapter 33

I stand as close to the edge as I dare, leaning forward slightly to see below. The sun is directly overhead, dodging between clouds. I feel its rays warming the top of my head as the sea winds blow my hair. I pull an elastic from my pocket and gather the wild mane into a ponytail. It's always windy at the cliffs, but it's my favorite place in the world.

I take a step back, shut my eyes, and breathe the air blowing in from the Atlantic. I keep my eyes shut and reflect on all that's happened since last summer. As I think, I wonder if the sunbeam shining on me now is Brad. Could Brad be letting me know he's still watching over me?

It's true, you never stop grieving, but over time, the grieving changes. I know he'd be proud. My photography hobby has become a full-fledged business. I applied my teaching skills to photography and created several online photography courses and videos. My website has grown and is generating revenue for me, even as I stand here on the Cliffs of Moher. The business is doing so well, I've decided to take next year off from teaching.

My friends' lives have changed too. Sue is transferring to another school in the district. She thought it would be wise to teach elsewhere when she and Mr. Payne started dating. They're engaged to be married in December.

Sorcha and Liam are expecting their first baby in five months. Liam's walking around like he's the prize bull. Virility is very important to the Tully men.

As for Paul and Deidre, Grandma fired Deidre the minute she found out about her and Paul. It was really more a show of solidarity with me on Grandma's part since I don't think Deidre would have dared set foot back in the taxi office again anyway.

Deidre admitted to Bernard Mullany she was the one who taped the note on the cottage door. She and Paul had hooked up in Cork that day after I left. After their little *romance* in Cork, they planned another rendezvous. Turns out, Liam's brother Kevin was spot on, he *had* seen the two of them that night at The Moorings in Knockvicar.

Deidre wanted Paul to be her boyfriend and hoped to scare me away from him, but her plan wasn't very well thought out. Last I heard, she moved to Cork and is working in an off-license.

I got over Paul quickly. It's funny when you find out someone isn't who you thought they were, you start to piece together all the inconsistencies. Little clues that at the time were insignificant start to add up once the lie is exposed. Sue said she thought she saw Paul sitting at the bar at Hell's Kitchen in Wilmington one night last winter, but if it was him, he didn't say hello.

The cryptic emails were coming from Paul's flatmate in Cork. Ashlyn told the police Paul confided in her about his *domestic situation* in America one night when they'd been out drinking the previous summer. When she found out he was coming back to teach and that we were dating, she sent the first email. After we met, she liked me and felt badly he wasn't being honest so she started sending more emails. She thought her warnings would encourage me to dig deeper and learn more about Paul. It would have been much easier and far less painful if she'd have been brutally honest from the start.

I dismiss all thoughts of last year and take another step back from the edge of the cliff and lean into Declan standing behind me. He wraps his arms around, holding me close, and keeping me warm.

Declan followed Maeve that night, but he returned to me. He knew the day we met in Galway he would fall hard for me, but I wasn't ready to fall in love with him, so he waited.

Seeing how Paul hurt me crushed Declan. Leaving me behind with his mother while he went after Maeve, he knew he'd waited long enough. He couldn't imagine life without me.

I turn around and face Declan, place my hands on his shoulders and smile up at his handsome face. I look again at the dazzling two and a half carat emerald shape diamond ring he placed on my finger when he proposed to me moments ago and I know I'm home again.

I wonder if that fey old lady in the bakery knew I was going to meet Declan. I wonder if Brad and Sheila had something to do with me and Declan finding each other.

The wind blows and its chill cuts through me. I start to shiver, but Declan pulls me in tighter and kisses my forehead. As his lips brush my skin, a sun beam warms the top of my head.

One thing I'm certain of; I was right. When Declan Gallagher loves, there's no in between - it's all or nothing. He doesn't know how to love less; once he's in love he only knows how to love more.

Author's Note

When I was a *twenty-something,* I traveled several summers to the town of my grandfather's birth. Boyle is located in County Roscommon, Ireland. I loved my visits and kept a travel journal to help me remember the details of my time in this beautiful part of the country. I always knew Boyle was the perfect backdrop for a story, I just needed to imagine it. *The Cottage on Lough Key* is the result of my time spent in Boyle and the imaginings in my mind.

On one of my visits, I was given a t-shirt and on the shirt was a drawing of Ireland with a red heart on the map where Boyle is located. Inside the heart was the town's name. The shirt read, *The Heart of Ireland.* I hope I've done a good job depicting the town I love, because I concur with the slogan on that t-shirt. Boyle **is** *The Heart of Ireland.*

Acknowledgements and Notes

I'd like to thank Linda Clopton for helping bring this book to fruition with your skilled eye and hand at editing. I'm honored you took on the challenge of editing my first novel.

Thanks also go to Joe Carlin my Create Space mentor. You made me believe I *can* do this!

Next, a big thank you to Maura Wiggs, my dear friend and very first beta-reader. Your friendship, good cheer, and encouragement kept me moving forward.

I'd also like to thank my friends at the Inis Cairde School of Irish Dance in Raleigh, North Carolina. Irish dancing keeps me sane and happy. I truly appreciate the island of friends that brings joy to my life.

To Pat and Agnes Harrington a special thank you. I always stayed at Glencarne House when visiting Boyle. The Harrington's welcomed me like I was family; never asking how long I'd stay, but always, "How long are you home?"

The cover art is a water color rendering of the Mullany home in Ireland, my ancestral home on my mother's side, by Cindy Strella. I asked her to paint it for my mother as a present many years ago and when Mom passed away, the picture returned to me. I feel blessed to have spent time there with my grand uncle. If I close my eyes, I can still smell the turf fire.

I extend a special thank you to the town of Boyle, Lough Key Forest Park and the village of Croghan in County Roscommon, Ireland. This beautiful part of the world holds a dear place in my heart and the memories I carry with me of my time spent here are priceless.

The Legend of Úna Bhán is a story I was told by a local on one of my visits to Boyle. I've heard different variations of the story, but I hope I've done an okay job conveying the legend through Gemma's recounting of the tale.

The Boyle Arts Festival is an actual event that takes please each summer. https://www.facebook.com/BoyleArtsFestival/?fref=ts

Fonts for chapter headings and titles are by James Shields of James' Fonts and SL Celtic Style by Sharon Loya.

In the story, one of William Shakespeare's sonnets is referenced. That sonnet is Sonnet 116 Let Me Not to the Marriage of True Minds.

I especially want to thank my family for their encouragement and belief in me. For the hours you left the house to allow me to write in peace, I'm appreciative. For listening to me read my story on a long car ride and for wanting me to *keep* reading - you're the best.

Finally, thank you to my handsome J, you are my muse and I love you.

To learn more about Anna Marie Jehorek, visit her websites;

AnnaMarieJehorek.com

PullOverandLetMeOut.com

TheCottageonLoughKey.com

Follow her on Twitter @AnnaMarieWrites

Find her on Facebook https://www.facebook.com/AnnaMarieWrites/